PRAISE FOR

ALMOST CRIMSON

"Dasha Kelly writes with equal parts sweetness and sadness about being a human. She writes about girls and women, family, friendship, and aching love. *Almost Crimson* offers a full teacup of emotions, past and present, delicately balanced on a wildly beating heart. This author, this novel–blessings to readers and storytellers alike."

—LEESA CROSS-SMITH, author of *Every Kiss a War*

"Dasha Kelly's *Almost Crimson* is a beautiful, poignant account of many lives, tremendous intersections, journeys to wholeness, and an exploration of love and community. This book rightly deserves a place alongside the works of Toni Morrison, Maya Angelou, and Toni Cade Bambara."

—SAMUEL THOMPSON, nationally-acclaimed
Afro-Classical violinist

"Dasha Kelly's novel *Almost Crimson* is almost perfect, its structural genius rivaled only by the depth and complexity of its characterizations, the candor and frequent beauty of its understated yet direct prose style, the simultaneous plausibility and unpredictability of its plot, and the importance of its message of survival, perseverance, and ultimate transcendence."

—PAUL MCCOMAS, Midwest Book Award-winning author of
Unplugged, Planet of the Dates, and *Unforgettable*

"Dasha Kelly's *Almost Crimson* is a debut of rare power and grace. Beautifully written, moving, and wonderfully paced. This book is a must read."

—ROB ROBERGE, musician and author of *The Cost of Living*

"*Almost Crimson* is what happens when a storyteller with the deft skills of a glassblower takes something as normal as words and transforms them into intricate works of art. Dasha Kelly has spun a vivid and timeless treasure, as only few writers can do."

—FREDDIE GUTIERREZ, screenwriter for MGM,
Nickelodeon and Warner Brothers

"This book drew me in with increasing power. I couldn't put it down. It's a story of survival and redemption, offering a spark of hope and poetic justice for all the kids that raise themselves from neglect and isolation, and those who dare to reach out with encouragement and generosity. Dasha enchants and ensnares the reader with wry wit, lush imagery, and measured cadence of a true storyteller."

—ASIA FREEMAN, Executive/Artistic Director of Alaska's
award-winning Bunnell Street Art Center

"Readers cannot help but root for CeCe as she struggles, hiding her pain behind grim determination and a strong habit of just putting one foot in front of another—walking onwards and upwards to new beginnings. Thumbs up to Dasha on this tour de force, coming-of-age novel!"

—KIMBERLY GRABA, librarian,
Wisconsin Department of Corrections

DASHA KELLY

ALMOST CRIMSON

A NOVEL

CURBSIDE  SPLENDOR

CURBSIDE SPLENDOR PUBLISHING

Published by Curbside Splendor Publishing, Inc., Chicago, Illinois in 2015.

First Edition
Copyright © 2015 by Dasha Kelly
Library of Congress Control Number: 2014953131

ISBN 978-1940430485
Edited by Karen Craigo
Designed by Alban Fischer
Cover artwork by Mary Osmundsen

Manufactured in the United States of America.

www.curbsidesplendor.com

for BabyCakes and SugarBug

ONE

YARN

CeCe felt her hip buzz. It was the third call. She knew her mother would start picking at that damn finger if she didn't answer one of these calls soon. The last infection was gruesome, and CeCe didn't want to deal with it again.

CeCe and her small team of coworkers stood in a carpeted intersection of their office suite holding what their boss called a flash-forward. According to him, the stand-up, bare-bones briefings saved them all from nearly four hours of bloated conference room meetings each week.

CeCe tugged at her purse strap as her hip vibrated again. She wanted to abandon this circle and escape into the elevator behind them, through the lobby, and into the downstairs diner. She needed to call her mother, and she needed a slice of cake. Now.

CeCe shifted her weight and tried to will a coworker into silence as she unwound a tangled ramble about missed calls, transposed numbers, keynote speaker contracts, and water chestnuts. CeCe tried to make eye contact with her boss to flash her impatience and annoyance. The blathering coworker was young and new and eager to counter every reality these truths might hold.

"Maybe we check out his booking fees through a different agency?" CeCe said, realizing no one was going to stop this child from speaking. Her boss was usually good at shepherding their small, nine-person team. He was being far too generous today, CeCe decided. "That way, we're on his calendar but not locked in to such a crazy high quote. Good thing you pulled those numbers early."

The young associate beamed, nodded and was quiet. The group dismissed and CeCe slipped into the elevator. She waved to the pair of security men as she walked the expansive lobby, breezed through the open doors of the Golden Goose diner, and headed toward a booth in the back. CeCe sat down and pried away her shoes. Beneath the table, she wiggled her toes.

"Heya, CeCe," her waitress, Misha, said from behind the counter. She wore long braid extensions this month, and her signature brilliant red lip gloss, which had too much blue undertone for her complexion. CeCe had tried lobbing cosmetic tips at Misha when she first started working in the building. Much of the advice had been new for CeCe then, too. She'd been eager to evangelize. Misha would always respond with enthusiasm and conviction. Four years later, Misha still sported homegrown experiments of quick weave, color streaks, iridescent makeup powders, and elaborately decorated nails. Like any new convert, CeCe got over herself and her newfound style scriptures and embraced Misha's good nature, red gloss and all.

"I'm good, Misha," CeCe said as her cell phone rang again. She pressed the talk button and spoke into the phone. "Yes, how are you?"

As Misha poured a cup of coffee, CeCe mouthed her order. Cake. CeCe counted on an extra thick slice.

"I know, Mama. I was in a meeting," CeCe said into the phone, digging in the small tray of sugar packets. "I'm sorry you worried."

CeCe emptied two packets and stirred while her mother recounted highlights from her news programs. She had taken to calling CeCe with leading stories or curious statistics, in case the news of Prescott

Public School closings, council meeting decisions, or book reviews might prove helpful in CeCe's work at the management consulting firm. CeCe often reminded her mother there were televisions at the office, but she remained undeterred. CeCe's best friend, Pam, had once pointed out that atonement arrives in many forms.

"Yeah, even Spencer voted for it," CeCe said into the phone, pointing and nodding as Misha stood near the cake domes waving her hand above the pound cake like a model from *The Price Is Right*. CeCe's mother was asking if she was busy after work.

"What do you need?" CeCe said, and mouthed a "thank you" as Misha placed the cake in front of her.

CeCe switched the phone to her other ear, picking up her fork. Her mother was talking about the new knitting class. Or was it crochet? CeCe used her tongue to flatten the bites of cake against the roof of her mouth. She didn't suckle the rich flavor. She let them rest, feeling the sweetness of indulgence ink into her.

"It's fine, Mama," CeCe said, sipping her coffee. She approached the golden edges of the cake, her favorite part. "Yes. It's fine. I'll get it. Yes. Don't worry about it. OK. I'll see you later. Yes. Bye."

CeCe disconnected the call and tucked the phone back into her purse pouch.

"Whatchu goin' to get?" Misha teased as she refilled CeCe's coffee cup. "Something sexy for yo' motorcycle man?"

CeCe snorted at the mention of the bike, and gave a theatrical sigh. "Nah, my mother needs green yarn."

Misha raised her dramatic penciled eyebrow. "Yarn?"

CeCe shrugged. "If green yarn will keep her off the ledge this week, then I need to get the woman green yarn. Everybody wins."

Misha laughed. CeCe ate her cake.

TWO

LIONS

As a small girl, Crimson would walk herself around the apartment, muttering rhyming words for the things she could name. Crimson, or CeCe, liked the way the letters sounded against each other, *couch . . . ouch . . . bed . . . head . . . key . . . see . . .*

Rhyming words. Mrs. Castellanos taught her the rhyme game, and they played it in the courtyard all the time. CeCe wondered if her mother knew about rhyming words. CeCe had learned a lot of things from Mrs. Castellanos that her mother didn't know, like the alphabet song, the Berenstain Bears, and gingersnaps. CeCe had rushed inside one day to tell Mama about the rainbow color no one could see.

"If they can't see it, how do they know it's there?" CeCe had asked.

CeCe's mother, Carla, sat in their kitchen with lake-water eyes fixed on the table. She nudged her left shoulder into a weak shrug.

"They just do, CrimsonBaby," her mother said.

CeCe couldn't remember when her mother became too weak to carry anything but tears. When the Sad started to come, pressing her mother to their bed, her mama cried slick, silent tears for a long, long time. Longer than a game of hopscotch. Longer than singing the alphabet in her head five times. Longer than a nap, even. The Sad made her mother cry all the time.

CeCe wasn't big enough to pry the Sad away from her mama.

Instead, she started to remember for them. After the building manager lady fussed at Mama about their overstuffed mailbox, CeCe remembered to pull the letters every day, even though Mama seldom opened them. When she snapped the last roll of toilet paper on its rod, CeCe remembered to pull the bills with the 20s on them from the bed stand and tuck them in her shoe for her walk to the store. When CeCe could see the Baker family through their apartment window leaving in their dress-up clothes, CeCe remembered to gather Mama's underwear with hers and cover them with soap bubbles in the bathtub.

CeCe remembered to make sandwiches and open cans of fruit cocktail for lunch; she snapped rubber bands and barrettes around thick handfuls of her hair; she whisked their floor with the broom; she sniffed the milk; she wiped the dishes; and she arranged her small troop of dolls into their corner each night.

CeCe's mother was slender with elfin features, to include a spray of cinnamon freckles across her light brown skin. She was not an animated woman by nature, but her density filled the house. When her mother was filled with air and words and winking, CeCe loved the way everything about her mother would soften. There were still exceptional days, like today, when her mother tickled and ate sandwiches with her. CeCe didn't hope for those days anymore, though. Hoping made her ache on the inside of her skin.

"I think there's extra sunshine out there today," her mother said, pulling her hair into its usual ponytail. "Let's go outside to get some!"

CeCe hadn't noticed any extra sun, but nodded in agreement anyway. She watched her mother at first. Ever since the flowers started to push up from the ground in the courtyard, her mother's light might only last a few minutes, instead of the whole morning. Definitely not the whole day anymore. Sometimes, her mother wouldn't last for a whole game of jacks.

CeCe counted to a hundred, listening to her mother chatter while she floated about the apartment—bedroom, kitchen, bathroom, kitchen again. When she reached 101 and her mother was dressed in jeans and a button-down, CeCe allowed the giggles to spread down her elbows and knees. She kept smiling as her mother snapped two Afro puff ponytails on the top of CeCe's head.

They decided to drag their two kitchen chairs out onto the porch slab to eat Cheerios with *extra* sugar. They watched the sun pull itself above the wall of their apartment complex. The residential building had been converted from a senior citizen community to low-income housing the year before CeCe was born. Some of the elderly residents remained, like Mrs. Castellanos, the second-floor widow who befriended CeCe. Most of the residents were young veterans, some with wives and preteens, some with screaming girlfriends, and many with only bottles and brown paper bags.

The building was fashioned like an old motel, an open rectangle lined with all their front doors. CeCe had counted twenty-four doors on the first floor one day and twenty-four doors on the second floor. She knew a little something about the households behind every door. For some, she could peek past their curtained windows when she walked her imaginary pet dragon or chased a toy. Others she observed from their porch slab or the window.

CeCe didn't know most of their neighbors' names, but she recognized all of their faces. Sometimes, the grown-ups said hello to her when they passed, but most had learned she would only reply with a stiff wave. She would have asked their names, but they were strangers. Speaking to them wasn't allowed. Waving, on the other hand, was different.

Her feet swinging beneath her chair, CeCe scooped her cereal and listened to her mother coo about fresh starts and bright beginnings and healing wounds and buried shadows and such. CeCe didn't know what these words would look like, but her mother had been waiting for them to show up for a long time. She was about to turn up her cereal bowl and drink down the sweetened milk when her mother took the bowl from her hands and declared they were going to pick some flowers along the courtyard square.

"You walk that way, and I'll walk this way," her mother said, standing.

Between watching her mother flit along the other side of the courtyard and searching the sidewalk cracks for flowers Mama called "Danny Lions," CeCe hadn't noticed one of their neighbors waving through the window. Mr. Big Mole on His Chin tapped on his windowpane to get her attention. CeCe liked Mr. Big Mole. He had thick auburn sideburns, sparkly eyeglasses, and the coolest bellbottom colors ever. CeCe thought there must be music playing inside his head when he walked, the way he bounced and bumped along their walkway. He didn't have children, but he did have a girlfriend who wore earrings so big, CeCe imagined them as Hula-Hoops. CeCe saw them kissing all the time.

Mr. Big Mole had his thumbs tucked under his armpits, flapping in a funky chicken dance. CeCe burst into tickles of laughter. CeCe looked over to see if her mother was laughing, too. She had rounded her second corner in the courtyard and was moving toward her daughter. Her eyes were cast to the ground, but it didn't look to CeCe like she was looking for flowers anymore. As CeCe got closer, she could see the light in her mother's face being consumed, once again, by textured shadows. When their eyes met, CeCe saw no trace of the smile that had greeted her an hour earlier.

The inside of CeCe's skin began to hurt again and the small clutch of "Danny Lions" seemed woefully misplaced inside her hand.

"Let's go inside now, CrimsonBaby," her mother said. As CeCe took her mother's hand, she looked over her shoulder to wave goodbye to Mr. Big Mole. He waved back, but his smile and funky chicken were gone.

While CeCe placed her clutch of dandelions into a small a Dixie Cup filled with tap water, her mother retreated to their room. CeCe could hear the mattress groan its familiar embrace while she put away the kitchen stepstool. CeCe brought in their chairs, rinsed and put away their cereal bowls, played with her toys, made lunch, walked her dragon, and came back inside to settle herself on the couch with one of the picture books Mrs. Castellanos had given her. CeCe fell asleep there. When she awoke from her nap, CeCe saw her mother next to her, folded into their old armchair with damp knots of tissue scattered around her like spent bullets.

CeCe said nothing, just rose from the couch to wrap her small arms around her mother's neck. Her mother didn't respond to her tight embrace. She never did. Not this version of her mother. CeCe kissed her mother's hair and went into the kitchen. She began her evening ritual of dragging one of the kitchen chairs to the fridge, reaching into the freezer for two frozen dinners, and climbing down to spin the oven dial to 4-2-5. Pushing the chair back to the table, CeCe noticed tufts of yellow winking at her from the garbage can. CeCe's skinned ached again. There was their sunshine morning, tossed in the trash.

Sitting at the table, CeCe finished her dinner while her mother picked absently at the plate compartments. Her mother had begun eating less and less.

"*Why were you sad today, Mama?*"

"*I just am, CrimsonBaby. I just am.*"

THREE

MOSS

CeCe circled the lot. She only parked the behemoth in corner spaces now. Her first month with Aunt Rosie's old Lincoln Town Car had earned CeCe four angry notes pinned beneath her windshield. They were bitter scribbles from drivers who had been forced to climb into back seats and out of windows to escape her car's imposing body. Once, she came out of the movies to find the front bumper hanging in defeat.

Besides negotiating parking lots and navigating the long chariot through traffic, CeCe also learned to ignore the bemusement of her small frame emerging from the oversized ride. Leaving the drug store, yarnless, CeCe heard the familiar cross-lot taunt about a booster seat. She wasn't even inclined to flip them the bird. The day had greeted her with an empty milk container in the fridge, a client ambush as a result of yet another one of Margolis' errors of enthusiasm, being stood up for happy hour, a screaming pinched toe from a pair of shoes that decided to hate her, and a scavenger hunt for green yarn—nylon not acrylic, moss not emerald.

Two stops later, CeCe finally stood in a checkout lane, frustrated that she hadn't driven out to the fabric store in the first place. As she left the register, her cell phone chimed. Looking down at the display screen, CeCe smiled for the first time all day.

"Doris!" she said, slipping sideways past two women blocking the automatic door with their baskets and chatter.

"Kiddo!" Doris replied, the edges of her voice still crumbling from decades of menthol cigarettes. CeCe had met Doris in the smoker's garden, a landscaped corner exclusively for mall employees. CeCe's smoking habit lasted less than three months, but her enchantment with Doris, a spirited middle-aged Jewish woman, would last beyond the years they worked at the mall. Even with Doris all the way in Florida, CeCe felt a welcome, comforting warmth at the sound of her friend's voice.

CeCe had worked at Hip Pocket, selling designer jeans to bony teenage girls and metrosexual college boys. At the other end of the mall, Doris hawked dishwashers and deep freezers at Sears. The two adopted each other straightaway, shifting their midpoint meetings from the smokers' garden to the food court. They ate lunch together every day for four years. A year after CeCe had left Hip Pocket and landed her current job, Doris had announced her move to Florida.

"You're taking a break from your sexy senior singles bingo game to call me?" CeCe teased, angling her car key into its lock.

"Honey, I told you I'm only hanging with the cool old ladies," Doris replied with a laugh, "and we do *not* do bingo."

CeCe could imagine Doris' head tilting back to let that enormous laugh escape, her eyeglass chain glinting in the sunlight. Doris once confessed that her silver chain gave her an edge over the other sales reps because it implied "grandmotherly wisdom."

"My bad," CeCe said, attaching her Bluetooth before turning over the Lincoln's engine. "How are the cool grannies doing? Did Maddie get her driver's license back?"

Doris told CeCe about the gossip and shenanigans of her retirement community and CeCe told Doris about wanting to lock

Margolis in the copy room. CeCe drove the long way home as they talked. They still were chatting incessantly by the time CeCe snaked through the labyrinth of duplexes and four-unit apartments buildings and stretched her car beneath the carport.

"What were you doing out?" Doris asked.

"Mama needed green yarn," CeCe said.

Doris let out another laugh, smaller this time. "Of course she did," she said. "Hey, can you get me from the airport tomorrow around ten forty-five?"

CeCe agreed, and the day's irritations melted away.

FOUR

THURSDAYS

CECE PLAYED IN THE COURTYARD while the lady with scuffed brown shoes talked inside with her mother. She lay on the wrought-iron bench, the front of her body dimpled by the hard lattice pattern. CeCe hung her head over the end of the bench to watch her sundress pucker through the spaces. Shuffling and scooting to align the print patterns on her dress with the crosshatch of the bench, CeCe didn't hear the screen door or the brown shoe footsteps. Just a voice.

"Do you mind if I join you?"

CeCe raised herself with a jump. She knew better than to let a stranger get so close to her. Snapping upright, CeCe could see that the voice belonged to Scuff Shoes. She relaxed a little. Scuff Shoes was technically a stranger, but had been talking with her mother for a long time now. CeCe edged to one side of the bench and smoothed the front of her dress. She watched the woman cautiously.

"What were you looking at?" she asked CeCe.

"My dress."

"What does is look like under there?" Scuff looked down to assess the bench.

"Waffles," CeCe said matter-of-factly.

"Waffles?" Scuff repeated, raising her eyebrows. "Clever girl, Crimson. Clever girl."

DASHA KELLY ‖ 19

Scuff was a stocky woman, sausaged into a maroon skirt suit. CeCe could see the bulge of her trying to leap from behind the buttoned shirt and blazer. Scuff introduced herself as Tanya Boylin, a social services agent who came to make sure CeCe would be enrolled for school.

"Like the big kids?" CeCe asked, wrinkling her nose and letting her heavy plaits pull her head to one side. She was the youngest person in the complex, but watched the older kids head off with their books and satchels.

"Crimson," Boylin continued, with a chuckle. "You *are* a big kid. That means you get to go to school, too."

CeCe felt her insides tingle. Some lost inner layer begin to warm. *School.*

"Am I going to school tomorrow?" CeCe asked, hopping down from the bench.

"Not tomorrow," Boylin said, smiling as she hoisted one thick leg over the other. "School isn't open yet, Crimson, but it will be soon. We want to make sure you're ready for the first day."

"How many Thursdays?" CeCe asked.

"Thursdays?" Boylin repeated, her cheery smile fading. "Do you mean how many weeks?"

"Thursdays," CeCe corrected, pulling her own short legs onto the bench and crossing her ankles into a pretzel. After a moment, CeCe remembered Mrs. Castellanos and tugged at her sundress to cover her panties. "I don't want to miss school when it opens, so I have to count my Thursday tabs."

Boylin regarded CeCe for a long time, reading her rounded, pecan features as if doing some kind of ancient calculations. Finally she asked, "Would you mind showing me your tabs, Crimson?"

Without another word, CeCe returned her sneakered feet to the dusty ground and headed toward the apartment door. Boylin followed. Carla sat with her arms folded atop their kitchen table, staring into a cup of coffee. She didn't look up when CeCe and Boylin walked by, but CeCe hadn't expected her to.

In the bedroom CeCe and Carla shared, she moved to stand beside a wall calendar from a neighborhood deli. "If you want the best, buy your meat from Burgess!" was scripted across the top with a photo of the butcher store's front window. Boylin commented that she passed the shop all the time when she came to visit other little kids in CeCe's neighborhood.

The complimentary calendar, with tear-pad sheets for each month, was from the previous year. December 1975 was the only square sheet still fastened to the thick cardboard. The rigid calendar sat on a slim strip of wall between the bed and the tall chest of drawers. Dangling from the same single nail holding the outdated calendar was a long chain of soda can tabs.

There was a blue milk crate on the floor in the corner. Boylin slowly entered the room as CeCe pulled out the crate and climbed on top. She still had to stretch her arms to reach a handle-less coffee cup resting on the otherwise bare dresser top. CeCe hooked her tiny wrists to the edge of this mammoth pine chest, her hands patient and relaxed as Boylin moved in closer.

"I have this many Thursdays," CeCe said, tipping the coffee cup toward Boylin to show its content of soda can pull tabs.

"Can you tell me about this cup and the Thursdays, Crimson?" Boylin asked, perplexed.

CeCe teetered on the blue crate to turn and face the nail in the wall, holding its outdated calendar and chain of soda pop tabs. CeCe was careful as a schoolteacher as she explained how she moved the tabs from the cup to the wall every Thursday, after walking with Mrs. Castellanos to the store for her lottery tickets and small groceries.

"When I have only one left, then I'll know to get ready for Santa," CeCe said, tapping the chain absently. Watching it swing, CeCe turned to Boylin, eyes wide with a sudden realization. "Do you know about Santa Claus?"

Boylin smiled and confirmed that, indeed, she knew all about Santa Claus.

"How did you hear about him?" Boylin asked.

"Ms. Cas-teanose."

"Mrs. Castellanos?"

CeCe nodded.

"She told me all about Santa after I missed him last time."

"You missed him, honey?" Boylin asked, amusement fading from her eyes.

"Mmmhmm," Cece replied, giving a small nod. "And he only comes one time every year, y'know."

"You make sure you ask for your mama's permission before you eat this, *dulce*," Mrs. Castellanos said each week before handing CeCe her weekly salary of fruit punch soda and a Chick-O-Stick for helping with her grocery bags.

"OK," CeCe said. They both knew CeCe's mother never heard about the treats.

CeCe enjoyed Mrs. Castellanos. She knew lots of songs and made up smart games. She had sat next to CeCe one day in the courtyard when she was four and stayed her friend ever since. CeCe didn't have any other friends, since the other kids were so much older and she and her mother didn't know any other kids. CeCe only waved at Mrs. Castellanos for a long time. When she introduced herself to CeCe, offering to read her a story the next day, CeCe had been thrilled.

Mrs. Castellanos read stories in her decorated accent, still waxed heavy with Puerto Rican roots. Sometimes, CeCe would play quietly on the bench next to her while Mrs. Castellanos read a newspaper. One week she didn't meet CeCe out in the courtyard and CeCe thought she had somehow made her friend angry.

"Last Thursday was Christmas, *dulce*," Mrs. Castellanos said, squatting next to CeCe on the dusty ground next to the bench. "Don't you remember when Santa came to visit?"

CeCe pinched her face together trying to remember a visit.

Mrs. Castellanos gasped a little. "*Dulce CeCe*, you didn't get anything from Santa for Christmas?" she asked.

CeCe shook her head slowly, beginning to wonder if she was in trouble somehow. She didn't know anything about this Claus.

CeCe sat with her friend until lunchtime, until CeCe's stomach was empty and her mind full of images of happy, fat men hauling around gifts with her name on them. Mrs. Castellanos told her good little girls were allowed to send their wishes to Santa, too. Having her mother back was CeCe's number one wish. Roller skates was her second.

"When is he coming back?" CeCe asked.

"We've got a ways to go, *dulce*," Mrs. Castellanos said, watching the cloud fill the child's face. "Christmas is always December twenty-fifth and that was only one week ago. We have to wait until next year."

CeCe considered.

"How long is that?"

"A year?" Mrs. Castellanos asked. "One year is the same as fifty-two weeks, *dulce*."

CeCe thought some more.

"Is that soon?"

Mrs. Castellanos took in a breath and thought. She crossed arms across her massive breasts and drummed her fingertips until an idea came to her.

"On Thursday when we walk to the store, that will be one week," she had said. "And the next Thursday will be another week—"

"—And after . . . fifty-two Thursdays Santa will come back?" CeCe chimed.

Mrs. Castellanos beamed. "Yes, *dulce*."

"Is fifty-two a long time?"

"It can feel like a long time sometimes, *dulce*," Mrs. Castellanos laughed.

Ms. Boylin now sat on the hard, square bed, facing CeCe and her rudimentary calendar. She could see now that December 25, 1975, had been circled.

"Did you do this, Crimson?"

"No," she said, unsettling her thick plaits with a shake. "Mama showed me where Christmas was after I told her about Santa. I don't think she knew about him either, because she cried about missing him, too."

"And, so, you count the Thursdays with this chain so you and your mama won't miss Santa, is that right, Crimson?"

Another rattle of braids.

"How many Thursdays are left in the cup?

"Thirty-three."

"How many Thursdays are on the chain?"

"Nineteen."

"That was a lot of fruit punch, huh?" Boylin said, with a wink.

CeCe ducked her head with a grin.

"You're a very bright girl to have figured this out all by yourself," Ms. Boylin said.

CeCe released her second broad smile of the morning. "Ms. Cas-teanose calls me 'bright,' too," she said. "I like it. Makes me feel like I have magic inside."

"Sweetheart, you *do* have magic inside you. You absolutely do."

CeCe returned to the courtyard bench while Ms. Boylin spoke with her mother again. She tried to press all of Ms. Boylin's words against her memory: bus stop, state law, gifted class, private school, scholarship, development, future, foster care. CeCe could tell these were all serious words, but she knew her mother wouldn't hear any of them. She had to remember.

Ms. Boylin came outside and walked to Cece on the bench. When she spoke, Cece was taken in by the warmth of her hazel eyes. Her lashes were long and her lips glistened pink. She had a tiny mole on her left temple, which CeCe hadn't noticed before. She wondered if all the extra nice grown-ups had moles.

"It was very nice to meet you, Crimson," she said. "I'm going to see you again in a week to make sure you're all ready for school, and then I'm going to see you again the week after that to tell you all about your class. We'll even make sure you have a new dress. How do you like that?"

CeCe beamed her approval.

"Will Mama get a new dress, too?" she asked after a moment.

"No, Crimson," Ms. Boylin said. "Only big kids like you can go to kindergarten. Grown-ups like me and your mama aren't allowed anymore."

CeCe's face began to cloud with a realization.

"She's gonna be all by herself?" CeCe asked. "The Sad doesn't let her remember stuff so good."

"Your mama's sad a lot, isn't she, Crimson?"

CeCe's braids rocked forward and back slowly.

"Does that make you scared?"

Side to side with the braids. Boylin grinned a little.

"You're a brave girl, Crimson. I tell you what, though, things are going to get better around here for you and your mother, OK? We're going to get you into school with other bright children, and we're also going to get someone to help your mother get rid of her sadness. How does that sound?"

CeCe felt a slow smile stretch between her ears.

"Like Christmas," she said.

FIVE

SQUISH

DORIS STOOD OUT LIKE A neon light amid the crowd of travelers jockeying for curb space. She was easy to spot, with her inflated ash-streaked hair, Christmas-red lips, and a face-eating brooch that Doris had pinned high on her shoulder instead of her lapel. She had always reveled in becoming a caricature of herself.

They embraced, young woman and old, before CeCe lowered Doris' overnight bag into the trunk.

"That's all?" CeCe said, standing by Doris' passenger door.

"I only needed my thong and a toothbrush," Doris said.

"No," CeCe laughed. "No. I do not approve."

"Stop being a hater," Doris said.

They cruised along the expressway, chatting about Doris' twins, now married, and CeCe's mother, now compelled by crafts projects at the independent living center. Dr. Harper told CeCe her mother responded well to the mixed company of the center, not just depressives. CeCe was about to ask for any updates on mall gossip when Doris interrupted.

"Get off on Parker," she said.

"What? No dim sum from the Emperor's Throne?" CeCe said.

Doris smiled. "Maybe tomorrow."

Doris' turn-by-turn directions carried them beyond the shopping center to a residential neighborhood of bungalows. CeCe parked in front of a gray house with lavender trim.

"Cute house," CeCe said. "You used to live out here, right?"

"Yep, right here," Doris said, looking past CeCe at the house.

CeCe parked on the curb and followed Doris up the walkway of flat granite circles. A black sedan was parked in the driveway and Doris stooped to brazenly peer inside. They continued past the empty car and reached the porch. CeCe was surprised when Doris pushed open the front door without even ringing the bell first.

CeCe hadn't expected to find the house empty. She knew Doris had always hated the idea of renting this little house to strangers, and remembered listening to her friend complain about the "trolls and cavemen" she'd been interviewing as tenants. She had asked CeCe to move in, but CeCe couldn't afford the rent and hadn't had transportation to get herself and her mother around from this end of the city. Now, her friend's tenant had skipped out on her. CeCe had witnessed plenty of couches, lamps, and laundry baskets filled with clothes sneaking away in the middle of the night in the final years at her and her mother's old apartment.

CeCe closed the door behind them as Doris' soft-sole shoes squished across the hardwood floor to the oversized window overlooking the back yard. CeCe knew how much Doris loved this little house. It had been a victory for her in every possible way: engineering a divorce from her philandering husband of nearly twenty years, and stumbling into an intimate clique of socialites who paid her handsomely to clean their condos and, ultimately, provide a bit of homespun therapy while they hunted for the next prenuptial agreement. Doris had bought this house, her first, with part of what she earned from the Ladies, as she called them. She never gave CeCe hard numbers, but CeCe had long estimated that Doris' job at Sears was simply for insurance and rainy-day money. She'd purchased other properties, her condo in Florida and homes for her sons, but this one was special, and CeCe was saddened for her friend.

CeCe fiddled awkwardly with her keys, not sure if Doris would want space or a hug. She watched Doris take in a slow, deep breath before turning around. Her face was full of light and whimsy.

"Take a look around, kiddo," Doris said with a smile. "I gotta go see a man about a horse."

"I'm a ranch hand now?" a man's voice called from the kitchen.

Doris laughed and squish-squished toward the kitchen door, saying, "You can be a cowboy, if that makes you feel better . . . "

CeCe shook her head as Doris disappeared into the doorway that held the man's voice. Whatever happened with her tenant, CeCe thought, Doris had it under control. CeCe couldn't be surprised. Since the day Doris had adopted her in the smokers' garden more than seven years ago, CeCe had always known Doris to have a plan. Whether convincing mall management to support a cross-store secret Santa tradition, helping her youngest son secure a grant for a conservation study in Belize, coaching CeCe through her first attempts at dating, or researching retirement communities in Florida, Doris was always thinking about the next move. Doris had once told Cece that after spending half of her life doing as she was told, she was now intent on creating her own pathways out of this world. CeCe often wondered what such an assembly of thoughts might feel like.

SIX

MONSTER

CeCe's stomach jumped and flipped beneath her new dress. It was green with a rainbow on the left edge of its hem. CeCe didn't even care that it had someone else's name written on the tag.

"Nobody will know but you, CrimsonBaby," her mother said.

CeCe was most excited that the Sad had released her mother for a day, long enough to go with CeCe to her new school. The two of them waited on the corner next to their building, on the side of the street with the record shop and not the side with the hardware store, as Ms. Boylin had instructed. The yellow bus drove past them on Kennedy without slowing down at all. CeCe and her mother watched the bus whisk by in gaped-mouth panic.

"It's coming around!" a man's voice called. Across the street, in front of the hardware store, a small gray-haired man at the newspaper stand perched on his stool with a daily relaxed in his hands. "The school buses aren't allowed to stop on the boulevard so the driver has to make his turn on Sixty-Fifth."

CeCe looked up to her mother and Carla nodded at the newspaperman. CeCe was relieved her mother was still here. The Sad could wrap itself around her so quickly. They turned toward the whine of bus brakes and watched it lumber around the corner.

"Thank you!" CeCe called out to the newspaperman as the bus pulled in front of them. The newspaperman nodded and waved.

The only passengers, CeCe and her mother settled themselves in a center seat, holding hands as they watched the familiar landmarks of their neighborhood unfold into new stretches of storefronts and rows of houses.

CeCe counted twelve stops between their corner and the school. There were thirty-two kids on their bus and six mothers. CeCe counted mostly big kids. The smallest ones, like CeCe, had their mothers by their sides, too. The kids exchanged terrified glances with CeCe, while the mothers looked in her direction with a flash of some different kind of fear, like finding a spider on the kitchen floor and then realizing it was just a sprig of yarn.

CeCe smiled wide at each mom. Most smiled back.

CeCe marveled at the bigger kids as if they were mythical wonders. The big kids in their building were older, high schoolers mostly. These were little kids, but still bigger than her. Their laughter boarded the bus before their bodies, and CeCe was mesmerized by the music of their banter about videos and bug bites and older sisters and lunch money. They all looked in CeCe's direction before choosing their seats, but none of them spoke. She didn't know the stranger rule applied to other kids.

CeCe looked up at her mother after the twelfth stop, to make sure her eyes were still looking at these close-up things. CeCe knew her mother was being held down by the Sad when her eyes seemed to be searching for only faraway things. Her mother's eyes were still seeing the close-up things. In fact, her mother's eyes were sharp, moving slowly from one passenger to the next. CeCe could tell from the hard lines of her jaw that her mother did not plan to love school like CeCe.

The bus rounded the corner of a lush, expansive park. The older children began to bristle with even more excited chatter. This must be it. Neil Armstrong Elementary School, where Ms. Boylin said CeCe would learn more numbers, the names for more colors, new places, and, most importantly, how to read. CeCe began to fidget in her seat, too, as they pulled into the yellow school bus queue.

The front of the school had a large, arched portico with letters that CeCe would later learn spelled "Neil Armstrong Elementary." The buses spilled children and mothers onto the pavement. Big kids raced under the archway and into the school. CeCe's feet wanted to run, too, but they were arrested with an unfamiliar panic. She didn't know what to do. Ms. Boylin said she would know what to do once she got to school, but she didn't. There weren't any instructions pressed into her brain. She started to get scared about her new school.

CeCe felt her mother give her hand a little squeeze and CeCe looked up to see her mother's eyes still sharp, looking down at her. CeCe felt better, less like a wind might sweep her away. She followed the gentle pull of her mother's hand away from the portico and toward a loose cluster of other mothers and kids. They were small, like CeCe, gathered around a tall man with a billow of sandy curls.

The fun-hair man was named Mr. Neumann. He was the principal, the person in charge of Neil Armstrong Elementary School, CeCe understood, the same way their apartment manager was in charge of all the mail and rent and shoveling and broken door handles. Mr. Neumann explained to the eager mothers how the vice principal usually welcomed the younger classes, but she'd fallen at home that morning and broken her ankle.

"I'll do my best to fill in for her," he was saying, "but I'll need to make sure the hallways are clear for the first bell. The upper elementary students are excitable on the first day."

Mr. Neumann was not as fun as his hair, CeCe thought. He wore brown slacks, a white dress shirt, and a steel-blue necktie, and she wondered how someone with such soft, springy hair didn't smile more. CeCe folded in closer to her mother and was relieved to feel her mother's hand rest on her bare shoulder. Looking around, CeCe noticed her classmates' stares. Their eyes were blue, hazel, amber-brown, and green. They didn't have any smiles in their eyes, either. CeCe pressed harder against her mother.

Mr. Neumann spoke stiffly to the mothers about pickups, parents' day, and the hours for the school nurse. Looking at his watch, he turned to walk toward the school, waving a hand for the small group to follow. They trailed him through the wide double doors and into the school. He stopped in front of a room with a number six affixed to the door. He rapped lightly before opening.

Inside, a slender young woman with long, wavy red hair kneeled beside a bin filled with colored blocks. As she stood to her full height, CeCe felt the woman's smile get bigger until it filled the room. CeCe felt her first surge of genuine excitement. This was her teacher. This was their classroom. CeCe was really in school.

CeCe entered the room with the rest of her class, stepping gingerly onto colorful tiles as if the floor might collapse beneath her tiny sneakers. She turned to see her mother halted at the door. Her eyes were moist. CeCe's smile froze.

Her mother raised her hand to CeCe and mouthed, "I'm OK." She smiled to CeCe, the biggest CeCe could remember in a long time. CeCe bolted toward the door and barreled into her mother with her very best hug. A few other kids did the same, and the mothers were pleased. Their teacher, Ms. Lapham, invited all of the children to join her at the front of the class, where they waved good-bye together to all the mothers.

At 12:15, as promised, Ms. Lapham's class wiggled in an almost-straight line on the sidewalk where Mr. Neumann had gathered them that morning. Mothers retrieved their progeny one by one, dispersing into station wagons and sedans and onto yellow buses. CeCe saw her mother waiting, picking absently at her fingernails until she spotted CeCe's caramel face in the row of vanilla crème.

CeCe's mother held out her hand and CeCe held tightly, and they walked to their bus in silence. Her mother had caught the city bus to the school, like she said she would, and CeCe was relieved to have her there. Once they were settled into their seats and the yellow bus had pulled itself around the ball field, CeCe's nestled into the crook of her mother's arm. They watched the green lawns peel away to concrete in silence until they dismounted in front of the record store once again. The newspaperman was already gone for the day.

"So . . . " her mother began once their feet were on the sidewalk, "how was your first day of school?"

"OK," CeCe replied, looking down at her sneakers peeking from beneath her green rainbow dress.

"Did you learn any new songs?"

CeCe shook her head no, her new green barrettes dancing above her shoulders.

"Was your teacher nice?"

CeCe nodded emphatically, shaking the green barrettes.

"Did you make a new friend?"

CeCe's barrettes quieted. They crossed through the small lobby of their apartment building and to their front door. CeCe knew her mother didn't move quickly anymore, but this time, she really wanted her mother to hurry. This time, CeCe needed her mother to move like the pee-pee dance. CeCe needed her to swing open their door so she could place her feet back on their floor. Sit on their couch. Hold her crayons. She didn't like being on this side of their door anymore.

As her mother fumbled with the lock, CeCe's small shoulders began to tremble. She felt the quiver work itself from inside her sneakers, up her knees, through her tummy, around the collar of her green dress, and into her thick plaits. She thought, again, of the block letters on her dress tag. Maybe the other kids had excluded her from games and turned their chairs away from her because they knew her dress really belonged to a girl named Lorraine. Her mother had said no one would know, but CeCe could tell they had figured it out.

The first fat tears rolled down CeCe's cheeks as her mother held open the door. CeCe wanted to race inside, but could not force her feet to move. She was seized by a gale of tears, and her mother had to take her hand to pull her into the apartment. CeCe collapsed onto the couch into her mother's lap. They stayed that way for a long time, until CeCe's peals diminished to whimpers. CeCe didn't know she had so many tears inside her.

Just like Mama.

As CeCe regained her breathing, she felt her mother's hands on her shoulders gently pulling her upright. Her mother's eyes weren't as sharp as they'd been that morning, but they were looking down at CeCe. Close up. With a smile hanging faintly on the tips of her lashes.

"What's the matter, CrimsonBaby?" her mother asked.

"Nobody wanted to be my friend," CeCe started, feeling her lip begin to pout again, the wails begin to mount again. "They were so mean, Mama. I didn't do anything to anybody!" CeCe's small brown face was slick with tears.

"Nobody, CrimsonBaby?" her mother asked. Her voice did not thicken, unaccustomed to the race of adrenaline, but her body responded to her child's tears. "Not even the other black children?"

Slow swing of barrettes.

"They said I was a . . . a . . . ghetto girl!" CeCe said, wailing. "I don't even know what that is!"

"Oh, CrimsonBaby," her mother said.

CeCe let her mother rock her side to side on their couch.

"It's going to be hard, but I want you to try not to stay angry with the kids in your class," she said. "A lot of them were taught the wrong way to treat people."

"They were?" CeCe asked, her brow crinkling at the thought of her mother or Mrs. Castellanos teaching her anything wrong or upside down.

CeCe's mother nodded, wiping away tears with the whole of her palm.

"Some grown-ups are rotten on the inside," her mother said. CeCe thought her mother's voice felt far away this time, instead of her eyes. "Still so full of hate and teaching it to their babies now. Monsters. Hateful monsters."

"Ms. Weathers?" a feathery voice lilted behind CeCe and her mother. It was Friday afternoon, the last day of their first week at Armstrong.

They turned to face Ms. Lapham, her long dark waves pulled back in one long French braid. CeCe beamed up at her teacher. Her mother, weary, responded with a faint and placid smile.

"You can call me Carla," CeCe's mother said, placing both hands on CeCe's shoulders.

"Oh, thanks, Carla," Ms. Lapham said, smiling sheepishly. "You'd be surprised at how many parents aren't comfortable with first names."

CeCe's mother raised her eyebrows and gave a slight nod. In spite of her soft tone, CeCe could feel her mother's fingers growing tense as the draped over her shoulders.

"Carla," Ms. Lapham continued, nervousness now lacing the edges of her voice. "Would you mind if we went inside to chat for a moment? There's something I'd like to discuss with you."

CeCe felt her mother begin to move and then decide not to commit. Her fingers were firm on CeCe's shoulders. CeCe looked up and saw her mother's head swivel slowly to look around them. Children were chasing one another beneath the portico, two teachers stood in the front doorway talking, parents were calling their children into station wagons, and a few mothers were standing close by, like they were hoping to hear a secret.

CeCe's mother turned to face Ms. Lapham.

"We can talk here."

"Oh," Ms. Lapham blinked. "Well, um . . . what I wanted to talk with you about, um, is that a, um . . . situation has unfolded this week."

CeCe's mother nodded for her to continue.

"It seems CeCe may have, um . . . taken something she, um . . . heard at home out of context and, um . . . it's become something of an, um . . . issue among the children."

As Ms. Lapham fidgeted with the drawstrings of her peasant blouse, CeCe turned toward the sound of movement. She watched the other mothers inching closer, trying to get nearer to the secret her mother was getting from Ms. Lapham.

CeCe's mother was quiet, but CeCe could feel her mother's body harden.

Ms. Lapham cleared her throat, her eyes also taking in the encroaching mothers.

"CeCe seems to think some of the other children are, um . . . half-monster, and it's turned into quite the firestorm with the other families."

CeCe's mother turned now, slowly, to face the other mothers. They were out, CeCe thought. Caught moving, like red light, green light.

"Nothing out of context," CeCe's mother spoke over her shoulder.

The other mothers were no longer pretending not to eavesdrop. CeCe watched them gasping, looking to one another, crossing their arms, moving ever closer. Ms. Lapham continued.

"Yes, well, the children were upset because CeCe was so . . . *convincing* . . . about the whole monster business. Many of them—"

"Let me guess," Carla interrupted, returning her focus to Ms. Lapham. "Many of them went home crying? Like my daughter has done every day?"

CeCe looked up at Ms. Lapham. She felt her stomach tighten in perverse anticipation, like knowing the jester would leap from the jack-in-the-box at any moment. One more crank of the handle. One more. One more.

The mothers bristled and mumbled. Ms. Lapham's face was a deep red.

"Here we go," huffed a mother's voice.

CeCe felt her mother's torso turn. CeCe turned with her to see the other black mother, Mrs. Johnson, yank her purse strap to her shoulder and summon for her kids, the twins in CeCe's class.

"Michael? Michelle?" the other mother called. "Let's go."

CeCe felt a low rumble against the back of her head. She felt her mother's hands leave her shoulders and turned to see her mother crossing her arms and turning to face Mrs. Johnson.

"Please go," CeCe's mother said. "You're the worst of them all."

"Excuse me?" Mrs. Johnson said, tugging again at her purse strap as she turned to face CeCe's mother.

"I expected these white folks to be themselves," CeCe's mother said without flourish, "but it's inexcusable that the *black* woman didn't teach her *black* children to embrace their only *black* classmate."

Mrs. Johnson leveled a look of contempt in their direction. "I don't have to—"

CeCe's mother slowly turned away. Her full back faced Mrs. Johnson and her hands returned to CeCe's shoulders.

"Is there anything else?" she asked Ms. Lapham in a slow, level tone.

"I suppose not," Ms. Lapham said with a swallow. CeCe watched her teacher's eyes flit from mother to mother. "I just, um . . . wanted to . . . um, that should be—"

"Don't turn your back when I'm talking to you!" Mrs. Johnson said, her barbed words lobbed from behind their heads and landing in the middle of them all with a thud. CeCe peeked past her mother's hip to see Mrs. Johnson moving toward them. She wasn't a big woman, but to CeCe she looked like she was filled with hard metals and glass. Her facial features and limbs jutted with sharp edges of bone. Even the corners of her eyes and mouth pulled upward into points. CeCe didn't doubt Mrs. Johnson had a monster inside of her.

"Who do you think you are?" Mrs. Johnson continued, stepping around them to assume the space where Ms. Lapham had stood. CeCe watched her teacher scurry into the school building. The circle of other mothers began to drift backwards.

CeCe's mother did not move. She kept her fading eyes on the woman.

"What makes you think—" Mrs. Johnson had raised a finger to continue her rant.

"No," CeCe's mother said, with a definitive, single shake of her head. "I'm not helping you dance for these people."

"Now, you listen to me," Mrs. Johnson began, her body wilting into a familiar curve of hands on hips and neck on a slow rotation. CeCe pressed herself into her mother's legs as Mrs. Johnson continued to raise her voice at her mother.

"I said no!" CeCe's mother shouted. "I'm not about to help you shuck and jive for these white folks!" CeCe snapped her chin upward to look at her mother. She'd never heard her mother yell before. Now she was afraid, not for what could happen next but for the final dregs of energy she knew had escaped her mother at that moment.

"Don't worry," CeCe's mother continued, reaching for CeCe's hand and leveling her voice again. "You can still be their token darkie."

The collective gasp inside the portico seemed to suck in all of the wind, weather, and energy circling the elementary school.

"Ladies!" a man's voice approached them. CeCe turned to see Mr. Neumann and Ms. Lapham dashing into their circle.

"You know-nothing bitch," growled Mrs. Johnson, glaring at CeCe's mother before turning toward the school building.

"I'm sure that's what your little friends call you behind your back," CeCe's mother said at full volume, "when they're not calling you 'nigger,' of course."

CeCe's eyes opened wide when Mrs. Johnson whirled around and shoved her mother's shoulders. CeCe's mother toppled backward to the ground.

"Mrs. Johnson!" Mr. Neumann shouted. CeCe watched as everyone around her covered their mouths.

Ms. Lapham rushed to CeCe while Mr. Neumann stepped in front of Mrs. Johnson. CeCe's mother raised herself onto her elbows, pausing to catch her breath. Before reaching for Mr. Neumann's outstretched hand, CeCe's mother looked up piteously at Mrs. Johnson and shook her head.

"But you want these people to believe *my* daughter is 'ghetto.'"

All heads, tsk-tsk-ing, turned to Mrs. Johnson and then looked away. Mr. Neumann helped CeCe's mother to her feet. She met CeCe's tearful gaze and nodded.

I'm OK, she mouthed to CeCe. CeCe allowed herself to breathe.

"Your mama is mean," the twin boy, Michael, said to CeCe as the three children waited inside the classroom. Their mothers, their teacher, and the principal were all in the office sorting things out. That's what Ms. Lapham had called it when she deposited CeCe and the twins in her classroom and spread out crayons, papers, and the big bin of blocks.

"No, she's not!" CeCe said. "*Your* mama is mean!"

CeCe and Michael sat on the floor in front of the storybooks with their short legs splayed in front of them. The other twin, Michelle, sat at a table on one of the tiny yellow chairs and cradled her sad face in her chunky little hands.

"Both our mamas are gonna get in trouble," Michelle said.

"Maybe," CeCe offered after a moment. "Maybe you only got a little monster in you."

Michael, whose skin was dark as espresso, turned toward CeCe. His mouth was tight with disapproval.

"I ain't got *no* monster in me," he said, stuffing his arms into an angry twist across his slight body. When splitting cells, he had assumed the thinness genes while his twin had staked claim on all the beauty.

"Yeah, we ain't no monsters," Michelle said, her tone still softer than her brother's. "We didn't know you was gonna get mad about living in the ghetto."

"But I don't live in the ghetto," CeCe said.

"How come none of us ever seen you before, huh?" Michael demanded. "You don't play at the park, you don't go to the church, you don't come to any of the birthday parties. My mama said you don't live around here. She said you were bussed from the ghetto."

"Your mama don't know what she's talking about," CeCe said. "I live at 6723 East Fountain Drive." CeCe announced her address proudly. She'd practiced memorizing it for more than a week.

The Johnson twins looked at each other, with surprise.

"That sounds nice," Michelle said, her face brightening a bit.

"Yeah, I guess so," Michael conceded, uncrossing his arms. He swallowed. "I'm sorry for calling you a ghetto kid."

"Me, too," said Michelle, moving to sit with CeCe and her brother on the floor.

CeCe beamed, and apologized for ever calling them monsters.

"I'll bring my jacks again tomorrow, if you want," CeCe said.

"Yeah!" said Michelle. "We keep losing the ball for our jacks."

"*You* keep losing the ball," Michael corrected.

"Shut up!" Michelle said.

CeCe laughed at them both.

By the time their mothers appeared in the classroom, the children were sprawled across the colorful carpet with sheets of paper scattered all about them like oversized squares of confetti. Each had a fistful of colored pencils, and they were pointing and swapping and challenging and laughing as five-year-olds should.

"Children," Ms. Lapham said, walking past the mothers. "Let's pick up our papers and put away the pencils, OK? It's time to go now."

The children obeyed their teacher and began cleaning up while they chattered and skipped throughout the room.

The afternoon classes had been combined and released onto the playground for an early recess, in light of the fracas that had consumed their teachers and rooms. These new faces were assembled into impressively straight lines under the portico. CeCe could see them through the glass door.

"Are those your afternoon kids, Miss Lapham?" Michelle asked.

"Yes, and I think they're ready to come inside now," Ms. Lapham said. "Why don't you kids do me a favor and hold the door open for them."

The twins raced the short distance to the school doors and wrestled them open. CeCe stayed behind to take her mother's hand.

"I wanted to let you know how sorry I am about this whole incident," Ms. Lapham said. "I feel horrible that I didn't recognize what was happening before it turned this . . . um . . . ugly."

The two mothers were standing several paces from one other in the hallway, forcing Ms. Lapham to pivot and speak to them.

"Ms. Weathers—"

"Carla."

The teacher smiled. "Carla, I'll be more attentive from this point forward about any, um . . . racial issues between the children. The only explanation I can offer is that, well, we haven't really experienced this kind of thing before."

Ms. Lapham spun to face Mrs. Johnson. "I mean, the children have been exposed to other, um . . . cultures before. It's just that most of these kids have known each other their whole lives. I can only presume those, um . . . issues were smoothed out elsewhere."

"Ms. Lapham—" CeCe's mother began.

"Heather."

"*Heather,*" CeCe's mother gave a weary smile to Ms. Lapham. "I doubt the issue was ever smoothed out, but we'll get there."

"I promise to do my part," Ms. Lapham said, extending a handshake to both mothers. CeCe's mother clasped her palm with both hands while Mrs. Johnson only offered a stiff pinch with the pads of her fingers.

As the Johnsons walked away, the twins turned to wave at CeCe while their mother moved like a rain cloud.

"Bye, Michael! Bye, Michelle!" she called.

CeCe felt her mother squeeze her hand and they left the school building and stepped into the warm autumn sun.

In the days and weeks following that first week of school, CeCe's mother retreated into the Sad. She didn't ride with CeCe to school, but walked her to the bus stop. By the time Christmas came, CeCe was walking to the bus stop alone. The newspaperman, Mr. Curtis, let her sit next to him while she waited. He let her read the funny pages, but she had to give them back when the bus came. CeCe liked Mr. Curtis. He didn't have lots of stories and questions, like Mrs. Castellanos, but his quiet was just as fun. CeCe would even visit Mr. Curtis' stand during the summers, too. By the time she was a second-grader, Mr. Curtis was letting CeCe keep the funny pages, and the word search. Mr. Curtis even told CeCe about the city bus.

"You can get all the books you want at the library," he said. "Just a five-minute ride. Straight down Kennedy."

When CeCe took the twenties from the nightstand for her grocery trips, she started to keep the change for her bus fare in a separate jar. Her mother would have said it was all right, but CeCe had stopped asking her mother things. Sometimes, CeCe would read her library books aloud to her mother's silhouette. Mostly, she read to herself while her mother let the hours and days and sunshine and music and holidays evaporate above their heads.

SEVEN

DEWEY

ON THE SECOND DAY OF third grade, a sixth-grader came into CeCe's new classroom with a note. Before the teacher called her name, CeCe knew to gather her notebook and pencil box. The sixth-grade emissaries had started coming for her at the end of first grade. The note usually directed CeCe to the vice principal's office, where she questioned CeCe about wearing summer dresses in cold weather, bringing a can of sardines for lunch, her father's place of work, and how often her mother read to her at night. In second grade, Armstrong Elementary welcomed a new person called a guidance counselor. During that year, CeCe's summons included this counselor and someone from outside the school, called a caseworker.

CeCe didn't mind the guidance counselor, Ms. Patterson, because she talked to CeCe about books and old movies and baking.

"I love to make the fancy cakes," Ms. Patterson said one day, "but the best ones to eat are the simple ones. Pound cake is my favorite."

CeCe didn't care as much for the caseworkers. They never had stories for her, only sly questions. CeCe didn't like how they asked questions, as if trying to be her friend, and then wrote down everything she said. Her other friends didn't scribble her words into folders. Mr. Curtis. Ms. Patterson. Mrs. Castellanos. They listened to her. Talked to her. Hugged her. Taught her things. These caseworkers weren't like that at all.

Worse, CeCe had a feeling they didn't like her, either. She asked Ms. Patterson one day why they came to pick on her, and did they talk to all the students.

"Not all the students," Ms. Patterson had said. "Just the ones we really care about and want to make extra sure they're OK."

CeCe had felt special. She answered their questions.

She hadn't expected the caseworker interviews to begin so early in the year. The first week of school wasn't even finished and CeCe was already heading to the front office. She took the hall pass and walked the hallway to Ms. Patterson's office. CeCe took her seat in the orange plastic chair and waited, humming the chorus of "Silent Night."

There was no secretary, like in the main office, just a row of chairs outside two closed doors. One door led to Ms. Patterson's office and the other was used for conferences, detention, and sitting with caseworkers.

The door to Ms. Patterson's office opened and another student left, clutching a stack of notebooks to her chest. It looked to CeCe like she'd been crying. Ms. Patterson, on the other hand, emerged with a wide-mouthed smile. She was a rectangular woman, with large heavy hands. She didn't wear much makeup, only color on her lips and mascara on her lashes, but she always wore a suit. She seemed tough at first but, to CeCe, had been soft as summer grass.

"CeCe! How's it going, sprite?" Ms. Patterson asked. CeCe said things were good and stood to let Ms. Patterson fold her into a one-arm hug. "Listen, I have an idea for you."

She told CeCe they'd hired a new librarian and the new librarian had requested a student assistant. The assistant, she explained, would help shelve the books, keep the library neat, help the younger grades find things, and help keep the card catalog straight.

"You were the first person we thought of," Ms. Patterson said. "Whaddya think?"

CeCe was gape-mouthed. Her mind couldn't hold all of the morsels Ms. Patterson had tossed at her: library, new, assistant, books, chosen. Her head nodded anyway.

"Great," Ms. Patterson said, clapping her hands together. "Let's go meet Mrs. Anderson. I think you'll like her, CeCe. She's pretty special."

CeCe stood beneath the mobile with *The Very Hungry Caterpillar, Curious George, Goodnight Moon,* and *Harry the Dirty Dog* while Ms. Patterson disappeared behind a narrow door. When she emerged, a tall black woman stood beside her with rolled posters tucked beneath her arm. The first thing CeCe noticed was her smile. The woman had long teeth, longer than most grown-ups', and one dimple. It was so deep, CeCe wondered if it pressed against the side of her tongue. CeCe like the woman's smile. It seemed like a real one.

"You must be CeCe," the woman said, walking to the big desk and dropping the paper tubes. CeCe waved absently, fixated by the woman's movements.

"I'm Mrs. Anderson. I'm very pleased to meet you."

CeCe stepped closer to accept Mrs. Anderson's extended hand. Ms. Patterson excused herself and Mrs. Anderson leaned back against the desk, returning her attention to CeCe.

"So, you like libraries, huh?"

CeCe nodded.

"What kind of stories do you like?"

"Umm, ones with princesses and wishes and magic and stuff," CeCe said.

Mrs. Anderson smiled. "I like those, too. Maybe I could show you some of my favorites and you could tell me yours?"

CeCe nodded again.

"It's important for librarians and library assistants to be familiar with the titles in their library," Mrs. Anderson said. She stood and gestured for CeCe to follow her toward the first shelf of books. CeCe could smell her skin. It wasn't sweet, like the perfume Ms. Patterson would wear, or strong, the way cigarette smoke lingered around Mr. Curtis. It reminded CeCe of summer nights and fireflies. Maybe that was the special thing Ms. Patterson talked about, that Mrs. Anderson's skin smelled like twilight.

Mrs. Anderson smiled her perfect smile and laughed. "You're grinning like you've just remembered something special, CeCe. Can I know what it is, too?"

CeCe reached up to touch her own face with her fingertips. She felt her cheeks warm, but couldn't stop the grinning.

"I figured out your special secret," CeCe said in a lowered voice.

Mrs. Anderson raised her eyebrows, amused. "You have?"

CeCe nodded. "It's your skin."

Mrs. Anderson leaned her head to one side, looking at CeCe for a long moment. "My skin?" she asked.

"Uh-huh. Ms. Patterson said you were 'something special,' but I thought you were gonna be regular," CeCe said, leaning toward her new friend. "Then I smelled your skin. It's like nighttime in summer. I never met nobody with skin that smells special like that."

Mrs. Anderson raised her hand to her mouth, unable to contain the giggle that escaped. CeCe could still see her teeth and her dimple. She returned the giggle and smile.

"CeCe, that's the sweetest thing I've heard in a long time. Thank you," Mrs. Anderson said.

CeCe beamed.

Mrs. Anderson glanced up at the wall clock. "You should probably head back to class now," Mrs. Anderson said. "Your position as the new librarian's assistant can start during tomorrow's recess. OK?"

"OK!" CeCe said, shaking Mrs. Anderson's hand again.

The next day, CeCe went to the library and Mrs. Anderson read to her *The Snowy Day*.

"What'd you think?" Mrs. Anderson asked.

"I like that story," CeCe said, flipping through the pages again.

"I thought about what you said when I got home last night," Mrs. Anderson said. CeCe looked up, unsure. "About being special?" CeCe remembered, and nodded.

"We're both special, did you know that?"

CeCe nodded.

Mrs. Anderson smiled. "Of course you did," she said. "Well, we special people have to look out for each other, because there are a lot of *un*special people who just won't understand us sometimes. It might make us sad. If that happens to one of us, we have to promise to come get a hug from the other one, OK?"

CeCe nodded and Mrs. Anderson flashed her dimple again.

They visited that way every day for the next week, and then CeCe went to the library only two or three times a week, wanting to play with the twins sometimes. CeCe redeemed at least a dozen of those hugs from Mrs. Anderson by the end of the school year.

By the time CeCe had advanced to the fourth grade, she was reading seventh-grade chapter books recommended by Mrs. Anderson and cashing in on a hug every day. CeCe's mother couldn't listen to CeCe's recounting of the books she read. Her eyes weren't seeing things close up anymore, and she hardly remembered anything CeCe told her about the light bill or the new pack of underwear or school field trips.

For the first time, CeCe was afraid. The newest caseworker asked different questions from the others, questions about living in other houses, with other families, other mothers. Mrs. Anderson assured CeCe that, as long as her mother did what was asked of her, CeCe wouldn't have to worry about living anywhere else.

"What was the word we learned?" Mrs. Anderson had asked.

"Compliance."

"Right," Mrs. Anderson said, not showing her dimple now. Over the past two years, CeCe had shared things with Mrs. Anderson she'd never told anyone else, especially the caseworkers. CeCe told Mrs. Anderson the truth about their empty refrigerator at home, about her imagined birthday gifts, about their laundry in the tub, about her mother's wrenching sobs at night.

Mrs. Anderson explained that everyone was just trying to make sure CeCe was safe, and her mother, too.

"Sometimes mamas need a little help," she said.

"Did you need help?" CeCe asked. Mrs. Anderson spoke to CeCe often about her teenagers.

"I sure did," Mrs. Anderson said, reaching out her hand for CeCe to place a book from the cart. CeCe had been relieved to be exempt from recess and become Mrs. Anderson's aide. The other children played with her, sometimes, but Mrs. Anderson talked to her kindly all the time. CeCe enjoyed her job, too. She'd been fascinated when Mrs. Anderson taught her the Dewey decimal system and thought it was honor when she'd been given the job of re-stocking the mislaid books.

CeCe handed her another book from the stack of 900s, history. From the looks of the titles, CeCe guessed one of the upper classes must have assignments about U.S. presidents.

"We had our first daughter right out of college," Mrs. Anderson said. "Being a mother is a lot of work, and I needed help figuring everything out. My own mother passed away when I was a young girl, so I relied on my aunties and a few ladies from church. It was really hard, but we finally got the hang of things."

CeCe was quiet, handing over the next book.

"Did you miss your mother?" CeCe asked.

"All the time," Mrs. Anderson said. "I was only thirteen when she died."

"I miss my mother a lot, too," CeCe said.

"I know, sweetheart," Mrs. Anderson said. "I know."

EIGHT

MAGIC

CeCe looked through the back window where Doris had stood. The yard was enclosed only because all three neighbors had a fence or a thicket around their properties. The stellar feature for this small yard was an arching tree in the corner with two thick trunks. CeCe had attended one of Doris' Fourth of July parties and remembered wanting to pull the library book from her bag and sprawl out beneath that tree.

CeCe started to walk through the house when the voices in the kitchen shifted from jovial banter to hushed, official tones. There were three small bedrooms, two baths, a dining room, and a living room. CeCe stood in the living room estimating how many books might fit into the wall's cubby shelves when she heard a voice behind her. She spun around, shrieking.

"I'm sorry, CeCe," the man said, stepping back and spreading his arms to draw CeCe's eyes to the round belly buttoned inside his salmon-colored shirt. "It's not often I'm able to sneak up on anyone."

CeCe held on to her chest, willing her heart to stop racing. She grinned at the short, portly man with a retreating hairline. She was arrested by his emerald green eyes, the way they smiled at her.

"I'm Brian Clark," he said. CeCe shook his outstretched hand as Doris soft-soled into the room.

"Well, we know who's not getting invited to any haunted houses," Doris said.

Everyone laughed. CeCe wondered if she'd actually heard this stranger call her by name.

There was a brief, clumsy silence, like would-be lovers uncertain of who should kiss who first.

"Doris has herself one helluva house, huh?" Brian said.

"Yeah," CeCe replied. "I've only been here once, but it was so full of people I really didn't get a chance to see all of her touches. I mostly remember the yard."

"The tree," Doris said. "That's right. I remember."

"I still feel like I know the house," CeCe said, looking around them. "Doris talked about it all the time. She loved this place."

Doris and Brian smiled at CeCe, then at one another.

"That's a high compliment, don't you think, Doris?"

Doris nodded, her eyes shining.

CeCe's antennae went up. This guy was no renter, but he wasn't a friend, either. She'd never heard Doris mention anyone named Brian Clark. CeCe looked at the dumpling of a man and hoped Doris wasn't trying her hand at playing Cupid again. Matchmaking was one area where her friend was not gifted, though she gave great advice once the connections were made. CeCe felt Doris' eyes on her and resolved to humor her dear friend for as much of the afternoon as she could bear. At least he had a sense of humor, CeCe thought. Their lunch date wouldn't be too painful.

"Tell me, CeCe," Brian said, slipping his hands into his pockets and talking at his shoes. CeCe braced herself for the awkward exchange. "Can you picture yourself in this house?"

CeCe's brows raised.

"Picture myself?" CeCe said, tilting her head to one side. "What do you mean?"

Brian looked to Doris, so CeCe did, too. Her friend's eyes were wide with anticipation and her bright berry lips were pursed together. CeCe could see her friend wanted to explode.

"I've known some pretty amazing women in my life," Doris said with a deep breath. Her hands were clasped together in front of her chest, like prayer. "In big ways and small ways, I wouldn't have been able to finally make the life I wanted for myself without them."

CeCe waited for another story about the Ladies, but Doris stepped forward and took CeCe's face in her hands. Doris had never positioned herself as a mother figure for CeCe, but they both had cherished the obvious opportunity for their friendship to fill aching spaces: Doris' miscarried baby girl so many years ago and CeCe's miscarried childhood. Doris' hands were soft and warm, like her eyes. CeCe didn't know why, but she wanted to cry.

"You're one of those amazing women, kiddo," Doris said, her voice plush and sweet. "You've got a good head on your shoulders and a great heart in your chest. From the first day I met you, I knew I was going to like you."

CeCe's tears began to brim. So much love they'd harvested in that food court. Doris had given her advice and confidence and reality checks and courage. She was humbled to know Doris had seen a fighter in her all along. Doris smiled at her and used her thumbs to wipe away her tears.

"When Doris called me about revising her will," Brian's voice broke in and the women took a step back, "naturally, I introduced a number of options for her properties. Her boys. Area nonprofits. We even talked about making it a free residence for college kids working at the mall through the summer."

CeCe frowned at the idea of keg parties spiraling out of control in Doris' back yard.

"Doris reminded me this is more than a house," Brian continued. "This home is the icon for freedom and success."

"Good God, Brian, you sound like you're delivering the Ten Commandments," Doris said. "Move, smarty-pants."

Brian dropped his head to hide a blush as Doris elbowed past him to take CeCe's hands again. Her eyes were soft and proud.

"On the outside, we don't have much in common, you and me," Doris said. "You know what's the same about us?"

CeCe shook her head.

"We're good-hearted people patiently waiting our turn for a little good luck, right?" CeCe turned it over in her head and conceded a nod and sideways smile. Doris tugged at their hands and pulled CeCe closer. Her expression turned serious.

"The other thing we have in common is that we never learned how to dream. I was never allowed to and you never had the luxury. Nothing like magic or good luck had ever blown our way before."

Doris clasped their hands together and pressed the knot of their fingers to her chest. CeCe was pulled off balance, startled by Doris' strength. She looked at her friend with confused anticipation, ready for another gut buster. The women stood eye to eye at five-foot-one, and Doris' eyes shone with tears and affection.

"I want you to have this house, CeCe," Doris said. "Have it. No money and no strings. Just some lucky magic to help you see that you are greater than your circumstances. You are stronger than the things in life that have made you afraid."

CeCe snatched her hands from Doris' grasp to try and catch the squeal rocketing from her throat. She couldn't believe the sounds her ears were taking in. Did Doris say she was *giving* her a house? A whole house?

"You could put the universe in your handbag, if you wanted to,"

Doris said, her eyes electric now, "but, kiddo, you gotta learn how to dream. You deserve to learn."

CeCe looked from Doris to Brian in disbelief and then around at the empty walls of the house. Her house. She couldn't intercept the wailing, not this time.

NINE

SPIDERS

CeCe clenched her fists until the crunch of gravel beneath the school bus' tires gave way to smooth, paved road. CeCe braced for a forgotten shoe or dental retainer, flat tire, anything that might turn them back. She exhaled after three highway exits, certain they all were finally free. CeCe leaned back, closed her eyes, and promised herself never to look forward to anything so desperately again.

Eight weeks earlier, CeCe and four dozen kids had ridden on another yellow bus along this stretch of highway from Prescott and onto the gravel road leading to Camp Onondaga. At that first sound of stones popping and spraying from beneath bus tires, CeCe had trembled with excitement. The bus rocked and bumped, all the kids' heads and shoulders moving in a wobbly choreography. This was the first day of summer camp for them all, and CeCe's first time away from her mother.

With her small, nervous hands gripping the seat beneath her knees, CeCe looked through the front windshield, taking in the approaching view. Brilliant bars of liquid sun reached through the canopy of forest, and the trees seemed to salute their passing bus in curved formation. Pushing deeper into the forest along the narrowing gravel road, the bus reached an open glen, where four handsome young people in matching blue T-shirts stood around a flagpole. They were the staff of camp counselors who, CeCe would learn, were mostly college students earning money for the summer. That they weren't driven to create lifelong memories for each camper—like the brochures said—would be the least of CeCe's disappointments.

CeCe had been skeptical about the idea of camp at first, mirroring her assessments of her newest social worker. She especially didn't like the way this one, Ms. Petrie, tried to scrape about by asking the same questions in six different ways. After one of their meetings in the second room of the guidance office, CeCe went directly to Mrs. Anderson with the Camp Onondaga brochure.

CeCe wanted to feel excited, but she was suspicious of Ms. Petrie. Or maybe she felt uneasy with the tendrils of guilt snaking around her ankles. Ms. Petrie said her mother would be in a special hospital and arrangements had been made for CeCe to have an extended registration at summer camp. Mrs. Anderson helped her decide what to do with the thoughts and feelings she couldn't name.

"I know it will be hard to think about having fun," Mrs. Anderson had said, leaning closer to CeCe, "but your mother will be getting the help she needs while you're gone. Having fun will be perfectly acceptable."

CeCe had come to rely a lot on Mrs. Anderson over the years. Books about puberty, recordings of Motown artists, decoding the condescension of some of her white teachers, and advice on how to keep the curl in her bangs. If it hadn't been for her reassurance, CeCe might not have made the bus. CeCe absorbed every one of those earliest impressions, because she wanted to tell Mrs. Anderson everything about her summer. CeCe filed away mental pictures of huge wooden stumps, big enough to sit on, and clusters of wood cabins situated on top of slats and stilts beneath voluptuous oak trees.

She'd tell her mother, too.

CeCe would remember the sound of creaking springs and slamming screen doors, as well as cheerful, young white people in matching polo shirts and whistles. CeCe's young white person was named Hoot. Or, that's what CeCe and the other five girls she'd been clustered with were instructed to call her. Other groups were led by Trout, Blaze, S'more, Bambi, Foxy, Rainbow, Mudslide, Whiskers, Thunder, and Moss.

Once Hoot had shown them to their cabin and around the grounds, the small troop made their way to the mess hall for the camp's official opening session. There were a hundred kids, all grouped by age. Most of them would board for a week or two. CeCe's extended registration would have her at camp for eight. By her third welcome session, however, the experience felt less like a sweet treat and more like repeated loops.

Back at the cabin, CeCe studied the other girls while Hoot chirped on about buddy systems, lights out, water safety, poison ivy, and keeping the latrine clean. All six of them were nine or ten years old, but the similarities ended there. They were African-American, Samoan, and white. Suburban, rural, and hood. They were broken. Naive. Jaded. Faithful. Each on her separate way to becoming debutante, valedictorian, underachiever, bully, innovator, and lost.

She listened to their banter while building the courage to join in and *take initiative*, like Mrs. Anderson had made her promise to do. Mrs. Castellanos had given her a winding lecture about using this summer as her time to bloom. Though CeCe liked the notion of being compared to a flower, she felt more like a radish or, maybe cabbage, nothing overtly beautiful, but still something that emerges from the earth completely intact and completely without interference.

"I have those same pajamas at home!" the Samoan girl said excitedly, spying the Smurfette PJs in the redheaded girl's open duffel bag.

"They're my favorites," Redhead said.

"I don't like the Smurfs anymore," said Portia, one of the other black girls. "I like the Care Bears. I got a Care Bear lunchbox at home."

From there, the conversation swirled around which of Strawberry Shortcake's friends was the best, which Super Friend was smarter, and whether *Ghostbusters* were real. They were unpacking their toiletries and sheeting their cots, while CeCe followed the bounce of their chatter from Ninja Turtles to New Edition to *ET*.

"You're awfully quiet, Crimson," Hoot said as she walked into their small cabin. "I think I could hear everyone talking about their favorite things except you. I'd like to hear about your favorite shows."

"CeCe."

"I'm sorry?" Hoot replied.

"I go by 'CeCe,'" she said.

"Oh," Hoot said, a relieved smile lighting her face. "CeCe, it is! What's one of your favorite things, CeCe?"

The other girls perched onto the ends of their cots, waiting for her to speak.

"Um . . . ," CeCe began, uncomfortable with the twelve eyeballs pointed her direction. "I don't watch much TV," she mumbled. "I like to read, mostly."

"Ain't you got a TV?" one asked.

"Yeah," CeCe said, lying. "I just don't watch it much, is all. I like books better."

"You like Judy Blume?" asked another from the next bunk.

CeCe hesitated, looking to Hoot. "I've read all of her books."

"Me, too," her bunk neighbor said.

CeCe felt optimistic. She hadn't been around unfamiliar kids since starting kindergarten at Neil Armstrong Elementary. She was a fourth-grader now, with years of compiled lessons on which classmates might turn their smiles on and off from day to day, which ones would mock her mix-and-match thrift-store clothes, and which ones would always call out a goodbye to her as their class spilled from the cloakroom. She couldn't yet know which labels to assign these new cabin mates and she felt anxious.

By the end of that following day, their first full day at camp, CeCe was convinced she'd boarded a big, yellow school bus to heaven. There was a brand new experience almost every hour; she engaged with kids from every walk of life. Hoot and the other counselors were unwavering in their excitement, and CeCe was stunned by the scenery around her. Her visits to the park were wholly unremarkable compared to this immersion in *nature*.

By the end of the second week, however, CeCe accepted that the other campers had not been eager to experience nature in the form of lilting wind songs, blinking jewels of sunlight, or sky-reaching trees. When the third arrival of cabin mates assumed the clique-ish and tittering obsessions of the departed first two groups, CeCe realized that other kids came to camp with an interest in the nature of boys.

"You should sit next to Brian at the campfire tonight," one girl said to another on their group's walk from the lake. "My brother is in his cabin and said Brian thinks you're cute."

CeCe considered herself average-looking and there were a fair number of boys her age, black, white, and a few Latino, for her to join her fawning peers. Instead, CeCe's skin tightened whenever the topic of boys came up, which was constantly. None of their bodies were blooming behind their shorts and tank tops, yet these other girls who occupied bunks each week all around CeCe were already painting their fingernails, wearing curlers in their hair and boasting encyclopedic knowledge on all things *boy*.

With each cohort, CeCe was one of a handful of other social misfits who actually poured effort and attention into weaving their dream catchers, roasting s'mores, discovering leaves on a hike, learning to wrap an ankle bandage. CeCe learned to maneuver around their giggling huddles in the arts-and-crafts tent, by the canoe docks, before and after meals. She let the crunch of twigs and leaves drown away their chatter as she walked another clipboard to the main office for Hoot or escaped into the quiet of a wooded path.

Befriending the girls made CeCe equally anxious. She couldn't tell when she was having a conversation or being sized up. CeCe was uncertain of Hoot, and the other counselors, as well. They didn't ask questions of her, the way Mrs. Anderson did. When they hugged her, the insides of their arms weren't warm, like Mrs. Castellanos'. They delivered spirited but unvaried welcomes at the camp kickoff week after week.

By CeCe's sixth week, she was all brood and silence. She was lonely, unhappy, and stuck. Hoot had given up on trying to legislate CeCe's good cheer and simply allowed her to wander the grounds, choose her own activities and exist along the periphery until their summer sentence could come to an end.

On a trek to retrieve oversized Band-Aids for Hoot, CeCe stopped along the trail to watch a rabbit. She stood in the middle of the pathway, quiet and still, when a boy's voice made her spin around. She knew his name was Dwayne, one of the most-discussed boys in her cabin. Two other boys flanked him, but CeCe didn't know their names.

"Chill out," Dwayne said. "We're not bears."

CeCe wanted to run, but forced her legs to settle themselves. It was easy to see why his name had taken root in the mouths of so many of her fellow campers. Dwayne was dark-complexioned and lean, with the promise of broad shoulders one day. His teeth overlapped and his smile glinted with mischief. More boys like Dwayne had started to join her student body at Neil Armstrong Elementary, now that the district was experimenting with expanded enrollment

requirements. Boys like Dwayne came to her school with crisp out-
fits and a fresh haircut every Monday morning. She acknowledged
the appeal of a boy like Dwayne in her innermost workings, but
simply had no idea what to do about it all.

CeCe intended to slip her hands into the pockets of her shorts
but missed. Again, she willed her body not to panic. Instead, she
heard herself mumble.

"You'd be some small bears."

"Small bears?" repeated one of the boys, his eyebrows raised in
surprised peaks. "Man, she said we'd be small bears."

Her chest seized. CeCe had seen how easily one lightly tossed
joke could detonate into playground wreckage. Dwayne looked to
his friend and back at CeCe.

"We'd be cute bears, though," Dwayne said, winking that smile at
her. "Girls like cute bears, don't you?"

She shrugged her shoulders, held her breath, and looked for
an escape.

"Where you going?" Dwayne asked as CeCe resumed a more deliberate march toward the medical cabin.

"Med. We need Band-Aids."

"Somebody got hurt?" Dwayne asked, his eyes light.

"Portia. A branch poked her in the arm."

"She bleedin' real bad?" one of the other boys asked, impish curiosity pushing aside his cool.

CeCe waved away their wide-eyed attention. "Just a flap of hanging skin. She's bleeding, but not bad."

The boys were visibly disappointed.

"Tonya is in your cabin, right?" Dwayne asked, taking steps toward the med cabin with her.

"Which one?" CeCe asked. "Tall Tonya is in Whisker's cabin.
Short Tonia is in mine."

Dwayne looking to the other guys for verification and confirmed, "Short Tonia."

"Yeah, she has the bunk below me," CeCe said, taking another step toward the medical cabin. The boys followed.

"You should tell her to meet me by the boating shed after lunch," Dwayne said.

"I don't know her like that," CeCe said, recoiling at the idea of initiating a conversation with one of the girls, let alone relay a message from Dwayne and embroil herself in the subsequent chatterfest.

"Get to know her like that," Dwayne said. "Come on, CeCe, please?"

CeCe's head snapped around at the sound of her name trumpeting from Dwayne's throat. How did he know her name? How had he chosen her of all the people at camp who would willfully do his bidding? Why was he smiling at her that way?

"Well," CeCe said, giving Dwayne a thin and bashful grin. "OK."

CeCe returned to their cabin area with the Band-Aids as her group lined up for the cantina. CeCe paced herself behind Tonia as she bantered with another girl.

"I'm having fun," Tonia was saying, "but I'll be glad to sleep in my own bed."

CeCe injected herself in their conversation, asking Tonia what her room was like. One of the nicer girls, Tonia didn't dismiss CeCe's fringe status and gave a bubbly description of her matching bedspread and curtains, new Cabbage Patch dolls, and wall posters of Diana Ross, Marilyn McCoo, and Thelma from *Good Times*.

CeCe waited for Tonia to exhaust the inventory of her room, so she could submit Dwayne's request. While Tonia rambled, CeCe wondered why Dwayne had picked this girl. She wasn't *that* cute. She definitely wasn't very bright. Confounded once again by the nature of boys, CeCe half-listened and half-waited while they walked the trodden path.

As they reached the edge of the woods, CeCe glimpsed the shimmer of an enormous spider's web stretched between two trees. CeCe sidestepped the tree and, before she could open her mouth, Tonia said, "Bread and butter! It's bad luck to split—"

Then Tonia screamed.

Before they left for dinner, Hoot gathered the girls to slice through the heavy tension of their small group with a discussion on "trust." The open forum devolved into a sharp indictment of CeCe's deliberate trick to scare Tonia.

"You know she's scared of spiders," one girl barked.

"You were just on that pathway, so you knew the spider web was there," insisted another.

"What if she had been bitten?" Hoot even asked.

"That's why don't nobody even like your weird butt," concluded another.

CeCe claimed her innocence once more and absorbed the rest of their accusations. She didn't bother mentioning Dwayne's request. She didn't see how it could help her plight. She spotted him outside the cantina when their group finally arrived for dinner and he waved a dismissive hand at her. CeCe was irritated with the girls for swelling the incident and angry with herself for being hurt by Dwayne's disappointment.

CeCe ate her dinner alone, as expected. She scraped her tray and went outside to sit in the grass. Staying with the group before and after meals was Hoot's only restriction to CeCe's camp haunting.

Sitting by herself, pulling blades of grass between her fingers, CeCe watched Tonia emerge from the cantina with Tall Tonya and a collection of other girls. They approached CeCe in a buzzing swarm.

"I heard you let my girl almost crash into a tree," said Tall Tonya.

"Tried to scare her," someone else said.

"Almost got her bit by a spider," called another voice.

"I already said it was an accident," CeCe said, willed her legs to lift her from the ground.

"I think you lyin'," Tall Tonya said. She was gangly, with long arms and sharp shoulders.

"I don't care what you think," CeCe said, her good sense betraying her. She looked at the underside of the girl's chin, the color buttermilk, as she approached CeCe with a threatening stance.

"Don't jump bad," Tall Tonya said, eclipsing the space between them.

"Don't get in my face," CeCe said, mimicking the girl's neck roll.

"Don't make me whoop your butt, *Crim-Son!*"

CeCe cringed at the way her name curdled inside Tall Tonya's mouth. CeCe's irritation ignited into fury, swelling every cavern and vessel inside her small body.

CeCe jammed the heel of her hands into Tall Tonya's shoulders, knocking the girl backwards. Tall Tonya recovered her balance and charged at CeCe with balled fists and flying curses. CeCe responded with flailing arms and a stutter of feet and knees. She was distantly aware of the shrieks and cheers, growing louder and thicker as more campers came out of the cantina to watch them fight. CeCe flung herself at the girl's neck, mouth, thighs, and felt Tonya's returning rain of pounds and smacks.

CeCe felt weightlessness between her feet and the ground as muscular arms clamped around her waist. Blaze, one of the counselors for the teen boys' groups, lifted CeCe and carried her rebellious limbs away from the fracas. He carried her to the far end of the field and dropped her to the ground.

Blaze hovered before her like a barricade, but CeCe had no intention of rushing back into the fray. As her breathing steadied, the brew of campers and counselors slowly dissipated. CeCe took in the aftermath like a spectator, as if she hadn't been the one to bloody Tonya's lip. As if she weren't the one all the counselors were shaking their heads and tsk-tsking about.

"I don't even know what to say, CeCe," the camp director said, ending her reprimand. By CeCe's count, she had been pinned with the word "disappointed" nine times that day.

The adults decided to move CeCe into the six-year-old units for her remaining two weeks. She could be a helper to the counselors there, if she chose, but was not to interact with her age group any longer. As Hoot helped carry out CeCe's duffel bags while the other girls painted pinecone owls, CeCe looked forward to the preschool chatter and, hopefully, being ignored for the rest of her time at Camp Onondaga.

CeCe also welcomed the fluidity of her anger. She sat on painted rocks behind the archery field where the six-year-olds tumbled and raced in the hot sun. CeCe allowed the rush of bitterness to course around inside her. CeCe didn't hold her breath to stop it. She didn't resist its steady leaning against her thoughts. She didn't reject the way her rage sated her. By the time she boarded the yellow bus departing Camp Onondaga, CeCe had fury tucked beneath her tongue.

TEN

AFFAIRS

BRIAN CLARK LED THE WOMEN back to the kitchen, where he had short stacks of papers neatly lined along the counter.

"The deed has already been transferred to your name," Doris said, motioning CeCe to the counter. "A trust has been set up for you through Brian's law firm—you know how those work—to cover routine repairs and maintenance for a while. My estate will pay the property taxes for two years."

"Three," Brian corrected.

"Three, really?" Doris said to Brian. She turned back to face CeCe. "I must really like you."

The women looked at each other silently. As was their way, CeCe and Doris held a two-hour conversation of soul-honest epiphanies and heartfelt thank-yous inside that flash of quiet. When the silence burst, CeCe lunged at Doris, wrapping arms around her friend's wide shoulders and sobbing into Doris' hair.

Doris rubbed CeCe's heaving back. "OK, honey," Doris said once CeCe had collected herself. "The bad news is Mr. Smarty Pants has lots of papers for you to sign."

CeCe separated herself, her laugh garbled with tears.

"I can't even begin to find enough words to thank you, Doris," CeCe managed to say, wiping her face with her fingers.

"Live your own life, and live it well, kiddo," Doris said. "That's how you thank me."

Doris touched CeCe's chin and left her to sign and clip forms with Brian. When CeCe emerged from the kitchen, she had a thick, white envelope filled with signed papers and a label on the front with her name already typed on it. CeCe gawked at the envelope between her fingers.

"The deal doesn't work without keys," Doris said. She stood in the center of the empty dining room dangling a ring with three shiny keys.

"When—" CeCe began.

"Right now," Doris said.

CeCe walked over with an outstretched palm and let Doris drop the keys into her hand. She clenched and unclenched her fists, savoring the bite of metal against her palm.

"Well, my work here is done," Doris said in a loud stage voice, fanning the air with a faux regal wave. "Brian, call my driver."

Brian said, "I *am* your driver."

"Oh, that's right." Doris tossed a wink at CeCe.

"You two made me love my job all over again. CeCe, congratulations again. My business card is inside your packet and I left another one on the counter. Doris, I'll be in the car. Please take your time."

"You really outdid yourself this time," CeCe said to Doris once Brian was outside.

"That's the idea, kiddo. Outdo yourself every chance you get."

"What happened to the tenants you had, though?"

"Serendipity, honey," Doris replied, her voice distant. "The husband secured a better-paying job and the wife found out they had twins on the way. When they called to let me know they were going to be house hunting soon, I knew it was time."

"Time?" CeCe said, grinning as she folded her arms over her chest. Doris was always into something. "Time for what?"

"Time to pull the trigger on these projects before I go," Doris said.

"Where are you going now?" CeCe asked, still opening and closing her hand around the keys. Knowing Doris, there would be a passport and a long journey involved.

Doris did not return CeCe's giddy grin. She blinked before locking eyes with CeCe, transcribing another silent volume.

"Everywhere," Doris said. More softly, she added, "I'm dying, honey. Ovarian cancer. Too far gone to try and fix at it anymore. I'm taking the boys and their families away for a few weeks. Then I'm traveling to all the places I've never been—which is a lot of places, I tell ya."

Breath trapped in CeCe's lungs. The euphoria she felt ten seconds ago seemed perverse and dirty now.

"I know, it's nuts, right?" Doris said, acknowledging the question marks in CeCe's eyes. Doris folded her arms across herself and CeCe noticed she was without her signature silver chain. "Just when I was finally getting my shit together . . . "

CeCe couldn't force her face to smile.

"Hey, I've known for a long time," Doris said, stepping back into CeCe's personal space. "Not about the cancer, but that I wanted you to have this house. Before the cancer, my plan was to give you a helluva deal on rent. Once I started thinking about *getting my affairs in order* and leaving legacies and all, the idea took on a life of its own. Don't you go feeling like you got a consolation prize, girlie. You've been on my heart since the day I met you. If it makes you feel any better, you're one of nearly a dozen."

"One of a dozen . . . what?" CeCe said, stepping back to let her tears slide down her face and hope for the picture window glass to keep her standing upright.

"Amazing young people I've met who needed a break and some luck," Doris said. She started to count off on her fingers. "There's you. There's the art teacher my boys had in middle school; he wants to study art therapy. My hair stylist struggles to care for her autistic daughter; the girl at my favorite bakery wants a tea shop; a young widower at the end of the block needs a live-in nanny and house-keeper to help with his six kids.

"And Brian," Doris continued, thumbing toward the open door. "He used to live around the corner. He would take my boys with him to play soccer, basketball, and all. His parents were alcoholics and my boys thought he was a godsend. I'm able to repay him for that. He's opening his own firm now."

CeCe threw her hands in the air, propelled by a sudden burst of anger. "Doris!" CeCe exclaimed. "You can't just—"

"Zip it, honey," Doris said, turning for the door. "This one is out of my hands. And yours. I've worked hard to be a gift to someone else for a change. And you've worked hard to deserve it. I know it's a lot to take in, but take it in, already."

She turned to push open the screen door, a smile dancing on her lips. CeCe put her hands on her hips and felt the keys nip at her flesh again. CeCe looked down at the keys. When she looked up, Doris had escaped out into the early summer air.

CeCe stared at the open door, listening to Brian's car reverse out of the driveway. CeCe looked around at the empty walls and hallways.

For the first time since receiving the house news, CeCe thought about her mother and swallowed.

ELEVEN

BLUE

WHEN CARLA ARRIVED ON MACMURRAY'S campus in 1967, she hardly noticed its manicured greenery, its white-steepled buildings, or the two thousand pairs of feet plodding the walkways all about her. Carla only wanted to climb her feet aboard a Greyhound bus heading back for home every Friday afternoon.

Uncle John protested after the second month, hearing her only speak of lectures, papers, and exams. Carla had nothing to offer when Uncle John asked about campus events, new friends—just her roommate, another Negro girl, from Rockford.

"I think she's planning to be a teacher," Carla had said, peeling sweet potatoes while Uncle John leaned into their kitchen over the open half of the Dutch door.

"You gals get along?" he asked.

"We get along all right."

"So how come you don't know 'bout her studies?"

"I don't know a lot of things about Sandra," Carla said, annoyance fringing the edge of her voice. "She doesn't spend much time in the room—"

"—and you spendin' too much time in it," Uncle John said.

Carla paused her peeling, but didn't look up. She knew her Uncle John would be cleaning his nails with a pocketknife, his bushy eyebrows raised and expecting a good answer. Carla had been governed by that eyebrow for most of her life. As a young girl, she learned how to respond to his persistent questions by paying attention to the loving way Aunt Margaret had handled him.

Uncle John and Aunt Margaret had taken Carla in as a young child. She came to them as a quiet little girl, with knocked knees, long lashes and a blue ribbon in her hair. She'd belonged to Margaret's twin sister, who gave birth to Carla the same year John and Margaret were married. Unable to conceive, watching Carla grow in those early years of their marriage had been a bittersweet test of John and Margaret's faith. After her sister's suicide, raising Carla proved to be a test of their humility. They welcomed her as a gift directly from God.

When anyone spoke of Margaret's sister, they described her as having "an affliction of the mind." She had acquired odd and increasingly outlandish behaviors around the time John and Margaret were courting. Neighbors whispered across laundry lines about her sister's bizarre outbursts, public spectacles, and wandering. It had become common for a shopkeeper, deacon, or neighbor to deliver her, disoriented, to their parents' doorstep. By the time Margaret married and moved to the nearby county with John, one of her sister's disappearances had produced a daughter. Shortly after their fifth wedding anniversary, her sister was found hanging from a pecan tree.

Carla grew and settled in her aunt and uncle's quiet routines. She was an obedient child and shy. Carla went to school and came home to study. She rode her bicycle to the library on Saturdays and helped Aunt Margaret with cooking, housekeeping, and doting on their beloved John.

Once Carla developed into a young woman, petite and doll-like, she could have easily had suitors. She had her mother and aunt's petite frame and caramel-colored skin. Her mouth was small but heavy like theirs, too. "Kissable," little Clarence had written in a note to her once in elementary school, with a backward "s."

Carla's nose and eyes, however, suggested her mother's mysterious tryst so many years ago might have been an exotic affair. Her nose was arrow straight, with a light spray of freckles, and her large eyes were sleepy and plush, with dark lashes that curled against themselves.

"I think you got an extra helping of eyelashes up there in Heaven," Aunt Rosie said to Carla one afternoon, her eyes pleading for an extra gingersnap. Aunt Rosie was John's oldest sister, the first of their clan to migrate north from Arkansas. Six of their eleven siblings had settled in Decatur, Illinois, by the time Carla had come around, and Aunt Rosie—also childless—had been a surrogate parent to them all.

Carla had taken her cookies to the porch swing, munching thoughtfully about the Heaven babies who didn't get enough eyelashes because of her.

As a preteen, Carla's "thoughtful munching" advanced to "skillful worrying." She worried about the supply of firewood during the winter. Laundry being snatched up by a heavy wind in the spring. Baking bread falling in the oven. Soloists forgetting their lyrics in church. The "what ifs," as Uncle John and Aunt Rosie called them, also kept Carla from straying into friendships with girls her age, or enjoying the 45 rpm records at Miss Sherry's Soda Bop.

The Soda Bop was a converted shed for young people in the area to gather. Miss Sherry had led the charge of keeping her kids from crossing paths with the law or drunken Klansmen on Saturday nights, and most parents in their rural community were glad to help her along by supplying the hangout each week with food, pies, and chaperones.

"A lot of these honkeys is wishin' they lived in Birmingham," Miss Sherry would say, constantly reminding the youth about the notoriously violent sundown towns surrounding Decatur: Loving-

ton, Monticello, Blue Mound, Mount Zion. "Black folks still gettin'
lynched twenty miles in every direction from here. Hate and evil
don't know nothin' 'bout North and South."

"I hear Miss Sherry's got a good thing goin' for you young folks,"
Uncle John had prompted one night at dinner. Carla was nearing
the end of high school, becoming a woman. Still, she flushed at the
blatant discussion of her social life, or lack thereof.

Aunt Margaret smiled and added, "We can take you whenever
you'd like."

Carla had thought about Miss Sherry's, overhearing Monday
morning reports at school all these years about the food, the music,
the clothes and the slow dancing. Every now and again, her chest
had pinched with intrigue. Aunt Margaret urged Carla to go just
once, just so she wouldn't have any regrets. Carla had agreed.

Then Aunt Margaret died. Their house, already draped in a lingering weariness, was thick once again with heavy sorrow. Carla was
only fifteen and there was so much Aunt Margaret hadn't taught her
yet. Like how to whip the meringue. How to backstitch heavy corduroy and keep the seams straight. How to revive the tomatoes. How
to turn around a bridge game with a false card or a flannery. How to
type. How to pin-curl her hair.

Carla and Uncle John trudged through her final year of high
school in dark quiet. While her classmates and cousins headed off
to college, factory floors, and wedding chapels, Carla's plans were
to live at home, get a job at the library, and take care of her Uncle
John. A few months after their extended family had thrown a celebration picnic for her in Aunt Rosie's back yard, Uncle John told
Carla about college.

She resisted, but Uncle John explained the arrangements had already been made. Margaret and Marjorie had been raised in a world
foreign from John and his siblings. In their world, Margaret's parents

had established something called a trust to pass on to their girls the earnings of their hard work and that of the Reconstruction relatives before them. In turn, Margaret, John learned, had continued the tradition, traveling by buggy across the river to consolidate her trust with her twin sister's to make a family trust and college fund for Carla. When John drove his dirt-smattered pickup across county lines to meet with the attorney, John asked the polished Negro lawyer if disbursements would last long enough for Carla to finish school. The attorney had chuckled kindly, assuring John that Carla's inheritance would support her well into adulthood.

Carla had steamed for several weeks at the idea of a conspiracy and being shipped away against her will. Uncle John had been patient with her anger, withholding a grin when Carla's excitement betrayed her when her registration materials arrived in the mail.

Only halfway through her first semester, Carla turned away from the sweet potatoes and steaming pots to face her uncle.

"I'm there to learn about literature, not about Sandra!" she spat.

John pursed his lips, restricting his words. He didn't want to upset her, but this was not a time for coddling. Margaret had always scolded him behind their bedroom doors that their job was to prepare Carla for the world as much as it was their privilege to shield her from it. He'd hated that truth then and it made his temples pulse now. Still, he knew it was best. He knew this beautiful girl—young woman—was headed for a lonely and gray-sky life if he didn't push her forward now.

Carla turned her back to him, lifting and fidgeting with pot lids, opening and closing the oven door. She was upset, he knew. It often amazed him that although Margaret hadn't birthed Carla, they'd come to be so much alike. John dropped his head to whisper a quick prayer and collect himself.

"Literature. I know, Bluebell," he said, floating his favorite pet name for her. He'd called her that ever since she arrived on their porch with that blue ribbon in her hair. "But your Aunt Margaret done told me how being a *college* woman means you gets to learn 'bout more than literature and the Greyhound."

Carla laid down the potato and the paring knife and Uncle John saw her shoulders slack, and then begin with the slightest bounce. He was through the door and next to her in a breath. Carla turned and cried into her uncle's chest. He'd often told her and Aunt Margaret he never knew what to do with a crying woman, except stand still and be quiet. She loved him for that. Loved him for his simplicity. Loved him for being a constant in her life when she'd come to expect chaos around every corner.

"You know better about tracking mud into my kitchen," she said once the gales had abated. She wiped her face. They both smiled at her small tribute to Aunt Margaret. John, raising his hands in mock surrender, retreated back outside. Once he fastened the bottom half of the Dutch door, he looked at Carla for a long moment.

"Your Aunt Margaret would have some real good words for you now. Make you feel better," he said. "You know I ain't never been the one good with words. I'm jus gon' tell ya that you gon' be all right. You smart, Bluebell. You gon' be a professor one day, just like you wantin' to, but you gots a lot of days 'tween now and then and you gots to live 'em all."

Carla's eyes began to brim again. She leaned against the counter with her arms folded across her apron. She let one fat tear fall, and she nodded.

"I promise, Uncle John," she said, smiling. "I promise."

Carla knew wandering into buildings alone wasn't what Uncle John had in mind when she'd promised to invest more of herself in becoming a *college woman.* MacMurray was a quaint campus settled against a vivid, pastoral landscape. The college had a 120-year history, and Carla had been walking past its noble ghosts in a daze. Carla's awkward fidgeting was magnified here. In Decatur she tugged at her hands whenever someone turned attention to her in class or at church. Here, with so many girls eager to talk and link elbows, Carla found herself picking at the cuticles of her fingers. She was not ready for socializing, but she intended to keep her word to Uncle John.

Carla read the bulletin boards in front of the library to learn about the events happening on campus. She scribbled dates and notes on an index card and made plans to attend two lectures, one play, and a Christmas chorale concert. Blanketed in the darkness of the music hall, Carla let herself melt away. Tears wet her cheeks as the soaring altos carried Carla back to Decatur, when she and Aunt Margaret would clean house with Marian Anderson playing on the record player.

After her holiday break and another pep talk from Uncle John, Carla returned to campus ready to brave the next phase of her transformation: people. Her MacMurray classmates herded her in the cafeteria, lecture halls, dorm lobby, and on the mall. She didn't know how to insert herself among them. She tasked herself to linger in the dining hall twice a week after dinner, rather than rushing back to the quiet of her room. She relocated herself out of the library corners to tables where passing chatter would force her to look up from her book every now and again. As she made eye contact and received acknowledging nods from familiar faces, Carla felt herself growing stronger and more confident.

The unease she felt here was different from what she felt in high school. Partly because the student body raced ahead with their studies and lives with or without her, unlike the pressure of conformity back home. Partly, Carla hoped, because they were mature young women now, no longer juvenile high school girls.

Largely, Carla knew, her boldness came from being at a women's college. There were no boys distracting her gaze in class, breathing on her bare shoulder in the lunch lines, brushing against her small body in the halls, giving her goose bumps, consuming her with a look from across the courtyard.

Just before spring midterms, Carla stood before the bulletin board and tried to convince herself to add activities with humans to the index cards this time. She swallowed hard at the thought, scanning notices for reading groups, sewing circles, volunteering, and a group wanting to head into town to see a movie. Carla was writing down the phone number for a small group seeking a bridge player when she heard her name.

Carla turned to see her roommate, Sandra, moving through the rotunda with a small group of girls. She said something to the group and they all turned to smile at Carla before walking through the library doors.

"You didn't have to leave your friends," Carla said.

Sandra glanced back toward the door as the group exited. She was tall and narrow, with pocked skin the color of sweet tea.

"That's just my study group," Sandra said. "I don't really have friends here."

Carla raised her eyebrows. "Really? You seem to keep pretty busy to me."

Sandra laughed. "Yes, I suppose I do. Got to stay in the mix if I'm gonna keep up with the flavor."

Carla nodded, amused by Sandra's wit. From the one-sided phone conversations Carla could hear from the dorm hallway and listening to Sandra talk herself through her studies each morning, Carla knew her roommate to be intense, comical, charismatic, and domineering. There were always women, black and white, waving into their room at Sandra if their door was open. Based on the array of handbills and pamphlets Carla would often glimpse on her roommate's bed, Sandra was clearly an even blend of style and substance. Still, Carla assessed Sandra to be likeable and outgoing, but deliberately unknowable. She thought of her roommate as one of the black holes she studied in science, undetectable but capable of coercing all matter of light, energy, and mass into its gravity.

"I almost didn't recognize you without your headscarf and housecoat," Sandra said, stopping beside Carla.

Carla felt her face heat and reflexively pulled her notebooks closer to her chest.

"Oh, I'm sorry, sister," Sandra said, nudging Carla's arm with hers. "I was only poking fun. I have a whole bag of head rags, and the only reason I don't wear my housecoat is because it has a huge rip in the ass."

Carla smiled as her neck and cheeks cooled.

"What are you doing?" Sandra said, turning her head to peer at the index cards on top of Carla's notebooks.

"Oh," Carla said, suddenly more embarrassed and less brave about her project. "I was—um—thinking about joining a bridge game."

Sandra kept her eyes on Carla, expectant. When Carla didn't laugh or wink, Sandra straightened and gave a small nod.

"I never learned to play bridge," Sandra said simply.

"It was my aunt's favorite game. She never found anyone to play with after—" Carla caught herself. "Until I got big enough to do the computations. We played two-handed games all the time."

"She's gone, your aunt?" Sandra asked.

"Yes," Carla said, clearing her throat. "When I was fifteen."

"What about your mother?"

"When I was five."

Sandra was quiet. Carla could tell she was deciding whether to continue.

"It's a long, morbid story," Carla offered, with a weak smile. "It's me and my Uncle John now."

Sandra returned Carla's smile and reached out one hand to cup her roommate's shoulder. "You've both been in very good hands." Sandra pointed her eyes skyward. Carla's heart was full. She was warm with thoughts of Aunt Margaret.

Walking back to their dorm, Sandra told Carla about her own family back in Rockford; huge, loving, religious, and from whom she couldn't wait to get away.

"They might call me their rebel child," Sandra said, sitting cross-legged on her bed. Carla's short legs were tucked beneath her, and her nightgown and housecoat were pulled over her knees and feet.

"You don't agree?" Carla asked. "You're not the rebel child?"

Sandra twisted curlers into her hair and paused. "I wore my white gloves to church on Sundays. Snapped beans on Saturdays. Said 'Yes ma'am' and 'No ma'am.' Brushed my teeth. Real dangerous stuff."

Carla laughed.

"I've always been well behaved," Sandra said, and Carla noted the smear of disdain across the words. "Thinking for myself has been the problem. Wanting more than a husband and babies has been the problem. Wanting to be a part of this revolution has been the problem."

"Revolution?" Carla asked. "In Rockford?" Her nightgown had become suddenly warm and itchy. Carla had heard this line of discussion devolve quickly on Sunday afternoons after service, young men home for the weekend squaring with older brothers and uncles in their church suits.

Sandra pointed a curler in Carla's direction. "Exactly!" she said. "Since no one is burning crosses in our front yard, my family wants to act like what's happening in Chicago and Detroit and Oakland doesn't apply to us. They think they're safe because they're quiet. I'm not interested in a scared, quiet life."

Carla shifted on her bed. She recalled herself nodding with the congregation as her own pastor had barked an entire sermon about blacks steering clear of trouble. God, he'd said, would command what would happen to His children, not protestors, looters, or so-called street soldiers with sinfully rebellious souls.

"I'm a little scared of it all," Carla admitted, looking down at the buttons on her gown.

"It's not all your fault," Sandra said. "They want us to be afraid."

"Who?" Carla asked.

"The oppressors."

"Our families?" Carla asked, curling her face in confusion.

Sandra sucked her teeth. "Naw, girl. The White Man."

Carla looked toward the closed door of their room, one pulse of panic ripping through her. She was quiet for a moment.

"I know a lot of decent white people," she finally said.

"So do I," Sandra replied, "but they're outnumbered by the treacherous ones who are trying to destroy our communities."

"How do you know what they're trying to do?"

"I read the papers, watch the news."

"So do I," Carla said, now agitated. "I read stories every day about Negroes trying to make a change by breaking the law. I don't see how that's supposed to solve anything. It certainly isn't making things any better."

"See? This is the kind of propaganda I'm talking about!" Sandra said, bounding from her bed to Carla's. She leaned in close and Carla could smell her toothpaste and hair grease. "First of all, sister, we're

Black, not Negroes. Second, they're not going to put pictures in the paper about our tutoring programs and food drives, only when we get arrested for protecting our communities from crooked cops. No one talks about falsified records, or buildings getting set on fire by government officials, or the CIA orchestrating the assassination of Malcolm X and, now, Dr. King—"

"What are you talking about?" Carla exclaimed. Sandra's hands had worked themselves into two spinning flurries while she raged.

Sandra calmed her hands and leaned against the wall, regarding Carla. Her tone was controlled and gentle when she spoke again. "We're in a war, Carla," she said. "The sooner we all start acting like that, the sooner Black people in the country can expect some peace."

Carla was quiet for a long moment, conflicted by her resistance to Sandra's ideas and embarrassed by her own naiveté. Carla's relatives had lived on the same stretch of land since her Aunt Rosie had unloaded her things from Arkansas in the forties. Dozens of other families filled in the young landscape at the edge of Decatur's new city with similar jigsaw houses and handmade road signs. It never occurred to Carla that her neighbors were all Black for any reason other than choosing to live together after clapping the red clay from their roots.

Listening to Sandra talk, Carla felt a small seed of understanding begin to split and yawn open inside her.

"What if this is just the way things are?" Carla asked, her voice small. She was surprised by the sob trying to push through her words.

"When something is fundamentally wrong," Sandra replied gently, "it doesn't matter how long it's been going on."

The morning birds had begun to chirp and peal outside. The girls had been talking all night, but would need to get at least a nap before heading into their classes that day. Carla had a few more questions.

"Why are you here?" she asked.

"I wanted to attend Chicago State, but my parents wanted me as far from the 'unrest' as possible," Sandra said with disgust. "And let's make it a women's college for good measure!"

The young women laughed, wearily now.

"What would you do if you were in Chicago?" Carla asked.

"I have no idea," Sandra admitted, looking young and vulnerable to Carla for the first time. "I just know I would be involved. I wouldn't be tiptoeing around in bobby socks and saddle shoes trying to pretend the struggle isn't real."

Carla stole a glance at the saddle shoes lined in front of her bureau. Sandra followed her eyes and the two young women exploded in laughter.

"I'm sorry, sister," Sandra said, wiping a tear from her eye. "I got on a roll."

They commented on the hour and the fading darkness and the classes they could not miss that day. Before sleep pulled her into the stillness of her blankets, CeCe asked one more question.

"What if you only know one way to be?"

"Sister, what you are and what you can become are two different stories."

TWELVE

UNZIP

CeCe didn't talk much about camp. Ms. Petrie's polite inquiries withered along their ride from the yellow bus's drop-off to CeCe's apartment. Her mother had been home for a week and looked forward to seeing her, according to Ms. Petrie, the newest social worker. CeCe insisted Ms. Petrie didn't need to walk her in. CeCe hefted her duffel bag from the trunk and waddled through the lobby and onto the courtyard, and then wedged her swollen duffel bag through their apartment door.

Her mother sat at the kitchen table. There was her coffee mug. There was her sweater. There was her quiet. CeCe turned to lock the door behind her. The metal click of the deadbolt shot through their silence, its authority usually clanging against every surface. This time, CeCe only heard a dull thud beneath the rattle and pulse in her head.

Her emancipation from Camp Onondaga was a bittersweet celebration, as CeCe began to inventory all that awaited her at home. CeCe thought of her mother, swallowed by their bed. She thought of milk spoiling in the fridge. Envelopes overflowing in their mail slot. The apartment manager would fuss again about the mailbox. He would also wonder about the rent. When her mother had stopped getting out of bed last year, the apartment manager had showed CeCe which envelope to open and have her mother scribble across the back. When CeCe started returning the endorsed check, the manager deducted their rent and returned the remaining cash.

When CeCe turned away from the locked door, she was surprised to see her mother standing at the kitchen table, not sitting, making eye contact with her. Her mother even wore the outline of a smile. CeCe eyed her mother as she maneuvered around the coffee table to drop her duffel bag. She walked across the room to hug her mother and then open the refrigerator door.

CeCe spent the first few days home assessing bills and the cupboards, washing and hanging laundry, making daily trips to the library. Her mother didn't ask many questions about camp, just kept her eyes on CeCe with that ill-fitting grin.

At the end of the week, before grabbing her tote bag and heading out to catch the bus for her library retreat, the phone rang. The rare clamor filled their small apartment, making them jump. CeCe lifted the receiver. It was Ms. Petrie. CeCe wished she were at the bus stop already.

"I wanted to make sure you and your mom were all set for tomorrow," Ms. Petrie said.

"Tomorrow?"

Ms. Petrie sighed into the phone and chirped, "So glad I called."

CeCe listened as the social worker described the therapy series her mother had been committed to attending for the next six months. She would need to catch the bus to a counselor whose office was across town.

"He's really one of the best to deal with her type of, um, issues," Ms. Petrie said. "Are you excited about your part?"

"What part?"

"I know you've been a big girl for a long time but, legally, we can't have you stay at the apartment alone for more than thirty minutes,"

Mrs. Petrie said. "So, instead of making you sit in the waiting room of the therapist's office, we were able to get you free piano lessons at a studio down the hall."

CeCe knew she was supposed to return Ms. Petrie's excitement, but there were too many other, darker emotions waiting in queue. CeCe felt the sludge filling her skull. She wanted this woman's voice out of her ear.

"What if I don't go?" CeCe asked.

"I'm sorry; you have to go. Otherwise, I could get in big trouble with my supervisor," she said, "and your mother could get arrested for endangerment."

CeCe was quiet. Her neck grew hot as she gripped the receiver. She wrote down the address and called the transit office for the bus routes. She heard her mother in the bedroom, adjusting herself on the mattress, and felt a headache pressing against her ears and the backs of her eyeballs. CeCe slammed the front door when she left.

"Let's go, Mama," CeCe said, standing in the doorway of their bedroom. Her mother had been moving in circles, smoothing the blanket, slipping on her shoes, straightening the stacks of papers on the dresser. "We can't miss the Kennedy bus."

Two bus transfers and an hour later, they arrived at a strip mall in the Birchdale neighborhood, a small enclave on the far-east end of the city. The property was modern and clean, with a video store, dry cleaners, and other small businesses. Between the insurance office and the shoe store, a nondescript glass door led to an upstairs maze of boxy, wood-paneled office spaces. A directory sign pointed to the music school at one end of the hallway and Dr. Carroll Harper at the other.

CeCe's piano lesson started thirty minutes later than her mother's session, though they would finish at the same time. CeCe walked with her mother to the doctor's office. A scent of spiced apples greeted them inside. The waiting area was small. There were four cushioned banquet chairs and another closed door with a wooden sign hung from a thick, orange ribbon: "In session. Please have a seat."

CeCe and her mother took a seat on each wall. Her mother closed her eyes. CeCe examined the room. In the center of the space, a coffee table had magazines and a bowl filled with large wooden balls and spirals. A small bookshelf, painted orange, offered playing cards, an incomplete set of encyclopedia books, and a basket of toddler's toys. Eight black-and-white photographs of trees and forest glens dotted the room, each image held in place with cream-and-orange matting. CeCe recognized these pictures were the only items in Dr. Harper's waiting room that had not come from a thrift store.

A chime sounded on the other side of the closed door, followed by rustling, movement, and a murmur of voices coming closer to the door. CeCe looked to her mother. Her eyes were still closed, but CeCe saw her mother force a nervous swallow. The office door pushed open, releasing a heavy woman with long red hair, her face ashen and blotched from crying. CeCe looked down as she passed.

"You must be Carla," croaked a man's voice. CeCe looked up again to see a short round man standing in the doorway. He was bald on top with a ring of white hair around his head and a full beard. CeCe half expected her mother's new psychologist to appear in a white lab coat and, perhaps, a bow tie. Instead, he wore jeans, Docksides and a button-down striped oxford. He reminded CeCe of a science teacher.

"And you must be Crimson—wait—CeCe, is it?"

CeCe nodded as Dr. Harper came closer to shake her hand and then her mother's. Dr. Harper gestured for her mother to follow him and moved aside for her passing.

"I promise to take excellent care of her," he said to CeCe before pulling his office door closed.

CeCe poked through the magazines, but there were only news, camping, and home decor. She took out her library book to read. After a few minutes, CeCe realized there wasn't a clock anywhere. She knew she wasn't allowed to interrupt Dr. Harper, but didn't want to be late for her piano lesson. Begrudgingly, CeCe gathered her book and her tote bag and left the office for Claire McKissick's School of Music.

CeCe pushed open the door at the opposite end of the hallway and found a similar setup as Dr. Harper's office, with a second door separating the "waiting" from the "working." CeCe took a seat in the plastic molded chairs. Instead of pastoral photography, these walls were covered in autographed photos of an elegant woman posing with an assortment of people. Famous musicians, CeCe presumed. Claire McKissick, she was certain.

She could hear muted instructions behind the closed door and someone mashing the keys. CeCe pulled out her book again, blocking out the wailing piano noise. Tuning out the world was one of CeCe's favorite perks of reading. A half hour had passed before she knew it and the door flew open. A large black woman came charging out, in mid-bellow.

" . . . And the next time we come here and you don't know those keys, that's yo' ass. You hear me? I'm not payin' all this money for you to come here and piss around with this woman's time! How many times . . . "

She was like a passing storm, not even noticing CeCe sitting there. The target of her rant came coasting behind. She was a thin, dark-complexioned girl with tight bangs and a ponytail on top of her head. The girl mm-hmmed and uh-huhed as she trailed the barking woman, but made a mocking cross-eyed face as she passed by CeCe. CeCe clapped a hand over her mouth to keep from squealing. Finally. She was not alone in the world of misfit mothers.

Every week, the girl and her mother left Claire McKissick's School of Music this way. CeCe would constrict the giggle squirming in her chest as soon as the rehearsal room door flew open and the mother's voice would invade the waiting area. CeCe kept her head in her book, waiting for the precise half-second when the girl would unzip her blank expression to flash a bucky beaver face or another cross-eyed smile. CeCe would squeeze shut her eyes to keep from exploding with laughter.

The girls' Saturday antics carried them through the start of a new school year, frozen dinner trays for Thanksgiving, and an early winter snow. On a particularly cold morning, the girl did not make a face. She followed her bellowing mother, as usual, but stopped to face CeCe before pulling up the hood on her coat.

"You dropped your magazine," the girl said, with a bit more volume than the small room required. Puzzled, CeCe followed the girl's gaze down to the *Right On!* magazine dropped on the floor. CeCe looked down at the magazine and then up, into the mouth of the girl's mother. She had turned back to make sure none of her fussing, neck swiveling, or ultimatums were being missed.

CeCe looked back to the girl. "Thank you," she said, also with a stage voice.

As the girl and her mother's voice retreated down the hall, CeCe held the magazine in her lap. Randy, Jermaine, and Janet Jackson looked back at her. Handwritten on little Janet's forehead read, "Open to page 16." CeCe did and found a folded sheet of lined paper. CeCe opened it and felt everything inside her breathe.

THIRTEEN

FLAGPOLE

WHEN HER FIRST YEAR OF college ended, Carla continued her discussions with Sandra about street soldiers and sideways politics with letters throughout the summer. By the Fourth of July, the two were trading letters weekly, Sandra with reports of her clandestine adventure in Chicago and Carla with quotes and historical misinformation she'd researched in the library.

When Uncle John delivered Carla to Greyhound for her return to campus in the fall, he pulled her suitcase from the truck bed and walked it into the depot. Hugging his niece, he wished her luck and told her again how proud he was of her.

"Don't you go scarin' them professors with all your revolution talk," Uncle John teased as Carla stood with her bag.

"I have more reason to be afraid of them and what they're trying *not* to teach me," Carla said, quite seriously, reaching up on her tiptoes to kiss her uncle on the cheek. He shook his head and chuckled, heading back to his truck.

Carla launched her sophomore year with a new confidence and more fervor than her freshman year. She greeted dormmates, joined study groups right away, even spread out a blanket on the mall some afternoons to read. Sandra wasn't on campus for the first two weeks. Her parents had discovered her summer had been spent campaigning and protesting in Chicago, and not attending a leadership camp in Milwaukee, as she'd led them to believe. They were undecided about allowing her to return to college until the last minute.

Carla was leaving the library with one of her study groups one afternoon when someone called her name from across the mall. She turned toward the voice and squinted at two figures near the flagpole. The woman's outline resembled Sandra's but was missing her roommate's signature bouffant. Moving towards one another, Carla could tell the second figure belonged to a man and the first, indeed, belonged to her roommate, with some sort of hat on her head.

As they closed the yardage between them, Carla could see it was the young man who wore the hat. He was compact and strong looking, like the cousin who might always be asked to help move wood and boxes, or the handy church member who was good at repairs. His skin was the color of molasses, and his face was stern. His eyes were dark and potent, like pot liquor.

"You'll see. She's solid," Sandy was saying, somewhat winded. The two friends embraced and pulled apart to regard one another: Carla's new rebellious slacks and Sandra's new afro.

"I think I love it," Carla said.

"Just wait 'til I get my hands on that head of yours," Sandra said.

Although Carla giggled with her friend, all of the nerves and pores and follicles and cells in her body were drawn to the man standing to the side of them.

"Carla, this is Q," Sandra said. "He worked Chicago this summer, too. Powerful, conscious brother. I wanted him to meet you before he had to go back to Detroit."

"Nice to meet you," Carla said. Extending her hand, she made sure her grip was confident and firm, the way Aunt Margaret had taught her.

A handshake tells a man whether he's meeting a damsel or a dame.

"Q," Sandra continued, "Carla is the brains behind all that material we used in the rally speeches."

Q accepted her handshake, casting down his black milk eyes to look at their clasped hands. He looked up at Carla again with a slight glimmer.

He must like dames.

"Thank you," Q said, releasing her hand. "You helped us make a powerful impact this summer."

A whip of electricity sailed between them, and Carla saw her roommate pinch a thin, knowing smile.

"If you can stand to be stuck in the heartland for a few more hours," Sandra said to Q, moving between them to link all of their elbows, "I say we go grab some burgers and tell Carla all about Chicago."

Carla's heart jumped.

Q's face remained stern, except for his eyes. Dark and intense, Carla felt the full wattage of his gaze ratchet between each and every one of her nerve endings. She wasn't sure what happened beneath that waving flag, but Carla felt the first stitch begin to unravel inside her.

Carla's Greyhound trips home went from weekly to monthly in that second year and, by the summer, she was gone. She'd told Uncle John about a summer internship she'd won and that she'd be staying on campus over the summer. John was wary but still proud of her.

"You gots to give yourself a rest from all your studies, don'tcha?" he'd asked.

"Not to get where I'm going, Uncle John," Carla told him. "Plus, I have to work twice as hard as these white people to get there."

These white people. That was the last conversation John had with his niece in person. She wrote a few letters from campus over the summer and fall, and then postcards came with no return address. The postcards and scant letters were filled with updates on marches, uprising, community service projects, and "we." He drove up to the college when the trees were bare to learn Carla had not returned to campus for her third year. John gave mumbled reports of her whereabouts at the family gatherings, but everyone stopped asking when they saw how much it was hurting him to talk about it.

After a year, when Carla would have been loading into his blue pickup for her senior year at MacMurray, a young man appeared on Uncle John's porch. He referred to himself as Carla's husband. He had extended his hand to John, like a new man, and John stared at him. How could this boy travel all this way, to his home, and not have Carla with him? What kind of man asks for a woman's hand in marriage after the ceremony? Without his bride?

The boy tried to explain Carla's instructions, that she didn't want to return to Decatur until she could explain it all; that she was afraid Uncle John and the rest of the family wouldn't understand; that there was still so much work to be done.

"What kind of work is more important than lettin' her family lay eyes on her after all this time?" John asked, his hands balled into fists. He wanted to snatch this boy by the collar, pull him close, let him smell the terror and venom on his breath, but the boy was only doing his niece's bidding. John knew this, remembered his own helpless surrender of loving Margaret.

As the boy spoke, in his book-polished tongue, John flashed to how his feet had trembled inside his church shoes on the Tuesday he went to meet Margaret's parents. John had prayed he didn't reek of the ranch where he worked dehorning bulls or that he didn't leak all of his Arkansas onto their polished floors. Margaret's parents had lace doilies on the couch and opera music playing on a record player. John had been alone, too. Margaret had wanted her father to see

John as a man, brave enough to face them on his own. She'd always believed in the core of him.

Carla must believe in this boy, John thought. He fought himself to listen to the boy, describing their work in *the struggle* and the life they wanted to build together. They would return to college after a year, they boy had said. They would also have a big church wedding then. Right now, they were in love; they were living in accordance to God; and they were committed to making a better world for blacks.

John didn't want to like this boy. Not one bit. But he did. He knew his Bluebell did, too.

"When is she coming home . . . to visit?" John asked, choking down the last part.

"We're planning to come home this summer," the boy had said. "Coming here and visiting my family in Detroit."

"Detroit?"

"Yessir," the boy said. "My parents have a small sundry shop. Pop is a deacon at the church. We know you all have worried, but I wanted to meet you and assure you face to face—man to man—that I am doing right by your niece and doing my very best to look after her."

John felt his temples and nostrils flare, but the boy did not flinch. He stood planted in his dress shoes and black slacks and thick Afro, waiting for John's worst. John took a deep breath and invited the boy inside. Through the evening, they talked about Motown, baseball, four-barrel carburetors, the Book of Revelation, and the man being the head of his home. They shared a few glasses of whiskey and a plate of fish. John insisted the boy wait until the morning to drive on.

"I suppose Carla don't want me to know where you's livin'?" John asked the following day, as the boy shook his hand on his porch.

"No, she doesn't," the boy said. "But I'll tell you we're still in Illinois, close enough and far enough away from Chicago and the state line. Neither one of us cared for Chicago as a place to live forever. We're thinking about our roots now, sir. Was able to find us a nice, clean apartment, and I'm making ends meet working nearby at a butcher shop. My daddy taught me a thing or two about carving meat."

John smiled at the boy, hearing an echo of his own appeal to Margaret's father so many years ago. Before he sent the boy on his way, he disappeared into his bedroom and came out with a tattered envelope, thick with papers.

"A lot of people in my wife's family done worked hard to make sure all they kin is provided for," John said to the boy, handing him the envelope. "I don't know 'bout yo' people, but I never knew of such a thing. I was grateful, by God, and blessed. Tell my Bluebell I will respect her wishes and wait until summertime to talk to her. Trusting you to keep her safe 'til then, Quentin."

John received a short letter from Carla within the week, thanking him for the insurance papers and gushing about her two favorite men. Summer came and went, and John never heard from either Carla or Quentin again. The rest of the McCalls sealed away Carla's name, even after John's death. It would be years before her name would be spoken again.

FOURTEEN

BALONEY

My name is Te'Pamela. I go by Pam. Welcome to the McKissick School of Torture. Your sentence is every Saturday for the rest of your life! What's your name? What grade are you in? I'm in fifth grade. I hate social studies. I get all As in math. What's your best subject? Are you an only child, too? I like not having brothers and sisters. Sometimes I wish there was another person for Mama to yell at. Haha! Where's your mother? OK. This is a whole bunch of questions. Write me back!

> *Pam*

. . .

My name is CeCe. My whole name is Crimson Celeste, but CeCe is easier. I'm in fifth grade, too. I go to Neil Armstrong Elementary. I don't live over here. I live on Fountain Drive. I don't have any brothers or sisters, either. I don't think I like it much anymore. Do you like to read? That's my best subject. Reading and English. I do OK in math. I just don't like it very much. What's your favorite color? Mine is yellow. When is your birthday? Mine was September 25. I'm really 11! I can't wait to be 18. That's when they say I can leave. Which Jackson do you like best?

> *CeCe*

. . .

I love the Sylvers! The Jacksons are good, too. Randy is so fine! Foster Sylver is the finest! I'm not allowed to listen to world music (what

*Mama calls music she doesn't like). Only clean songs. Sylvers, Os-
monds, gospel, old Motown, stuff like that. Does your mother let you
listen to the radio? I can't wait to be 18 either! I'm going to college,
then I'm moving to Paris. They love Black people in Paris. I heard that
in a movie. I don't mind reading. It just takes me a long time to read a
whole book. I don't always like to sit still for so long. I can sit still for
a movie though! I love movies. Mama lets me watch movies on TV. On
Friday nights, they play the big movies. With no cussing. I don't know
what's so wrong with cussing. I'm not a baby! I can hear SHIT FUCK
HELL DAMN. My birthday is April 11. You just had a birthday! Now
that we're friends, I can be invited to your party next year! Ha! Ha! Do
you like piano?*

    Pam

• • •

*Piano is OK. It's hard though. I thought Ms. McKissick was going to be
mean. She's nice. I'd rather learn to paint or pottery or something. I like
making things. I went to camp this summer (yuck!) and we made stuff
every day. I liked that part. I liked the lake, too. I liked walking in the
woods. That's it. Everything else about camp was terrible. You're going
to college? Are you rich? Maybe I can visit your mansion one day! I
don't watch movies. I bet I'd like them. I don't do a lot of things. I want
to. I never thought about living in another country. Not even another
state. I would be scared. Are you scared of anything? I hate spiders.*

    CeCe

• • •

*I'm not scared of spiders or mice or stuff like that. Mama makes me
kill the bugs that get in the apartment. She's so big and bad but can't
step on a spider! She makes me laugh. That's why I don't pay her any
attention, most of the time. She's been yelling and bossing me around
ever since I was a little kid. I remember when she wasn't so big and
bad. I remember when she was just bad. We had a really rough life*

before she got saved. We had lots of secrets and stuff. Made my stomach hurt all the time. When she started going to church, I started to feel better. She changed from being scary to being saved. Both were hard on me! Haha! But I'd choose this every time. You didn't answer me about your mother. I hope she didn't die. I'm sorry, if she did. Do you live with your father? You should curl your hair. We're too big for two ponytails.

Pam

· · ·

I never tried to curl my hair before. Do I look dumb? I didn't know how to make anything else but ponytails. A lady in my building showed me how to make curlers from paper bags. It was pretty easy, but my mother said I have to leave them in overnight for the curls to stay. Funny. She hasn't taught me many things. This therapy stuff must be working. See? She's not dead. She's just been acting like it on the inside. She sees a brain doctor while I'm at piano. Three more months. I didn't know my daddy. He died in Vietnam. My mama misses him a lot. Makes her so sad she can't get out of bed some days. It gets worse every year. I don't remember her being like this when I was little. She used to make me laugh and give me big hugs. I like what you said about being glad things are getting better, but not forgetting that things weren't always this way. I'm glad she's getting help from Dr. Harper, but it's been so hard and so unfair for such a long time. I try really hard not to be mad all the time. Yeah, secrets suck! Haha! I'll keep your secrets safe, though. You'll keep mine too, right? Does your school dress up for Halloween? I might be a movie star or something.

CeCe

· · ·

I'm sorry about your daddy. I don't know mine. He's part of my mother's "bad" years, I guess. I'm not allowed to ask about him anymore.

She said I wouldn't like him very much anyway. This might be mean, but I don't think she knows who he is. She would tell me different things. He was a teacher, then he was a drummer, then he was dark-skinned, then he was light-skinned. There was always a new uncle coming around when I was little. Not really. She just told me to call them uncle. Another secret . . . my mother used to do drugs and stuff. It was always scary then. Strange people. Strange apartments. Strange everything. We even lived in a shelter for homeless people once. That place was so nasty. Someone who worked there said the state would make me live in foster care. My mother started to change. We went to a special house for women and their kids. She met with a therapist, too. It helped her stop doing drugs. She started going to church. Then someone got her a job at a dentist's office. We moved away from the city all the way out to Birchwood. She always says, "You have to do different to be different." She says smart stuff like that all time, when she's not yelling about something. Haha! Don't worry about your mother. She's gonna be OK. We have costumes at school. I'm not allowed. Mama said it's devil worship. Oh well . . . Hey, your hair looks good!

Pam

* * *

I can't believe we have so much in common! Maybe we're twins! Haha! I'm already sad about ending piano lessons. (Well, not piano . . .) Mama only has two more months left of her therapy. Do you have a phone? Are you allowed to talk on the phone?

CeCe

* * *

Yes! We have a phone. I'm allowed to talk after I do my homework. Here's my number: 683-9821. Call me on Tuesday. We have choir practice on Tuesday. She's always in a good mood when she gets to have choir practice.

Pam

* * *

It was cool to talk to you on the phone. Your voice is deep like a grown-up! You didn't get in trouble, did you? Sounded like your mother was mad. Are you a good singer? I sing like Whitney Houston . . . but only in the shower. Haha! What did you ask for Christmas?

CeCe

* * *

I got my Atari! A good report card spends like money! Remember that, CeCe!! Haha! I had another great idea (you know me, girlfriend)—let's have a sleepover!!! I think Mama will say yes. Christmastime makes her loosen up. Hallelujah! I love you CeCe! I'm so glad you're my best friend! Did you get your best gift?

Pam

* * *

I'm glad you're my best friend too. A slumber party???!!!??? Yes, I just got my best gift.

CeCe

* * *

CeCe spent the night at Pam's house at least once a month for the next year. On a slumber weekend before the end of the school year, CeCe and Pam admired their experimental hairdos when Pam's mother called from the den.

"Te'Pamela," she called, "what's the name of that new Richard Pryor movie?"

"Umm . . . " Pam called back, staring at the wall separating her from her mother's voice. CeCe watched Pam drum the barrel of the curling iron, visibly straining her memory for a movie title. CeCe continued to pack up the barrettes, bobby pins, and gels.

"Bustin' Out?" Pam said.

"Loose," her mother yelled back through the wall. "Bustin' Loose." Pam and CeCe heard her mother repeat the movie title to someone on the phone. Pam said her mother had been on the phone a lot lately.

"I don't know who Mama's been gabbing to," Pam said, "but they're keeping her off my ass."

"Maybe we should start handing out your number to strangers and install a switchboard," CeCe whispered back, launching the two girls into a giggling fit of pantomimes and half-finished sentences.

While they clutched their stomachs, trying to steady their breath, CeCe smiled at their visual. Best friends laughing heartily after an afternoon of beautifying and girl talk, relaxed and worry-free.

Once in the family room, the girls bunkered in with chips, Kool-Aid, and pizza, less the four slices Pam's mother always took first as the "pizza sponsor." The girls stretched on the floor in front for TV waiting for the Friday night movie to start. A commercial interrupted their banter:

"I don't know, Becky," one woman said, leaning conspiratorially to her friend across a small cafe table. "Sometimes I don't feel . . . fresh."

"I know what you mean," the friend said in a confident whisper. "I have those days, too. But you know what I use . . . "

CeCe and Pam giggled.

"She just nasty," CeCe said, angling a pizza slice into her mouth.

Pam laughed, taking a sip from her cup. "It's not nasty," she said to CeCe. "it's—uh—natural."

Pam kept her eyes on the screen and CeCe kept her eyes peeled on Pam. Both girls started to smile the longer Pam pretended to ignore CeCe's glare.

CeCe finally shoved Pam in the shoulder, toppling her over. "Come off it!" CeCe commanded.

Pam's mother bellowed from her bedroom. "Y'all better not be tearing up nothin' in there."

"No, ma'am," Pam called back, suppressing a laugh as CeCe shoved her again.

"Give it up, I said," CeCe said.

"OK, OK," Pam said, rolling away from CeCe's third shove. "Well, ever since I started my period I worry about smelling bad."

CeCe wrinkled her nose. "You smell bad?"

"No, but I don't want to," Pam said. "The school nurse said our bodies have natural odors. Women have a scent that's natural. She said it's the fluids that, y'know, coat our—y'know, stuff."

"Like bicycle oil?" CeCe teased.

They laughed. "I guess so," Pam said.

"If it doesn't smell bad," CeCe said, "then what's it like?"

Pam munched on her pizza while she considered. "Baloney."

CeCe stared. "Baloney?" she said. "Like . . . baloney?"

Pam nodded, and the girls howled with laughter.

The two kept laughing and talking until the feature movie began to play. Their conversation shifted from school nurses to school rules to school dances to, of course, boys. Hours after the movie ended and the network had signed off, the girls were nudged awake and herded, half-sleeping, into Pam's room.

The next morning, CeCe was dropped off at home while Pam and her mother went on to church. It used to be the rule for CeCe to attend with them, if she stayed the night on a Saturday instead of their usual Friday.

CeCe hadn't been to church enough to decide whether or not she liked it. Mrs. Anderson had taken CeCe to her church once. That had been nice. It reminded her of the white clapboard churches described in *The Color Purple*. Going to church with Pam and her mother was different. Pam's mother entered the massive building like a battlefield. They stopped, first, by the hallway bulletin board, where she would jot down names from the "Sick and Shut-in" list.

Pam explained her mother would always say extra prayers for them, the way strangers had to have said prayers for them once upon a time.

This morning, Pam's mother allowed additional time to detour and take CeCe home.

"She said she couldn't stand watching you sit comatose through another service," Pam said as they slipped on their shoes. "She said if you haven't taken to it by now, it's not her place to make you."

"Oh," CeCe replied. It was true she tended to zone out after the choir's first selection. "Was she mad?"

"Not really," Pam said, smoothing the edge of her blanket. "I guess she thought she was helping, since your mother doesn't, y'know, take you to church."

Stung, CeCe said, "My mother doesn't take me shopping, either. Tell Gwen she can jump on that, too, if she really wants to help out."

"Slow your roll, cowgirl," Pam said with a warning in her voice. "You know Mama was only looking out. She's not dissing your mother."

CeCe let out a slow breath and mumbled an apology. She wondered when the knee-jerk protection for her mother would calm itself.

"So, now that she's saved me from hell," CeCe said, deliberately upbeat, "will she let us go to the movies by ourselves?"

Pam laughed. "She said she'll think about it, which sounded like a 'no' to me."

"Keep the faith, sister, keep the faith."

FIFTEEN

HAZY

CeCe couldn't account for the hours between locking Doris' old house and stepping into her apartment. She had returned to work and sat through a meeting and picked up dish detergent on the way home, but her attention had been anchored to the thick envelope of signed documents in her car.

It was 7 p.m. and her mother had showered already for bed. In spite of her own evolution over the years, CeCe's mother still went to bed incredibly early. CeCe didn't mind her mother's twelve and fourteen hours of sleep now that her waking hours were spent out of bed.

CeCe rinsed suds from the pot and laid it down in the dish rack. She hung the dishrag over the edge of the sink to keep it from smelling sour, the way Aunt Rosie had shown her their first summer together. CeCe turned to lean against the sink. She still had on pantyhose and her work clothes, and her feet wanted to slide across the tile. CeCe remembered playing that game in her socks as a child. She'd slipped and banged her head against the cabinet once, frightened when she woke up minutes later on the kitchen floor. She hadn't known how long she'd been there, sprawled like a rag doll against their sink, but CeCe had been sure her mother hadn't noticed.

Today, CeCe wasn't even annoyed with her mother's worried

calls. She'd planned to stay late at the office to offset her time with Doris, until her mother started calling, asking if CeCe was on her way home and asking her to please be careful. Her mother didn't have much conversation for CeCe once she arrived home, but was visibly at ease.

CeCe once seethed at this latent care and concern but, in recent years, she accepted her mother's development for what it was: too late and not about her.

When Dr. Harper recommended the social programs at the Stringer Center, CeCe had been skeptical. How could a woman afraid of talking and breathing become social, she had asked. Dr. Harper had taken great care to explain the concepts of parallel play, initially observed in toddlers, but also useful in helping his adult patients re-enter their lives.

"They don't have to interact," Dr. Harper had explained, "but pursuing a shared activity goal together lends a critical social context. Baby steps, if you will."

Her mother's first *shared activity goal* had been beads. Then collages. Then herb plants. Now it was crochet. With each project, CeCe would nod in appeasement as if her mother were a preschooler with fragile self-confidence.

"You've been the parent in this relationship since forever," Pam reminded her when CeCe used to complain about her mother's art classes at the Center. "Now you and your little one have entered the arts-and-crafts stage."

For all Pam knew about little ones, CeCe would tease. Pam had been adamant since she and CeCe been children themselves about never having kids, and she managed to marry a man who didn't want children, either. Pam lived in Seattle now, where she and her husband had moved after grad school four years ago. CeCe had only seen her friend on Christmases since. She'd been invited again and again to visit them in Seattle, but CeCe couldn't imagine boarding a plane without being consumed with worry about her mother and grease fires. Confused bus routes. Finger picking. Backsliding.

"Look, you know I get it, but you're being fucking ridiculous now," Pam snapped into the phone when CeCe called to say she couldn't travel for her friend's twenty-fifth birthday bash. "Caring for your mother does not have to mean forfeiting your own life, CeCe. You need to call that Dr. Hampton dude and figure out a new game plan."

"Harper," CeCe had said, trying to redirect the pulsing in her head. "Dr. Harper."

"What the fuck ever."

CeCe missed the party and she and Pam had gone a few weeks—a record—without calling. CeCe knew her friend was right, but didn't want to admit she was afraid. Scaffolding a thin existence around the care of her mother was all CeCe had ever known. The eighteen months she had spent living on her own had been traumatic for them both. CeCe's social handicaps were glaring and frightening and, on her own for the first time in two decades, her mother had not recognized the multitude of ways she had begun to waste away through the years.

Leaning against the kitchen sink, not letting her stocking feet slide along the tile squares, CeCe jumped when her cell phone rang. She had only been able to give Pam a bulleted account before Pam's work meeting. CeCe greeted her friend while slipping on her shoes to step outside. Leaning against the Lincoln, CeCe recounted the morning.

"Why are you whispering?" Pam interrupted.

"I don't want my voice to carry," CeCe said.

"Are you telling me you actually have company?" Pam asked.

"Company?"

Pam's laugh throttled through the phone. "Yes, company," Pam said. "That's what it's called when people who don't live in your house come visit you at your house."

"Forget you, Te'Pamela," CeCe said, grinding out the syllables. Pam hated her full name.

Pam halted their banter with a gasp. "You didn't tell Ms. Carla about the house, did you?"

CeCe swallowed. "Not yet. I wanted to—"

"You're thinking about moving without her, aren't you?"

"Don't say it like that."

"Like what?" Pam asked.

"Like I'm abandoning her," CeCe said.

Pam was quiet. CeCe could hear her friend's tone shift and settle. "Don't do that, CeCe," she said. "'Abandon' is a word I wouldn't dare use with you. You better not either."

"I should be excited, but all I feel is this knot in my stomach," CeCe said, looking down at her feet, bare and ashen inside her commuter flats. Pam had taught her that trick, too, wearing flat shoes when she drove to prevent floor mat scuffs on the backs of her leather pumps. Although CeCe's height actually had her working the car pedals with her toes, she liked the ritual. The simple act of changing her shoes reminded her every day that she was a full-fledged, professional, grown woman. Right now, with her eyes rimming with tears, CeCe felt less than grown up. Right now, she felt the weight of the universe on her five-year-old shoulders all over again.

"My own house, Pam," CeCe continued, rolling a jagged rock beneath one foot. A hot tear streamed her cheek. "A house. For me! But I know how selfish that sounds. I'm angry for feeling ashamed that I want it all to myself. I can't trust if I'm choosing with my brain or my emotions. I don't know what to do."

"Pack your shit. That's what you do," Pam said. "Your mama has taken the bus by herself for a while now, and she's memorizing the evening news report, painting stained glass, making out with lesbians and shit. She is going to be fine."

"They did not make out," CeCe said, shaking her head at the phone. CeCe's mother had walked into the apartment across the hall once, disoriented from using the rear entrance and confusing left side and right side. She'd interrupted the lesbian couple who lived there by standing by as they had sex in their kitchen.

"Hey," Pam said, "if you watch, you're involved."

"She was in shock, Pam. Stop it," CeCe said, kicking away the rock. "You're supposed to be giving me advice right now."

The dusky summer sky turned dark. CeCe leaned back against the car and looked up to the changing heavens. No matter how intently she watched a sunset, CeCe could never detect their surrender, the moment when hazy hues of orange and violet would give way to the resolute darkness of nighttime.

"My best advice is to breathe," Pam said. "You don't have to figure anything out tomorrow. That place can stay vacant forever, if you want. It's yours."

CeCe looked back toward the apartment and the square of light glaring through the window of her mother's bedroom. She let out a weighted breath.

"OK," Pam said. "Tell me about the back yard again."

SIXTEEN

YELLOW

He was waiting for her again, next to the mailbox, hands jammed in his pockets like always. He wasn't there every day, not at first. His appearances were random, seemingly governed by unseen forces rather than time. CeCe first noticed him two weeks ago when she'd been peering out of the library windows at the darkening stretch of sky. The early summer had begun to unwind itself in spasms of rain showers and CeCe found herself waiting out a downpour. Her bus stop was directly across the street, but had no shelter or awning. It was just wide open to the rain.

CeCe watched from the library window as people hunched and scattered, but the dark-skinned man didn't budge. When the first drops fell, fat and heavy, the dark-skinned man never even looked up to the swelling clouds. The man didn't look to CeCe like one of the "crazies" Mr. Curtis had warned her about at the newsstand. CeCe had imagined the crazies would stumble like drunks or have ghoulish skin and tattered clothes. The dark-skinned man looked like he was waiting for someone, for something to happen.

CeCe pressed her cheek to the glass. At the far end of the boulevard, she could see the westbound Kennedy bus lumbering around the corner at Market Street. CeCe bounded from the window, past the librarian's desk, through the front lobby, down the concrete steps and across the street to meet the bus before it sighed to a stop.

CeCe gloated from moving so fast. So fast, she hardly got wet. So fast, even the wind had whispered her name. CeCe dropped into an open seat and the bus lurched forward. She smiled at her reflection in the window. As the bus pulled away, the dark-skinned man smiled, too.

He was there again the next day. The municipal plaza, a smooth concrete streetscape connecting the library, post office, and city hall, stood brilliant in the summer sun. Businessmen strolled in twos, women whisked by on bicycles, children danced on the long and palatial library steps. Like a black bird, the dark-skinned man perched beside the mailbox, facing the library steps. CeCe turned from the window and tried to concentrate on her magazines. The more pages she flipped and the longer he stood at his post, still and resolute, the more curious CeCe grew.

Abandoning magazines, CeCe inched toward the window to watch the Bird Man. He wore another long-sleeved shirt, in spite of the humid weather. CeCe could tell he was short, like her, and his body was squat and strong, like crates stacked atop one another. CeCe wondered what he waited for all these days. The part of her mind that knew things for no reason, the part Mrs. Anderson called *intuition*, knew she should say something to the Bird Man, knew he wasn't one of the crazies.

CeCe moved to the couches but still couldn't sink into her book. She helped the librarian scoop and shelve stray books, but the Bird Man pulled her to the window. CeCe decided to collect her things and make her way outside. When she reached the top of the library steps, the Bird Man faced the street. Clutching her denim tote bag, CeCe descended the long stone steps. She kept her eyes on her sneakers until she reached the bottom and didn't stop moving her feet until she stood several feet behind him. Bird Man concentrated on concentrating, turning his head slowly to scan the boulevard. CeCe could see the muscles of his jaws grinding and churning.

"What are you looking for?" CeCe asked, holding her tote now with both hands. A bus pulled away from the corner, its passengers emptied into the summer heat. The man continued to face the street and CeCe was unsure of her fresh bravery.

"My name is CeCe," she tried again.

"Nice to meet you, CeCe," Bird Man said, turning only his head to speak to her in profile. His hands stayed jammed in his pockets. His face stayed pointed to the sidewalk.

CeCe waited. Her *intuition* told her to wait.

"What does CeCe stand for?" the Bird Man asked, angling his dark eyes to look up at her.

"Crimson," she said, rolling her eyes. "Crimson *Celeste*."

The man laughed. He turned to face her, hands still in his pocket.

"You don't like your name?" he asked.

"It's a little weird," she said, shrugging. "I don't have to explain so much with CeCe."

The Bird Man jutted his chin in agreement. "That makes sense," he said.

The Bird Man and CeCe faced one another on the plaza. Mid-morning traffic and pedestrians buzzed around them, oblivious to the wavelengths stretching between them.

"You're not going to tell me your name?" CeCe asked.

"Please, forgive my manners," he said, placing a hand on his chest. "My name is Q."

Q did not extend his hand or entreat her any further. CeCe liked that.

"That's OK," she said, dropping the tote bag to hang between her feet. She swung the denim bag like a pendulum, waiting for him to speak.

"You're not afraid to talk to me?" he finally asked.

CeCe shook her head, watching him search the sidewalk for words.

"Well, I've been afraid to talk to you, Bluebell," Q said, making CeCe and her tote bag freeze.

Her memory skipped through scraps and torn corners to locate this name. Bluebell. It was familiar, like watery images in a dream. CeCe's feet wound slowly backwards, away from Q and onto the library staircase. Maybe it was her intuition again.

"Please don't be scared," Q said, hands flying from his pockets now. He kept them low at his sides, but his fingers were still fanned wide and pleading. "Please don't be scared."

"Who told you to call me that?" CeCe asked. She was six steps away from him now. Passersby began to look twice.

"Crimson," he started, seemingly unsure of how to string together his words. "I used to know your family. Your Uncle John called your mother Bluebell when she was little. Did you know that?"

CeCe stopped moving backwards. Q relaxed his hands.

Bluebell. Before her mother's Sad became impenetrable, CeCe remembered her mother washing her hair, dragging a fingertip heavy with thick grease along her scalp, and twisting her coarse locks into braids with a rattle of blue baubles and barrettes. Ever since she'd been doing her own hair, CeCe only managed to wrestle her hair into two angry knots or braids. Bluebell was one of the few details CeCe's mother had shared about her youth. She knew her mother came from a place called Decatur and before her Aunt Margaret and Uncle John had died, they called her Bluebell. CeCe looked at Q and crossed her narrow arms.

"How do you know my mother?" she asked. "Does she know you?"

"Yes," Q said, slipping his hands back into his pockets. "She knows me."

CeCe squinted an eye at him. Her intuition asked, "What's the Q for?"

The Bird Man hesitated. "Quentin."

CeCe felt her feet and hands turn to lead.

"Quentin what?"

"Weathers."

CeCe's mind couldn't work fast enough. Grown-ups, she knew, had a tough time saying what they meant. She looked at the Bird Man and waited for the weight of Quentin Weathers to crush her shoulders. She moved toward him again, step six, five, four, three. CeCe peered at him, tried to add up his angles. Step two.

"Mama said my daddy's name was Quentin Weathers," she said

Q kept his hands in his pockets but his eyes on her face. "Yes, Crimson," he said, his voice a whisper. "That's me."

CeCe felt her arms pump and her feet slapping against the concrete, propelling her small body off of the last step, past Quentin and threads of passersby, across the thickening current of taxis, mopeds, and sedans, and onto the curb across the street where a bus was approaching. It wasn't the Kennedy line, but CeCe climbed aboard anyway.

Her chest heaved as she watched the divided wake of onlookers examining their bumped elbows, adjusting handbags, looking around for more. Quentin was gone, and her tote bag. CeCe turned to watch the city approach her through the bus window. Four blocks away, still engorged with adrenaline, her hands trembled. CeCe pulled the cord and got off for a transfer at Marshall Avenue. By the time she reached their apartment, CeCe had compiled a list of questions in her head for her mother.

CeCe found her mother at this time of the afternoon sitting on the couch staring out the window instead of the kitchen table. CeCe walked in without speaking, waiting for her mother's voice to arrest her as she made her way down the hall.

Where have you been, young lady?

Do you know what time it is?

Where is your book bag?

How was your day?

Nothing.

CeCe walked the short hallway to the bathroom. She closed the door and leaned against it, still listening for some reprimand to call out to her from the living room. She faced the full-length mirror behind the door. It had been discarded in the courtyard last fall, its frame cracked and unsightly. The apartment manager allowed CeCe to keep it and watched through his office window as she tussled the awkward plank into her house.

She examined herself. The way her short legs were beginning to lengthen, the musculature of her arms, the inactivity behind her tank top. CeCe touched the slim scar on her collarbone where she'd fallen on a wedge of broken glass during a first-grade field trip. She'd been a terrifying mess of blood that day. She felt like a terrifying mess again today. Just no blood.

CeCe peered at her face, at her dark, onyx eyes. Everything else on her face came from her mother—the small and heavy lips, the dark, plush lashes, and the peanut butter color of her skin. Her eyes were of something else.

Someone else.

CeCe leaned in closer, thinking of Quentin. His eyes had been sad, but kind. They were also dark as oil. Like hers. She had asked about him many times before, but her mother hadn't offered much. Quentin Weathers had been her boyfriend a long time ago. Quentin Weathers died in Vietnam. Quentin Weathers was her father.

CeCe opened the bathroom door and walked into the kitchen. Her mother was rinsing her coffeepot and mug. CeCe sat at their small table and watched her mother's movements. Fill pot with water. Two drops of detergent. Wash and rinse. Place on the rack. Pick up mug. Wash. Rinse. Stack. Wipe hands. The same movements. Every day.

CeCe watched her mother's slow gestures, holding her breath. For the second time in this past hour and for only the hundredth time this week, CeCe hoped for a skip in this groove. She'd once read a story about a geneticist racing to thwart a renegade band of test subjects and the book had left CeCe thinking often about mutations, hoping an aberration would bring her mother back to her.

Her mother's eyes floated to CeCe's as she retreated to their bedroom. CeCe forced a faint grin and her mother nodded back at her. CeCe watched the afternoon soon follow her mother out of the kitchen and into the hall. Twenty-six steps. The groan of the bureau drawer. Surrender of mattress springs. Settling of sheets. Every day.

CeCe ignored the tears as they plummeted to the table. Nothing was different today from yesterday, or last week, or when she was seven, or since she could remember. CeCe was angry with her foolishness, but couldn't help hoping for a link in their chain to snap.

CeCe waited for four days. She began to worry that Quentin would never return to his mailbox perch. She was at a table leaning over a *Mad* magazine. Her attention had long abandoned the pages in *Right On!* and *Ebony* and now Stephen King, her favorite author. CeCe would skim a few pages and crane her neck toward the window. When she saw him, CeCe scrambled to her feet and, for the first time ever, bolted from the library without clearing the table and returning all of her items to the librarian's desk.

She bounded down the stairs, her high tops skipping the long cement steps. CeCe stopped at the third step. He wore another button-down shirt, tucked neatly into blue jeans this time. CeCe could tell he'd been holding his breath while she galloped down the long staircase. He released and relaxed his shoulders when she spoke.

"Hi," she said.

He swallowed. "Hi."

"I looked for you," she said.

His back straightened, "You did?" he asked. "I wanted to come right back, but . . . I didn't feel so good."

"You were scared, a little?" CeCe asked.

Quentin lowered his head and chuckled. "Yeah, Crimson," he said, "I was."

CeCe noticed her book bag leaning against the mailbox next to his feet. He picked it up and held it out between them. CeCe accepted it.

"Mama said you died," CeCe said, pulling her book bag onto her shoulder. Quentin flinched, as if the blunt statement slapped at his face.

"I did, kind of," he said.

CeCe squinted at him quizzically. "They brought you back to life, like Frankenstein?"

"Not exactly," Quentin said, "but I did spend a lot of time with a lot of doctors."

"Mad scientist doctors?"

Another quiet laugh. "It felt that way sometimes."

CeCe gripped her book bag. Quentin slipped his hands back into his pockets.

"Are you still scared?"

"Not as much."

"Me neither."

Quentin gave a thin smile.

"I bet you have a lot of questions," he asked.

CeCe patted the back pocket of her painter's pants. "I made a list."

Quentin laughed out loud this time, a resonant rumbling that reminded CeCe of heavy furniture being moved around in the apartment upstairs. CeCe imagined him laughing so loud the ground beneath them would tremor, causing the people walking by to stagger. She decided she liked his laugh very much.

"I'll answer any questions you ask me, Crimson," Quentin said. "We can sit right here on the steps, if you like, so everyone can see. I won't sit close—"

"Uuhhh!" CeCe said, turning up her nose. "People spit on these steps. Let's go by the bus stop. There's a bench in front of the flower shop."

CeCe tipped down the steps in her white high tops, leading them across the street. Quentin followed at a distance, as promised, and stood awkwardly near the curb when CeCe plopped down on the bench. She slid to the edge of the bench, making room for him.

"I think I'll stand over here for a while," he said. "I'm more comfortable standing."

CeCe regarded him for a moment, and shrugged. She placed her book bag on the ground between her feet and dug into her pocket. Her two plaits pointed behind her like tusks as she read from her neatly written sheet.

"OK," CeCe began. "Why did you go to Vietnam?"

With hands anchored in his pockets, Quentin said, "My number got pulled. I had to go."

"Your phone number?" CeCe asked, tilting her head to the side.

"My draft number. All the men who were eighteen and older got numbers according to our birthdays. I had a pretty high number and didn't have to go my first year. My second year . . . " Quentin's voice trailed off as he looked away from CeCe. "Turns out I had only been almost lucky."

They held the silence between them until CeCe said, "We had to do the Presidential Fitness Test one time and I faked a stomachache so I wouldn't have to. I'm good at the sit-ups, but I can't climb up the rope. Maybe you should've faked a stomachache."

Quentin rumbled another laugh. "I didn't think of that."

"How old were you?" CeCe asked.

"Only nineteen," Quentin said. "By the time I turned twenty, I was already in Vietnam."

CeCe thought of the apartment manager's son, nineteen and home from college for the summer. CeCe found him sitting against the wall near the Dumpsters once, listening to his Walkman instead of working. He'd let CeCe listen to the screaming guitars inside his headphones. Skinny and pimple-faced, he was scared of his dad. She tried to imagine the manager's son in a war movie, but couldn't.

"I bet you were really scared, huh?" CeCe asked, tucking her feet beneath the bench.

"We were all scared," Quentin said. "So many of us were dying over there, and most of us didn't even know why we were fighting."

CeCe scrunched her nose again.

"They didn't tell you?" she asked.

"They didn't tell us the truth," Quentin said, a fervor in his voice.

CeCe leaned back against the bench. "My teacher says lying is the worst bad habit of all."

Quentin looked to the sky, as if noticing it for first time, and let out a deep breath. "Your teacher is right. When you lie, you compromise your integrity. And when you compromise your integrity, you devalue your word. When you devalue your word, you undermine your character. When you undermine your character, you limit your greatness."

CeCe blinked.

Quentin laughed.

"I'm sorry," he said. "That was kind of heavy. Do you want me to explain it?"

CeCe blinked again, and smiled. "You mean lying makes people not trust you, and when people don't trust you, you won't get help for all your goals?"

Quentin's face burst open with light. CeCe's heart thumped with pride knowing she could make him smile this way.

"That's exactly right, Crimson," Quentin said. "I guess I shouldn't be surprised. Your mother is the smartest woman I've ever met."

CeCe's entire face crinkled at that.

"*Mama?*"

Quentin's face twisted this time, stripping the smile from his face. "You don't think your mother is smart, Crimson?"

CeCe shrugged. "Deep down she's smart, I guess."

"Deep down?" Quentin repeated. Pulling his hands from his pockets and folding his arms across his chest, his face became stern. "What do you mean?"

CeCe shrugged again. "I mean, she doesn't say smart stuff like you just did. She doesn't say anything, really."

Quentin's face was a blend of confusion and concern. A trail of pedestrians passed between them, excusing themselves and pulling close their satchels and handbags. Once they passed, Quentin gestured to the bench and CeCe slid over for him to sit. He smoothed the front of his shirt and positioned himself on the far edge of the bench. CeCe pulled one knee onto the bench to face him sideways.

"Why don't you put your feet right here," Quentin said, tapping the pocket of his pants. "Don't worry about the dirt. It's more important for you to sit like the little lady I know you are."

It took a moment for CeCe to register his instructions, but then she remembered Mrs. Castellanos' long-ago reminders about little ladies and pinched knees. CeCe thought the rule only applied to skirts, but pulled both feet to the bench anyway. The wrought-iron railing pressed hard against her back. CeCe remembered her book bag and propped it behind her. Her sheet of questions fell to the ground and Quentin scooped it up, scanning the page.

"You have a lot of questions about killing and dying here, Crimson," Quentin said, looking at her careful, cursive letters. "You don't want to know what I was like as a kid? Or my favorite color? Or how I met your mother?"

"I guess I'm not so good at interviews and stuff," CeCe said, embarrassed. "I could only think of asking about what you were doing while me and Mama were here by ourselves."

Quentin fell quiet and so did CeCe. He looked from her to face the street and CeCe looked down to her short fingers. A lunch rush of people and traffic buzzed all around them as they traveled backwards in time. The trees netted a canopy above them, sprinkling honeysuckle flowers on the sidewalk.

"What's your favorite color?" CeCe asked. "Mine is yellow."

"I don't think I've ever heard yellow as a favorite color," Quentin said. "Mine is red."

CeCe's face lit up. "Like my name!"

"Exactly like your name," Quentin said, grinning. "Carla knew how to put the right word in the right place in just the right way. She was real exact about words, too. She'd written 'crimson' in a speech once and I changed it to 'red.' I told her it didn't matter. She snapped at me and said if it didn't matter, there wouldn't be a dozen words for red. We laughed about that a lot."

CeCe smiled at the idea of her mother getting snappy. She thought of Mrs. Johnson and the first day of school.

"She told me, huh?" Q said, a grin returning to his face.

CeCe giggled, sitting up higher on their bench.

"What did you and mama give speeches about?" she asked.

"We were organizers with the Movement," Quentin said. "I was one of the field officers who spoke at rallies and block meetings. Your mother helped write many of our speeches."

CeCe stared at him, slack-jawed.

"You never ask your mother about herself?" Quentin asked.

"Mama doesn't do so much with her words now."

Quentin refolded the sheet of paper and handed it back to CeCe. He turned to focus on CeCe.

"What do you mean, Crimson?"

CeCe swallowed. At school, she'd been conditioned to be wary of open-ended probes. Full disclosure would prompt a social worker's visit. At the corner store or the teller's window, sharing more details than necessary filled eyes with either pity or disdain. In case Quentin also campaigned to take her away from her mother, CeCe decided to deflect instead.

"I mean, she doesn't have a lot to say like she used to with you," CeCe said, crossing her legs at the ankle. "Why didn't you come see her, since you liked her so much?"

Quentin drew in a long, slow full breath. He leaned forward, resting his elbows on his knees. CeCe watched his fingers thread in and out of themselves while he built the momentum to speak.

"I couldn't, Crimson," he began. "When I got back from 'Nam I was in bad shape. That place was hell on Earth, and good men aren't supposed to suffer hell, Bluebell." Quentin turned to her. "Is that OK, if I call you that?"

CeCe nodded. She liked the idea of a nickname, even one she shared with her mother.

"I couldn't sleep when I got back," Quentin said. "Couldn't be around people. Couldn't be inside buildings for too long. I had spent four hundred and fifty-three days straight days in jungle warfare. I was messed up. Really bad."

CeCe was careful with her question. "You were . . . crazy?"

"Yes, Crimson," he said, still looking down at his thick fingers. "I was. I felt like everything inside my head and my soul had been rotted out. That war made me—"

Quentin stopped himself and looked at her.

"Made me different," he finished.

"Is that when you went to the mad scientist doctor?"

Quentin scratched the side of his jaw, relaxing his face. "Yeah," he said again. "A lot of us had to stay in the hospital for a while before we could try being civilians again. Plus, I had to get this taken care of."

Quentin stretched out his arm and rolled back his shirtsleeve. Tentacles of a scar stretched from his forearm toward his wrist. As he kept unrolling—all the way past his elbow—they looked down together at a blackened forearm with a mire of gnarled and charred skin.

"VC buried mines everywhere," he explained. "The cat walking next to me, Jake from Salt Lake, stepped on a Bouncing Betty, that's what we called them. I'll never forget his eyes when he heard the click. I knew what had happened before he said it. He tried to hold still while the rest of us crept away, but we couldn't move too fast either in case there were other mines. He couldn't hold his balance and the trap sprang up into the air. The explosion chased us in every direction. If it had been made like it was supposed to, I would've died. I got a dead arm, instead."

CeCe watched the side of Quentin's head as he spoke.

"Did Jake die?"

"Yes. He did."

"Does your arm work now?"

"Hmmm, it works for writing and picking stuff up," Quentin said. "I won't be playing basketball anytime soon. And I can't feel anything. Go ahead. Hit me."

CeCe looked at Quentin's arm, and tried to conceal her impulsive delight.

"Go ahead."

CeCe smacked Quentin's forearm as hard as she could. The sound snatched the attention of a mother walking by pushing a stroller. Quentin shrugged, with a grin. "See? Nothing. It's ugly," he said, rolling down his sleeve, "but this is what finally got me sent home. I was already over duty and this got me sent to a real military hospital. Letterman in San Diego. I thought I couldn't wait to get stateside."

"They weren't nice in the hospital?"

Quentin gave small nods. "Sure, they took good care of us, even the ones who couldn't really be helped."

"Like who? CeCe asked.

Quentin paused. "Like me."

CeCe hugged her knees, sitting up now. "But they let you leave the hospital," she said. "So they fixed you, right?"

Quentin was quiet and his fingers stilled.

"I ran away from the hospital," he said. He drew in a deep breath, closed his eyes, and continued.

"I choked a nurse," Quentin said. He took another slow breath. "I felt her near my bed. Forgot where I was."

CeCe quieted as Quentin seemed to retreat into the past.

"I jumped on her, pinned her to the wall by her neck," Quentin said. "I almost killed her."

CeCe was still. Quentin's fingers began to tap again.

"Crimson, I'm a good man," he said. "I didn't mean to hurt that woman. I could never do something like that. I sang in the choir as a kid. Wrote poetry in high school. Got myself into college. Tried to make a difference. I hate what that war turned me into."

CeCe shivered.

"Where did you go?"

"I hid in alleys and slept behind a Dumpster that night. Before I knew it, years had passed and I was just another homeless guy."

CeCe looked past him to the other men on their library perches. The other crazies. She looked back to Quentin. His face was drawn.

"Do you live behind the library?"

"No, no," Quentin said, clearing his throat. "I got some help a long time ago. A woman used to come to the viaducts looking for us veterans."

Quentin told CeCe all about the halfway house, the job at the grocery store, the doctors and therapy. It took him more than two years, he said, to sleep through the night without nightmares. Without weeping.

"I still use night-lights," he whispered.

"Me, too," CeCe whispered back.

Quentin smiled at CeCe and looked up again to the honeysuckle sky.

"One thing that kept me on this side of the grass was thinking of your mother in her wedding dress. Simple and beautiful, like her. She was so happy that day. I was so proud."

CeCe's face loosened like a drawstring, unveiling her shock and awe.

"You and Mama got *married*?"

Slow nod to the sky.

CeCe watched his face, lost on some distant memory. The afternoon sun reached down to them through the trees, spotting their limbs and the ground with light.

"You didn't want to come home?" CeCe asked.

Quentin opened his eyes and looked up to the dappling trees. He spoke his words, CeCe thought, to God first.

"I loved your mother with my whole soul, Crimson. She deserved better than what I had become. If I had been a whole person, I would've come to her sooner."

CeCe's voice was small when she finally spoke. "What about me?" she asked. "Did you think about me?"

CeCe focused her eyes on the knobs of her knees, away from the single stream of tears traveling the weathered curves of his face, like crystals against black velvet. He turned to her, insisting on her eyes.

"Bluebell, I didn't know about you. Carla's letters stopped during my first year over there. Two years ago, I was fresh off the streets. From living in that viaduct. I got up the nerve to call our old number. You answered the phone, and I knew. I will never forget how small and perfect your voice sounded. I knew I had to get stronger. I knew I had to be ready to meet you."

CeCe let her questions flatten and fall away from her tongue. She watched the Quentin clasp his hands together, not looking at her. She could see the tips of his fingers whiten beneath his own grip.

CeCe lowered her feet to the sidewalk. She slid closer to him, keeping her hands pinned beneath her knees. Tentatively, she leaned her cheek against his shoulder. They were quiet for some time. CeCe felt warm through her skin and inside her bones. Quentin felt solid next to her, while her mother always felt like a paper crane, ready to collapse at any moment. CeCe burrowed closer to Quentin, her father. She looked up to smile at him and her face crumbled into a landslide of tears.

"Sir?" a woman's voice floated behind them. CeCe and Quentin wiped, sniffled and turned to find a tall, elderly woman holding a clutch of tissues.

"I'm so sorry to intrude," she said. "The door to my flower shop was open and, well, I thought you two could use these."

The woman leaned in with a bony hand.

"Thank you," Quentin said, humbly, taking the tissues and handing some to CeCe.

"Thank *you* for everything you sacrificed for this country," the woman said, looking fondly at CeCe. "I wish I could offer more." CeCe saw his chest expand a little as he accepted the woman's praise. He raised his chin as he looked at her.

"If it wouldn't be going too far, do you think you could give my daughter one of your prettiest yellow flowers?"

The woman beamed and disappeared into her shop.

As CeCe's bus approached, she hugged her father tightly. Quentin lifted the vase of flowers to her once she had climbed the three short steps. He'd offered to ride home with her, but CeCe knew her mother would be under the comforter by this time of the afternoon. He did not wave from the sidewalk as CeCe's bus pulled away, but she could see his heart leaping. CeCe could see it in his eyes.

CeCe gazed at her flowers all the way home, turning the vase around and around in her lap. The shopkeeper had filled a small fish bowl with yellow snapdragons, roses, gazania, and daffodils. There was even a yellow ribbon tied around the lip.

CeCe pulled the arrangement close to her face and breathed in. She never wanted to forget this moment, this smell, these exact shades of sunshine, lemon, maize, construction hat, yolk, taxi, sunflower, bumblebee, mustard . . .

SEVENTEEN

GHOST

CeCe needed the fresh air of a drive after talking with Pam and decided to drive to the grocery to pick up a few items. Her cart was empty, but for a carton of milk, a bag of oranges, and a packet of chicken breast, when she spotted him somewhere between cereal and canned fruit. His maroon T-shirt, long plaid shorts, and white sneakers floated by like a vision.

She planted in the middle of the aisle trying to harness her galloping heartbeat. CeCe had seen Rocky only a handful of times since he moved back from Nashville. She'd gotten accustomed to missing him, but the pang was sharp on days like today. Pam was her go-to friend for strategy and tough love, but this situation called for Rocky's wisdom and philosophy.

CeCe walked in front of the deli cases, accelerating a bit after peering down each empty aisle. Careening past the floor cleaners and light bulbs, CeCe's neck stretched around the corner before her cart. She glimpsed the maroon shirt and tilted her cart into the aisle of coffee filters and seasonings. An unwelcome panic tightened around her chest.

"I've listened to you complain about your mother since we were sophomores," Rocky had said to her nearly nine years prior. It was the night they graduated from high school, when their affectionate bickering had sliced their friendship wide open. Rocky made another impassioned plea for her to apply to schools and leave Prescott. CeCe had stammered through her justifications before whipping back accusations of Rocky being arrogant, selfish, unsupportive, and an insincere friend.

"All I'm saying," Rocky had hissed, leveling his auburn eyes on her, "is if you're so miserable, but still *choose* to stay here, then you're as fucking crazy as her."

Now, CeCe scanned the store aisle with wide eyes. She wanted to yell out his name. After all these years, she wanted to, finally, yell out his name.

"Miss, are you alright?" said a man's voice, so startlingly close that it spun CeCe around to face him with a gasp.

"I didn't mean to scare you," he said, taking a small step back from his own cart. He was an average-sized guy but well toned, so he materialized to CeCe like a brick wall.

"You just looked like you might need some help," he said.

CeCe nodded and mumbled acknowledgements to his blue warm-ups and brilliant white shirt as her eyes darted up and down the aisle. The core of her continued to radar its signals for Rocky.

"Is someone following you?" the man asked. "Did you lose somebody?"

Over his shoulder, at the bank of registers, CeCe saw a pattern of plaid maroon slide into the express checkout. Her heart dashed around in erratic, painful circles. It wasn't Rocky. CeCe's heart collapsed, like an extinguished star.

CeCe gave a quick shake of her head, allowing her to rest her attention on the stranger. He was decent looking, with skin and eyes the color of warm molasses. Language found her again.

"I'm sorry; I thought I saw an old friend," she said.

The syrupy brown man looked behind him, followed her searching gaze, then settled a concerned look on her. He said, "Looked more like you saw a ghost, but as long as you feel OK . . . "

The stranger was, actually, quite handsome in the way ordinary features can assemble themselves into an extraordinary portrait. His jaw and forehead were broad. His skin was healthy and clean. His lips were symmetrical and supple and the facial hair well groomed. CeCe could tell his hair was freshly clipped, too. His black waves faded flawlessly into smooth brown flesh. Her father, in one of his instructional letters to her as a young girl, had listed at least a dozen signs for sifting out "trifling" men. A neat and crisp haircut was one of them.

"My name is Eric," he said. CeCe reached across their carts, side by side, to shake his extended hand.

CeCe declined his number, giving him hers instead (another commandment from her father's letters) and insisted walking to her car without his escort. As soon as she slid the key into the ignition, her phone rang.

"I'm on my way, Mama."

EIGHTEEN

WHISK

CeCe entered the apartment unit, marching the corridor to their front door. The grocery store bags swung by her sides. She felt emboldened. CeCe recalled earning a sales award once and being called to the front of a conference room at a district meeting. Her inner-city store had never been expected to outperform the affluent suburban locations. It only happened twice during her five years there, but it did happen and she never forgot the way her shoulders pulled upward as she walked to the front of the room and the patter of applause that followed her.

CeCe moved down the hall and into her apartment with the same strident walk. Cable news anchors murmured at the end of the hall, where CeCe knew she would find her mother propped in the arm-chair. When her mother began to emerge from her fugue eight years ago, ravenous for headlines and news stories, CeCe thought it was her mother's effort to reclaim lost years.

When she moved her mother into this four-unit, CeCe made sure their cable package had every possible news channel. Dr. Harper had advised CeCe against further codependency. The relationship with her mother was more habit than necessity by that point, he'd said. CeCe had insisted the therapist was wrong, citing her mother's shredded and infected cuticles. Dr. Harper reminded CeCe that the injury had been an isolated episode of anxiety. Pam had co-signed with Dr. Harper, saying it had become hard to tell who was enabling whom. Rocky had called her a tragic coward.

But things would be different, now. Doris' house had given CeCe a rare second chance, like Halley's Comet blazing across her sky. The resentment she'd clutched to her chest for so many years felt unwieldy for the first time. She was ready to seize that streak of fire now. They both were.

CeCe moved toward the clipped and manicured television voices. Her mother sat in the armchair, her narrow shoulders not even touching the wings of the tall chair. She reminded CeCe of a hand-carved figurine, her brown elfin features dulled from anguish and age. Her mother was still an attractive woman, CeCe thought, though hollowed and distant. CeCe looked at her mother, soaking in the news footage and anchor banter like nourishment. She looked tiny bathed in the world's news. CeCe's mother's life, she knew, was neither of their faults. The plastic bags of groceries hung in silence at CeCe's side.

NINETEEN

WOLVES

At Armstrong Elementary, CeCe first realized her life was different from her classmates', with their show-and-tell turtles, birthday parties, and mothers who took turns volunteering in their school library. In meeting her mother's family, however, CeCe realized her life was an aberration outside of Armstrong, too. Her aunts' and uncles' gentle questions and tentative rubs on her shoulder confirmed for CeCe that little girls weren't supposed to fetch groceries, soak laundry in the bathtub, or keep count of their mother's heavy tears.

Their blank stares and nervous swallowing made her skin feel small and tight across her bones. As her new family's collective enthusiasm melted into quick and familiar pity, CeCe resorted to the edited telling of her life, the tidied versions she reserved for prying teachers and social workers. Before Ms. Petrie, most had been intent on moving CeCe to a new house with a new mother. CeCe's mother wasn't like others', but she still didn't want a replacement.

CeCe shaved their details to soften her new family's stunned dismay. She played in her courtyard; she didn't play by herself. She watched *Little House on the Prairie*; she didn't overhear her classmates discussing the episodes. Her favorite sandwich was tuna salad; it wasn't a sole option that she spooned from the huge bowl she made every week. She and her mother read in bed together every night; she didn't ramble excitedly to the librarians and catch the bus home to a silent house.

For these people, the McCalls, CeCe and her mother were urban legends come to life. The elders remembered her mother, the quiet and bookish girl, but no one could give an accounting of her after those first few years at MacMurray. Carla seemed to have been swallowed by the sixties.

"How do you disappear from this nosy family?" asked one of the college-aged great-nieces.

"We ain't nosy, girl," Aunt Rosie said, sucking her teeth in mock disgust. "We *concerned.*"

The co-ed laughed as she pulled a stem of grapes from the crisper. "Well, I'm glad y'all got somebody new to be concerned about now."

The cousin noticed CeCe standing in the kitchen doorway as she closed the refrigerator door. She was petite like CeCe, like all of the women who trailed into this house, but carried a different set of facial features. The McCalls all favored one another, even if they didn't resemble one another. The cousin tried to swallow her laughter and Aunt Rosie popped her on the shoulder.

"Look at ya," Aunt Rosie said. "How 'bout you try making yo' *cousin* feel at home."

The cousin moved across the expansive kitchen with open arms to give CeCe a hug. CeCe's arms were stiff and awkward.

She had been at Aunt Rosie's for three days now. She was the only one of the clan who was not small-framed. She was, in fact, a mammoth, like her clapboard house, which seemed to stand as the central hub for their family. CeCe spent the first day in Aunt Rosie's house holding her breath and restricting her tears. She would release them when she was tucked inside the bathroom, where she would sit on the fuzzy blue toilet seat and rock herself back to silence. Quentin stood outside the door when she emerged the first time, offering his hand for her to hold.

"You'll be fine here, Crimson," he said to her when they stood together on Rosie's enormous porch. "Aunt Rosie was good to your mother when she was a little girl, too. I have to go back and meet with her psychiatrist in the morning. I'll be back for you next week."

He didn't come back. Aunt Rosie sat next to CeCe on the porch swing one morning and announced that her mother would be staying at the clinic for a while and Quentin was going back to San Diego. CeCe was furious to learn her father had swooped into her life, plucked her from the library steps, ruffled her mother into a catatonic trance upon hearing him speak her name after so many years, and carried her to this brood of strangers. Aunt Rosie said CeCe shouldn't be so angry, that being human sometimes gets in the way of doing what's best.

"Seein' yo' mama fall apart the way she did got all dem ghosts and memories jumpin' on him again," Aunt Rosie said.

CeCe was dizzy from deciphering Aunt Rosie's clipped words and hybrid idioms. Irritated, CeCe wondered how the woman's speech could be so firmly rooted in Arkansas dirt after more than twenty-five years in Illinois.

"He didn't have to leave me again." CeCe mumbled, leaning back against the swing. She tilted and rocked her end with the tips of her sneakers.

"He done you right," Aunt Rosie said, her large feet planted evenly on the porch. "You gon' be alright, baby. You got you plenty family now. We gon' take care of you while you mama and daddy take care of theyself."

CeCe didn't want this new family. She wanted the one she almost had with Quentin and her mother. Her mother's relatives had been generous and kind to her, but CeCe couldn't help but feel like a zoo exhibit. They popped by Aunt Rosie's every day to spy the exotic animal. They often came with clothes or food, but always with fascination on their faces.

The rough count in CeCe's head totaled two uncles, three aunts, eleven adult cousins, and nineteen first cousins between the ages of eleven—like her—and twenty-five. And there were another twenty-five who either still lived in Arkansas or moved to other cities. They linked their introductions to which uncle was their father or which sister was youngest. CeCe figured there were more people in this family than tenants in her apartment complex.

CeCe stopped trying to keep track of names. After a month, she also stopped asking when she could go home. Aunt Rosie had started a string of phone conversations to enroll CeCe in school for her upcoming sixth-grade year.

CeCe's head throbbed relentlessly.

Her favorite relative, after Aunt Rosie, was cousin Coretta. Coretta wasn't as sugary as the other adult relatives who came to meet her. Coretta had two daughters CeCe's age and took them all roller-skating and bowling, but she did not coo at CeCe or issue spontaneous hugs and sentiment. CeCe found she appreciated her cousin's appraising eye and plain talk.

In mid-August, when CeCe had been in Decatur for six weeks, she was at Coretta's house playing with her cousins, Tremaine and Corinne. Rain had forced the girls into the basement to re-imagine their favorite yard games. The washing machine became a wolf den, and balled up black socks from the laundry hamper became wolf pups the warrior girls were stealing to their village. Crouched next to the dryer, looking around furtively for imaginary wolves, they heard CeCe's name come tumbling down an air vent from an upstairs room.

"I don't know what we're supposed to do with her," Coretta was saying, presumably into the phone, since no other voices came down. "Carla is supposed to be released in a few weeks, but if things just go back to the way they were, the girl ain't in no better shape . . . yeah . . . been playin' the mama all these years . . . seriously, paying the phone bill, signing school papers . . . the girl's whole life, apparently . . . real bright, a little awkward, maybe . . . ten, same age as Tremaine . . . I know . . . don't forget about Carla's mother, too . . . no, something different . . . maybe some kind of crazy gene . . . "

CeCe slid to the laundry room floor and forced the air from her chest. Her cousins flanked her on either side. Corinne, the younger cousin who was eight, burrowed the top of her head into CeCe's shoulder. Tremaine turned to curl her knees against CeCe and clutch her hand. Coretta found the three of them wailing against the dryer, hysterical that CeCe might spontaneously lose her speech and her appetite and her mind. Coretta led them all upstairs and told them about Carla.

TWENTY

FLOODGATES

CECE SAT AT HER DESK, trading attention between a desktop calendar, a calculator, two printed spreadsheets, and a legal pad covered with figures and scribbles.

"You don't have to keep pretending; I know you all don't do any work when I'm gone," a man's voice spoke from her office door.

"You should be impressed I'm using props," CeCe replied without looking up.

CeCe adored her boss. Kester Williams had been an enigma to her when she started four years ago, with his eclectic reading lists, couture socks, and bottles of hot sauce in his office. Following him around that first year, she learned the breathing definition of "dynamic." Kester could negotiate contracts against blue-chip attorneys, consult with caterers about Moroccan versus Lebanese couscous, wage debates about cap and trade or redistricting or boxing or the best coffeehouses in the city. He was strategic, sophisticated, successful, and incredibly sexy with his rectangular spectacles, gleaming bald head, and skin as dark and rich as chocolate cake. He was also twenty years her senior and concretely devoted to his wife, but CeCe appreciated the view just the same.

Mostly, Kester had taken a risk in hiring CeCe. She'd been clumsy and unconvincing in her interview, a debacle he enjoyed referencing now and again, as she'd long since advanced from his personal assistant to the management firm's accounts manager. He'd never been anything but direct and demanding and managed to extract a brand of excellence CeCe hadn't even realized she possessed.

"You made a triple play, I see," Kester said, his crisp cologne and deep baritone filling her small office. He stepped in to slide her cell phone on the desk. "You left this in the conference room. It's been ringing in there all morning."

CeCe hadn't even realized her phone was missing, but she had been unconsciously grateful for the quiet. She scrolled through the call list while Kester peered down at one of the spreadsheets. Eric, Brian Clark, and Rocky.

"*All morning,* Kester?" CeCe said, giving her boss a scolding side eye. "Three calls."

"I know. I was the one trapped inside the noise chamber," Kester said, raising three manicured fingers. "Eric and Brian. Who are they? Rocky, I know."

CeCe was accustomed to Kester's intrusions. He had counseled her through her makeover, selecting life insurance, dumping a cheating almost-boyfriend, transferring her mother's trust-fund accounts, the circus of being a bridesmaid in her cousin Tremaine's wedding, and discovering Rocky was back in town.

"Eric," CeCe said, counting off with her fingers, just as Kester had done, "is a guy I met at the grocery story yesterday. Brian Clark is an attorney. I've sort of pre-inherited a house. I've been waiting for you to come in."

Kester's eyebrows shot up above his purple eyeglass frames. CeCe registered at least half a dozen instant questions in his face. She didn't expect the single question he chose: "Rocky. What'd he want?"

CeCe took a deep breath. She knew Kester wasn't a fan. "He's returning my call," she said, not looking into Kester's face. He had not been impressed with the way Rocky handled his homecoming to Prescott. "I wanted his opinion on the same thing I'm about to ask you."

Kester pursed his lips, accepting her deflection. "What's going on?" he asked, folding his arms.

"I want the house," CeCe said, her voice shrinking as she finished, "to myself."

She looked up to scan Kester's face for a reaction. His eyebrows were peaked above his frames again, and she wasn't sure if it was shock or disappointment. In any event, CeCe was awash with shame all over again. Kester turned to close her office door, sealing them both in as her floodgates broke free.

TWENTY-ONE

CANDY

WHEN CECE LEFT AUNT ROSIE that first summer, she was clutching a promise in her heart. Once home, however, CeCe found the only way to honor her word to Aunt Rosie of being kind to her mother was to be quiet around her mother. She arrived in Prescott three weeks after school started; in the fourth week her mother had been in the apartment on her own. CeCe layered the still of their apartment with her own new brand of quiet.

CeCe peered at her mother over the edges of her novels and textbooks, searching for signs her mother might laugh, or speak a full paragraph, or stay awake past twilight. She wanted proof her mother was cured. Nothing. Her mother was more mobile now, CeCe noted, bringing in the mail, sweeping the kitchen floor, adding the courtyard bench to her rotation of gazing sites. The one intriguing habit her mother had assumed was going out to the corner store on Sundays to buy a newspaper. Throughout the week, CeCe watched her peel open a new section and slowly consume the pages. CeCe was surprised, but disappointed that the results of her mother's eight weeks of treatment weren't closer to astounding.

CeCe intended to tell Dr. Harper how unimpressed she was with his work. She sat in the waiting area of his office, kicking at his coffee table with the toe of her sneakers. Ms. Petrie, her social worker, sat two chairs away, ignoring CeCe's irritated foot. She stood to shake Dr. Harper's hand when he emerged from his office. CeCe walked past him without speaking as he and Ms. Petrie exchanged pleasantries.

When Dr. Harper took his seat across from CeCe, he gave her a warm smile and opened his mouth to speak.

"What's wrong with her brain?" CeCe said before Dr. Harper could vocalize his warm-up to her.

They sat in high-backed leather chairs with their knees pointing at one another. Three empty chairs lined the wall behind CeCe and four framed photographs of forests lined the wall behind Dr. Harper. CeCe had been on this side of his office door only two other times, once when Dr. Harper had invited her to choose a piece of candy from his credenza and once when she had had to sit in on one of her mother's sessions. Witnessing how her mother's silence had followed them into these expensive leather chairs all the way from their apartment, aboard two buses and up a long, narrow flight of stairs, had confounded CeCe. If her mother had scant words for Dr. Harper as well, how was she supposed to get fixed?'

"Her brain is fine, CeCe," Dr. Harper said, unaffected by her abruptness. "It's the chemicals that regulate her moods we needed to adjust."

"Well, what's wrong with her 'chemicals,' then?"

"Your mother has a dysthemia, which means she has a form of depression that will always be present and always need to be managed," he said. "The problem is that she went undiagnosed and untreated for so many years, her mind and body have been stuck in what's called a major episode. The trauma of seeing your father after mourning him all these years pushed her over the edge. Treating her will be trickier now. Possible, but trickier."

Dr. Harper's desk was positioned in front of the far wall. This room was larger than the waiting area, as though the front-room seating had been an afterthought. Soft light from the floor lamp that sat between their tall chairs and the desk made Dr. Harper's bald top gleam. Between their chairs was a low, narrow table holding a box of tissues and the bowl of hard candy. Dr. Harper reached in to the bowl for a piece. CeCe declined.

CeCe listened to the crackle of cellophane instead of Dr. Harper's descriptions of her mother's treatment and prescriptions and long-term therapy goals. She watched as he worked his long words around the pebble of candy.

"When is she going to be regular?" CeCe interrupted again.

Dr. Harper paused for a beat, seeming to weigh his response. "I think she'll be better than ever," he said.

Dr. Harper offered a robust smile, intended to convey his confidence and reassure her, she knew, but CeCe didn't like his smile. Or his bald spot. Or the way he leaned forward in his chair to talk to her. CeCe wanted him to admit the real reason he'd wanted to talk to her.

"I need the medicine, too?" CeCe asked, challenging him with her eyes. "I have it too, right? Her chemical thing?"

Dr. Harper relaxed the tension in his jaw, understanding settling across his face. CeCe thought he looked real for the first time. All of his plastic smiling and forced cheer melted away. He crossed one leg over the other and leaned back. CeCe rested her hands on the armrests, like him, and braced for his reply.

"CeCe, mental illness doesn't work the same way as other inherited traits, like eye color or height." Dr. Harper said. "Yes, it's true family history plays a part, but it's not a guarantee. It gives us something to watch for."

CeCe considered his words. She felt his eyes warm on her while she thought.

"So, I have to wait to catch it?" she asked.

"It's not something you catch, CeCe," Dr. Harper said. "It's like a wrinkle in a paper map. You and your mother may have the same map, but that doesn't mean your map has the same wrinkle."

"But I might," CeCe said, tilting her head. "The same way her mother had a wrinkle, right?"

"It's possible we all do, CeCe," Dr. Harper said, reaching for a second piece of candy. "We just can't screen for mental illness. We can only treat it if it happens."

CeCe stared at him as he popped the candy into his mouth. It rolled around and in between his advice about managing stress and opening up and watching for signs and asking for help. CeCe crossed her arms, trying to pin herself still against the chair. Her head throbbed.

"You seem upset," Dr. Harper was saying. "Can you tell me what you're thinking right now?"

"I'm *thinking*," CeCe said, wedging her words through her clenching teeth, "you're telling me to be honest about my feelings, but you're lying to me."

Dr. Harper did not flinch from her flung words. He stilled the candy that had been dancing in his mouth, giving a single nod for her to continue, instead.

"Why don't you just say it: she got the crazy gene from *her* mother and I'll get the crazy gene from her," CeCe said. She sat straight up. The pulsing behind her skull was relentless.

"CeCe, I know you—"

"You don't know anything!" CeCe screamed, leaping from the tall chair to her feet. Her hands were knotted into small, brown fists and she leaned over the candy bowl at him. "You don't even know how to fix her!"

"CeCe—"

"Shut up!"

CeCe lifted the candy dish and threw it across the room. Candy gems rained across the beige carpet in muted thuds and the glass bowl exploded against the front wall. CeCe heaved, and Dr. Harper gazed coolly at the empty space on the table where the candy had been sitting.

There was a knock at the door, and he stood.

"Everything OK?" Ms. Petrie called through the door.

"Yes, everything's fine, Jeannette. Thank you."

Dr. Harper didn't look at CeCe or betray his impassive expression. He walked around his chair. He scratched at his silver beard before clasping his hands together and leaning his forearms over the back of his seat. He kept his eyes on his hands and CeCe kept her eyes on him. Still breathing heavily, she did not try to filter the rage gurgling through her veins.

She immersed herself in the feeling for the first time since Camp Onondaga. CeCe was furious all the time now, like she'd been the previous summer at camp. The events of this summer had awakened her darkest, densest rage. When she was mandated to return to her mother after starting school with her cousins in Decatur, CeCe strained to keep this bigger and heavier anger pinned in place. She was relieved to let it growl at Dr. Harper, to hurl dishes and watch them smash against the wall.

In the extended quiet, CeCe's fingers loosened and she was aware of the sting where her nails had bitten into her palms. Dr. Harper stood casually, as if waiting for her to tie her shoes. He still did not look up from his hands. CeCe watched his hands, too, and then her eyes moved to the wall and down to the shrapnel of glass and wrapped candy. CeCe's heartbeat quickened as the pulsing in her head subsided.

"Better?" she heard Dr. Harper ask.

CeCe looked at Dr. Harper, who met her eyes now. She was nervous to respond, but Dr. Harper stepped around his chair to sit again. CeCe followed suit.

"CeCe, you had to carry a tremendous amount of responsibility when most kids were learning to ride bicycles, playing kickball, and having sleepovers with their friends," Dr. Harper said. He crossed his legs and returned his folded hands to his lap. "I imagine that might make you angry."

Dr. Harper looked to the trail of candy and back to CeCe with a small smile. "Really angry."

CeCe flushed and a small grin winked from the corners of her mouth.

"You're also scared," Dr. Harper said. "You don't know what's going to happen next to you or your mother. And you feel like you're all alone."

CeCe listened as Dr. Harper plucked her thoughts from the air and strung them together like a beaded necklace. He fit words around her every dark emotion. Her head filled with light and air for the first time. She wanted to spring from her tall chair and tie her arms around Dr. Harper's shoulders and cry. Her body stayed pressed to the chair. Tears fell anyway.

"How do you know all that?" she asked.

"I don't *know* anything, like you said," Dr. Harper said, leaning forward in his chair. His face was soft and amused. "I *understand* how your situation can affect the way you feel. My job is to help you figure out how to keep the way they feel from disrupting the way you want to live your life. Does that make sense, CeCe?"

CeCe nodded. Dr. Harper sat with her for a short while longer, saying anger was an important emotion and CeCe would have to work at facing her feelings instead of trying not to feel them.

"I'll bet you have painful headaches," Dr. Harper said.

CeCe's eyes went wide. Dr. Harper grinned.

"I bet you want a piece of my candy now, too."

CeCe grinned back at him.

TWENTY-TWO

GUT

"HI, BRIAN, THIS IS CECE Weathers. I got your message and wanted to let you know I talked with the agency that writes my renter's insurance. They'll be able to write the house policy, too. Thanks for the other number, though. I'll send a copy of the certificate once I get it."

CeCe placed the cell phone on top of the spreadsheets on her desk. She hadn't gotten much work done after Kester popped into her office earlier and made her cry. Her office door was closed now and the hallway blinds drawn, both rare gestures in their office and universally respected as Do Not Disturb Unless You're Kester.

CeCe picked up her tea and cupped the mug with both hands. She rested the rim against her chin, letting the steam scale her face. CeCe loved the ritual of tea, selecting new flavors, steeping the water, breathing in the exotic aromas. Her old roommate, Terri, had converted her from coffee to tea.

Terri.

CeCe scanned her phone directory for Terri's number. They'd traded random texts from time to time, but hadn't had a long, leisurely conversation since Terri's birthday party earlier in the year. Terri had been busy with her new job as an art therapy instructor as well as planning for her own exhibit later in the year. Terri would always be CeCe's unofficial big sister, something she desperately needed right now.

She answered right away with her usual cheer. CeCe could hear the wind flicking at Terri's earphones. She had caught Terri on her daily walk.

"Call me back when you're done?" CeCe asked.

"No, sis, this is good. I thought about you the other day," Terri said, her voice strained but steady. "What are you up to?"

"Having a cup of tea," CeCe said, looking down into her mug. She listened to the rhythm in Terri's breathing.

"Really?" Terri said, her voice full of humor. "I just knew you would go back to coffee."

"Nope. I'm hardcore, now," CeCe said. "I even buy the expensive stuff."

Terri laughed. "Your body thanks you."

"And I thank you," CeCe said.

"Again," Terri said, a large truck rumbling by in the background, "what are you up to?"

"I'm moving out," CeCe said.

"I thought you loved that place," Terri said.

She was right. When CeCe had first moved into their apartment, Terri had been entertained to watch CeCe bask in a newfound independence. CeCe had been twenty-three, restless and dumbfounded by the reality of freedom.

"I did love the apartment. I mean, I do," CeCe said. "I got a house this week."

"A house? You bought a house?"

"No," CeCe said, "Doris—remember Doris from the mall? She gave me her house in a kind of pre-bequeathing."

"Get out of here!" Terri exclaimed, then CeCe heard her mumble an apologetic disclaimer to a passerby. "I guess that's great news and terrible news all at once. What's wrong with her?"

"Cancer," CeCe said. She thought of Doris standing in front of the naked window then, filled with pride and illness. "Said she's done with treatments. Gonna spend the remaining year or two traveling."

Terri was quiet. CeCe closed her eyes, knowing her friend was sending up a quick prayer.

Terri spoke again, "You feel guilty about the house? About Doris being sick?"

"Yes, I feel guilty about the house, but not so much because of Doris. She's working on one helluva bucket list. I'm grateful I was on it."

"So . . . what's—" Terri caught herself. "Oh. Is this about your mother?"

"Yes." CeCe's throat tightened again.

"She doesn't want to move . . . ?" Terri asked.

The sob snagged against CeCe's voice. "She doesn't know about the move yet."

Terri was quiet while CeCe gurgled and gabbed. Finally, she said, "Let's do logistics, then we'll get to the real stuff, OK?"

CeCe consented and sniffled.

"Can she afford the rent on her own?"

"Yes," CeCe said. "The trust will sunset in about three years, but she's also been getting SSI payments and back military pay of my father's. Of course, I'll continue to help her."

"OK. What about living on her own?" Terri asked. "Is it safe for her to be by herself?"

CeCe thought of her mother in their living room, sitting in the recliner. This evolved version of her mother consumed news, spoke a fistful of sentences every day, and ventured out by city transit to the Stringer Center each week to attend her activity group. CeCe hadn't allowed herself to marvel at this reincarnation in quite some time.

"She's safe," CeCe said.

Terri asked CeCe to hold on. CeCe listened to bursts of hard breath as Terri sprinted the last block of her workout.

"OK," Terri said, heaving her words now, "so you're not worried about leaving your mother in the apartment; you feel guilty. Is that right?"

CeCe turned her chair away from her office door and window, as if the fresh stream of tears might be detectable through the blinds. "I know I'm not wrong, but I feel wrong," CeCe said into the cell phone. "I want a regular life for myself, and I feel like the worst human alive for it."

"And, if she moves with you?" Terri prompted.

"It would be more of the same, with more space," CeCe said. "It wouldn't be awful. I mean, at this point, it's all we know."

Terri's breathing fell easy now. CeCe could tell she was still outdoors, maybe on the front steps of her new high-rise apartment building. Or maybe Terri had already made it up to her apartment and was standing out on the balcony. CeCe had sat near its sliding doors the night of Terri's birthday party. "Is this what you want," Terri said, "or what you think you're supposed to want?"

CeCe thought for a moment. "Both."

"When you visualize yourself in the house, do you imagine yourself alone or with your mother there?"

"Alone, but—," CeCe said, hesitating, "I kinda know Mama is there, somehow. Like she's always in another room."

Terri was quiet a moment before she spoke. "Sis, I don't think guilt is what has you stuck. I think it's fear. Pure, intense, and unadulterated fear."

CeCe stopped flipping the paperclip on her desk. She looked at it, pinned between her fingers, as if it were as foreign as the suggestion Terri had made. CeCe couldn't list many things she'd ever been afraid of. Uneasy? Uncomfortable? Uncertain? Absolutely. All the time. But fear? She'd never had the luxury of being afraid. CeCe'd had to be brave and make complicated decisions for both of them her whole life. The threat of being ferreted away by social workers had made her afraid until she figured out how to answer their questions. CeCe hadn't been afraid of much since.

"Think about it," Terri continued. "Your mother isn't the only one who's been shaped by this life you've shared. When you first moved in, with all your lists and notes and routines, you lived like someone who'd just gotten out of military school. And you were so awkward, bless your heart."

CeCe laughed with Terri, remembering their apartment's steady stream of artists, activists, entrepreneurs, and grad students whose personalities spanned the spectrum of "eccentric." After hiding in her room during the first few months, not wanting to infect Terri's frequent gatherings with her inexperience, CeCe realized no one was interested in her broken pieces. They all had their own. All of them. CeCe had been grateful to test her social wings with Terri's circle of brilliant misfits.

"Awkward doesn't make me scared," CeCe said.

"Girl, ain't nothing wrong with being scared," Terri said. "You're talking about untangling a lifelong codependency. With your mother. Not a small feat."

CeCe was quiet. She wasn't crying anymore. The imagery of their lives in a tangle resonated with her. Codependency? Until now, CeCe had seen herself as the straight rod with her mother's frailties winding themselves around her. It hadn't occurred to her that they could entangle each other. Codependency. The term felt vast in her head, full of echoes. How could she be dependent when she had always been the same? Their address changed, the severity of her mother's depression changed, the presence of family changed, but CeCe had remained the same. Methodical, reliable, resourceful, and furious. Their life had kept CeCe consistently the same.

CeCe couldn't imagine herself any differently. Trudging through life had prepared her to build the humble life before her. Her logistical mindset had made her invaluable to Kester's firm, had siphoned a modest pot of "rainy day" funds from their trust. Her rigid reasoning had also kept her distant from new people, second-guessing their friendliness or affections. Mostly, CeCe's thoughts were always on cooking the next meal, scheduling the next appointment, researching the next pharmaceutical trial, or cushioning them for the next time her mother might implode.

As a kid, CeCe had always been told being a grown-up meant she could do whatever she wanted, all the time. Not really, she discovered. Grown-ups had more options, but couldn't choose most of them. It was only as an adult that CeCe could smooth the edges of her resentment. Most of her mother's life options had been chosen for her by death, war, and injustice. Even her mother's mental illness had been a life defense chosen by genetics, CeCe knew.

How could her own life be different, CeCe wondered again. She hadn't known anything else. Maybe she wasn't meant to be anything else. She laid the paper clip on the desk. What if she wasn't meant to be free?

"You still with me?" Terri said. Her voice wasn't surrounded by the sounds of outside anymore.

CeCe blew out a breath. "Yeah, I'm here," she said. "I was just thinking you might be right. I don't know anything but this, and I don't know what that means. What it says about me."

"Says a lot," Terri said. "There were a half-dozen people who wanted to move in to that apartment when I left, but you chose Carla."

"She was—"

"I know," Terri said, cutting off CeCe's explanation. "The old apartment was going downhill and you wanted her safe. I know. Again, I'm not judging. I'm just saying. You used to roll your eyes, grumble about the errands you had to run for her, but never missed a Sunday going to sit with her. I think you were relieved to move her in back then, for your sake as much as hers."

CeCe groaned, falling onto her forearm. Her voice sounded trapped in tunnel when she spoke. "Oh my God," CeCe moaned. "I am a walking tragedy."

Terri laughed. "Join the club," she said. "Good news is, you get to decide what that looks like from this point forward. Let go of the notion that you can make a wrong decision. You can't. I keep telling you, follow your gut. It won't steer you wrong."

TWENTY-THREE

BOOBIES

CECE SLID A HAND DOWN her dress, working her fingers until she'd gathered a small clutch of fabric on either side of her hips. The stockings were crawling away from her waist again. More accurately, away from the new threat of her butt.

Cousin Coretta told her she should be glad to grow a booty. "It's beautiful, powerful, and dangerous, all at the same time," Coretta had said, laughing. "You'll see."

All CeCe could tell about her new curves was that they caused problems. First, it was the tight fit of her favorite jeans. Then there was the anonymous pinch at the bus stop. Now, at the end of the school year, CeCe had to buy ladies' nylons for the completion ceremony instead of girls' tights.

In addition to her physical reshaping, CeCe experienced shades of change all around her that year: Pam took her to get her ears pierced for her birthday; she started painting her fingernails and toes; her mother had her order them a television set; her father's letters came from Detroit instead of San Francisco; the new neighbors in their apartment building were louder, rougher, and younger; Dr. Harper kept monthly appointments for her now; and she received weekly phone calls from her family in Decatur, which CeCe regarded as call-ins from heaven.

At school, CeCe had to share her library assistant job. She was hurt, at first, until Mrs. Anderson explained that CeCe would help train the new assistant before leaving for middle school.

"Like a boss?" CeCe asked.

"Well, I'm still the boss," Mrs. Anderson had said, smiling, "but you're like my manager. So, think of everything you've learned to make you such a good library assistant."

CeCe's smile was broad. "I should write it down?"

"That would be fantastic."

CeCe had looked forward to their completion ceremony for weeks. She hadn't felt this good in school since her kindergarten year, and she was excited to stand in front of the auditorium and be handed her certificate and applause from the attending crowd. Plus, she got to dress up. Her dress had arrived in the mail with a note card tucked inside that read: "Special dress, special occasion, very special young lady! Congratulations. Love, Rosie, Coretta, and Family."

Family. CeCe liked the way this word felt in her head.

CeCe gave the hosiery another fierce tug, panning the small orchestral room to make sure the other students weren't watching her behind the piano.

"Bathroom," a voice whispered, startling CeCe. Before she could turn to see who it was, Michelle had hooked her arm and begun pulling her toward the door.

"Dang, Michelle," CeCe said, stumbling to keep her balance. "You gonna make me run my stockings."

"Come on," Michelle said, steering CeCe from the their chattering classmates, through the hallway, and into the girls' room. Michelle was swift, CeCe realized, even though she'd gained quite a bit of weight. Her twin, Michael, was still slim and promising to have an athletic build. Some girls even thought he was cute, but CeCe and Michelle only saw the saucer-eared boy obsessed with Matchbox cars.

Michelle bolted straight for one of the stalls once they reached the bathroom. CeCe watched the door rattle as Michelle locked it from the inside. She stared at the closed door for a moment, wondering why Michelle had pulled her into the bathroom instead of one of her closer friends, Marissa or Bethanne. CeCe turned to the mirror to check her hair. She'd styled it in a half-mushroom, with one side pulled up in with a sparkly hair comb. She'd slept in hard curlers and everything, just the way cousin Coretta had taught her during Easter vacation. CeCe turned on the faucet and ran water over the tips of her fingers, which she smoothed against the edges of her hairline.

She stepped back, admiring her work for the day—the hair, the dress, the lip gloss, the pantyhose—when she heard a muffled whimper coming from Michelle's stall.

"Michelle?" CeCe said, turning to walk toward the stall. "You OK?"

More whimpers.

"Open the door," CeCe said. She couldn't remember the last time she'd seen Michelle cry. Their friendship had ranged from hues of fierce to convenient since kindergarten, but it was always an honest alliance. Considering their bonding moment was the horror of watching their mothers get into a catfight in front of their school, they had no choice but to have each other's back.

"Open the door," CeCe said again, giving the metal door a push. She could hear Michelle moving and shuffling inside the stall. When the door opened, Michelle stepped out and CeCe stepped aside, looking at her friend's stricken face.

Michelle took long, slow steps to the sink and began to wash her hands. CeCe was used to her dramatic flair and, for a moment, prepared for a wail about chipped nails or someone looking at her funny. As Michelle dabbed at her face, CeCe calculated how long they'd been away from the orchestra room and whether they might be missing the processional lineup.

When Michelle crumbled into fresh torrent of tears, CeCe forgot the ceremony march. Michelle sank the heels of her wet hands into her eyes and turned to face CeCe.

"Michelle, you're scaring me now," CeCe said. "What's wrong?" CeCe placed her hands on her friend's shoulders and waited. She'd seen teachers do this in the hallways many times. It always seemed to make the students stop crying.

"What's going on?" CeCe repeated to the back of Michelle's hands. Right before CeCe's patience expired, Michelle lowered her hands and began to speak.

"I want to die, CeCe," Michelle said, her voice was thin and her lips hardly moved.

"What are you talking about?" CeCe said, grabbing her chin. "Don't say that."

"But I do," Michelle said, unshaken by CeCe's bark. Her gaze stretched far from them in that bathroom, the same way Mrs. Castellanos' did before moving to the hospice last year. CeCe knew these were not theatrics.

"You can't die," CeCe said, folding her arms across her chest. She didn't know what else to say. In the after-school movies, the friend always offered the perfect uplifting speech. CeCe had nothing else.

"You can't die," she said again, even more gently.

"Yes, I—," Michelle began, melting into more warm tears. "You can't tell anybody, CeCe."

"OK," CeCe said.

Michelle took a deep breath, looking toward the ceiling, and then down to her shoes.

"Papa," Michelle said to the tops of her black wedge pumps. "He comes in my room."

CeCe thought how pretty they looked today, Michelle wearing a turquoise-and-navy panel dress and CeCe in the soft gray dress with its thin pink vinyl belt. Everyone looked so grown up tonight.

"When?" CeCe said, more like a rush of air than a word. "Did he hurt you? Did he—?"

So grown up.

"Last summer was the first time," Michelle said, alternating her attention from her shoes to the turquoise fabric pinched between her fingers to CeCe's eyes and back to her shoes. "I woke up and he was rubbing on my chest. It felt . . . it felt nice. So I fell back to sleep."

CeCe crinkled her nose.

"When your boobies come in all the way, you'll see," Michelle said. "They'll be sore and stuff. I thought he was helping 'em not hurt so much. He came in my room all the time after that. My boobs stopped hurting and grew really fast."

CeCe nodded, trying not to look at the heaping bosom Michelle had now.

"Did you tell your mother?"

"No," Michelle said, her eyes starting to swell again. "Papa said it would hurt her feelings that she hadn't figured out how to stop me from being sore."

The bathroom door opened, breaching Michelle's confessional with the girlish giggles of two classmates. CeCe grabbed Michelle's hand and led her friend into the open hallway, down a short corridor and inside a stairwell.

Seated on the hard stairs, Michelle told CeCe how her father kept coming into her room at night to reach under her covers and under her nightgown to rub her breasts. By Halloween, Michelle said her breasts weren't swollen anymore and she told her father she was OK.

"He didn't stop?" CeCe asked.

"He stopped rubbing my boobs," Michelle said, shrugging one

shoulder and looking down to her shoes again. "He told me to lift my gown and breathe slow, like a music bar."

Michelle demonstrated four staccato intakes of breath, and one slow four-count to exhale. CeCe knew Michelle loved to sing. She tried to understand her friend doing vocal warm-ups in bed with her nightgown lifted.

"He had his finger in me," Michelle said. "He would move it in and out when I breathed."

Michelle told CeCe how her father's visits escalated from his finger to his cock. He promised Michelle it would only hurt the first time but would help his aches go away, like he'd done for her. For two days after that first time, Michelle said, she felt like she'd fallen on the cross bar of Michael's bike. Her father rubbed baby oil on her bottom for the next few nights, holding her and singing to her like a preschooler again. She thought it was over, until he maneuvered her onto his lap in the middle of a lullaby one night. Michelle said he came into her room almost every night after that.

"I made Michael sleep in my room every night during Christmas break," she said.

"Did you tell him?" CeCe asked, her face wide with surprise.

Michelle nodded. "He didn't believe me at first, but when he saw Papa peeking in at night, he did."

"Were you scared?" CeCe asked, feeling herself tremble in the cold stairway with these chilling secrets swirling around them.

"We both were," she said. "Remember that *Amelia* movie they made us watch last year, the one with the guy from *Cheers* and he went to prison? CeCe, I don't want my Papa to go to prison. I knew he would stop one day ... "

Michelle's voice trailed off. Her arms were folded across her knees and she dropped her head onto them. She cried again. CeCe's eyes welled, too.

"He didn't stop, CeCe!" Michelle wailed. "He didn't stop! I hate him! I hate him! He didn't stop!"

Michelle's cries had turned beastly and CeCe began to tremble.

"He even made me sit in his lap today," Michelle whispered hoarsely, once her sobs were under control. "Mama took Michael to get a new pair of shoes and we were alone. He made me do it in the daytime, CeCe. I still have creamy stuff coming out of me. I hate him, but if he goes to prison, my mother and my brother will hate me back. That's why I want to die."

CeCe had tears rolling down her face now. She felt desperate, scared, and helpless. She didn't want breasts anymore, either.

"You can't die, Michelle," CeCe said, sniffling. "I'll go with you to tell somebody. You gotta tell somebody."

Michelle swung her head back and forth while tears poured down her round cheeks.

"We have to," CeCe said, hearing how she'd included herself in the solution. "That's what the counselor said to do after the movie. It's not your fault and you gotta tell if you want it to stop."

Michelle was quiet, head on her arms. Knees and ankles tucked tight.

"You want it to stop, right?" CeCe asked.

Michelle's head bolted up, her brown eyes ignited with rage. She leaned in dangerously close to CeCe's face and exploded, "You think I *like* having my own daddy put his nasty dick inside me?"

Neither of the girls heard the footsteps coming up the stairs. Mr. Markeweiz, the social studies teacher, stood frozen on the landing behind them. Only CeCe turned to face him. Michelle buried her face and cried out again. Stuttering, Mr. Markeweiz explained the class was lining up and he had been sent to look for them.

"CeCe," he said, "why don't you head to the office and wait for me there. I'll let your mother know where you are."

"She's not here," CeCe said, remembering her own home woes. Worse, Mr. Markeweiz gave CeCe an "of course not" nod. CeCe had Mr. Markeweiz for social studies. He was corny but nice and seemed to own corduroy pants in a hundred different colors. He wore the forest green pair tonight.

"Can I stay with Michelle?" she asked.

"That's up to Michelle," Mr. Markeweiz said, turning his soft eyes to Michelle. "I've got to be upfront with you, Michelle. I have to go and pull your parents out of that auditorium."

Michelle's face contracted into a painful wince. "No!" she screamed. "They'll put Papa in jail!"

Mr. Markeweiz's face went ashen. He smoothed his hands over the pockets of his corduroys and CeCe could tell he was uncomfortable. A strand from his comb-over fell onto his forehead as he looked from CeCe and then back to Michelle.

"Honey," he said, leaning on the stair railing, "I am so, so sorry for what has happened to you. You're a smart, talented young lady and you don't deserve this. But I'm sorry; if I don't report this, then I'm committing a crime, too."

For the rest of their graduation night, CeCe, Michelle, and Michelle's mother and Mr. Markeweiz were in the office talking to Mrs. Patterson, the guidance counselor. Michelle's father had been left inside the gym to watch her twin brother, Michael, accept his lapel pin. He'd been told Michelle was having awful cramps and asking for her mother.

In the office, CeCe watched Mr. Markeweiz twist at his wedding band while he relayed his disturbing discovery and prompted Michelle to tell her mother what was happening to her at night.

CeCe sat on the floor next to Michelle, holding her hand the entire time. CeCe would squeeze her friend's trembling fingers each time Michelle had to say "my chest" and "his finger" and "inside me." Mrs. Johnson's face remained stoic and framed, as CeCe had always known her to be, but her thick makeup was streaked with tears. CeCe knew now that everyone, even icy queens like Mrs. Johnson, had a breaking point.

The police detectives came before the end of the ceremony. The vice principal had asked them to send plainclothes officers, because of the graduation. CeCe hovered near Michelle for the rest of the evening, although Mrs. Johnson had finally embraced her daughter. Every now and again, she'd catch CeCe's eye. CeCe felt badly for her. She knew how much Mrs. Johnson liked to brag about their "middle-class" family. CeCe wondered which she resented more, having a crack in their foundation exposed or seeing her daughter cry.

Mr. Johnson was discreetly escorted into the science lab and confronted by the detectives. CeCe was dismissed from the office, but was allowed to dispense one hug to Michelle.

"You promised, CeCe," Michelle whispered into her ear.

"I won't tell," CeCe whispered back.

Walking back to orchestra room for her jacket, CeCe saw Michael and Mr. Markeweiz in the hall. Mr. Markeweiz had his hand on Michael's shoulder as they walked and CeCe could see Michael fume. Their eyes locked. CeCe gave him a sympathetic look.

"This is all your goddamn fault!" Michael yelled. Mr. Markeweiz clamped his hands on Michael's shoulders and whispered into his ear as he guided Michael past CeCe and toward the office.

CeCe froze in her steps, mouth agape and arms lifted to the side. Moroseness coated her bones. She was tired. She was sad. And she'd missed her own commencement ceremony. As she turned around, back toward the orchestra room and her jacket, she saw two boys standing near the band door.

"Never heard him cuss like that," the redhead said.

"Yeah," said the smaller boy, his mouth too small for all the metal brackets inside. He turned a steely stare to CeCe and asked, "What the fuck did you do?"

CeCe didn't know the redhead very well. Only that his name was Scott. The shorter boy, with the braces, was Jesse. Jesse had been in the same fifth grade class with CeCe and now was in the same math block this year. Jesse was more of a taunt than a bully, a housefly buzzing in and out of the curtains. CeCe had never been significant enough for Jesse's sights, but she avoided his flight patterns anyway.

"Nothing," CeCe mumbled, walking past them and into the orchestra room. She scanned the scattering of empty chairs and cups for her jacket.

"What's 'all your fault,' then?" Jesse asked from the doorway.

"Nothing," CeCe said, more forcefully. She spotted the windbreaker draped over the piano bench and moved toward it.

"You were down at the office for a super long time," Jesse said. "Something happened."

"My dad said he saw a police car outside," said Scott, still in the hallway.

Jesse's eyes winked with mischief and he asked, "You and your *homeboy* getting arrested?"

CeCe folded her jacket over her arm and walked toward the doorway. The boys had already disheveled their black slacks and white button-down shirts. As she moved to walk past them, Jesse said in a low voice, "I'll find out what you did, *Crimson*."

"I didn't get in trouble," CeCe said, moving past them.

"So why was a police car here?" asked Jesse.

"Yeah," Scott said. Both boys followed CeCe down the hall. "Why are police at our school, *Crimson*? We never had police cars here before, *Crimson*."

"You niggers did something," Jesse said. "My dad said you always do."

CeCe's breath caught behind her tongue and felt the flood beginning to rise in her skull. She wanted to spin around and spit on them, throw her hard, dressy shoes, punch at their faces. Instead, she walked more swiftly. The boys did not continue to follow her, but their hollow laughter did. CeCe didn't think she could get outside, down the block to her bus stop, and across town to her bed fast enough.

"CeCe," Mr. Markeweiz called. He was in the center of the hallway, in front of the guidance office door, gesturing for her.

Reluctantly, CeCe walked over to Mr. Markeweiz. She felt worked up and worn out at the same time. She didn't want to talk anymore. She didn't want to listen anymore. She wanted to go home.

Mr. Markeweiz placed a hand on her shoulder when she stood close enough and CeCe could see Ms. Patterson standing in her office. Her eyes softened at the sight of CeCe.

"I have your pin and certificate," she said, handing them to CeCe. "I'm sorry you had to miss your ceremony."

"You helped Michelle do a very brave thing," Mr. Markeweiz added. "I'm so impressed with what a good friend you were for her tonight."

CeCe's mind flashed to the pinched fury in Michael's face. *All her fault.*

Once one tear got away from CeCe, she couldn't make the rest of them stop. Couldn't temper her wails. Couldn't stop her shoulders from heaving. Michelle. Michael. Ms. Johnson. Scott and Jesse. Even the fact that her mother hadn't come to the ceremony tonight.

"Talk to me, CeCe?" Ms. Patterson said, holding CeCe by one shoulder. "Tell me what else is going on for you right now."

"No!" CeCe said, hysteria beginning to tinge her voice. "They already think it's my fault. That I told. But I didn't. I promised I wouldn't tell. Now they think I did. Calling me names. I didn't tell!"

"Who is calling you names?" asked Ms. Patterson.

"Who said you told?" asked Mr. Markeweiz.

CeCe threw up her hands and covered her face. She wanted to disappear from their close-range questions, remove herself from the linoleum hallway, undo the weighted conversations of this long, long evening.

Mr. Markeweiz's hand was on her right shoulder and, now, Ms. Patterson's hand was on the left. CeCe fought to wrangle herself back under control. They all heard the boys' dress shoes approaching in the hall.

"I should've known," Ms. Patterson said under her breath.

CeCe turned from her wet palms to see Jesse and Scott stuck in their steps. Ms. Patterson moved toward them, demanding to know where they had been, why were they still in the building, what time were Scott's parents expecting them to make the two-block walk to his house, and why were they attacking CeCe?

"We didn't attack her!" Jesse snapped.

"Words can be attack weapons, too, Jesse," Mr. Markeweiz called to them from where he stood holding CeCe's shoulders.

Grown-ups can be corny at the worst possible times, CeCe thought.

"I didn't call her a nigger! Jesse said that!" Scott said.

The word ricocheted on the walls, the floor, the ceiling, and their stunned faces.

"Let's go," Ms. Patterson said, gesturing the boys into the dark office. "We're calling your parents *now*."

CeCe glued her eyes to her slick hands, although she felt Jesse's flash in her direction as he and Scott walked past her. Mr. Markeweiz gave her shoulder a small squeeze.

"Let's skip the bus this time," he said. "I can give you a ride home, if you don't think your mother would mind. Should we call her?"

CeCe shook her head. "She won't mind," she said in a small voice.

Once at the apartment, CeCe felt she had just enough energy to drag herself through the courtyard and through her front door. She dropped her windbreaker on the arm of the couch and walked the short hallway to the bathroom. CeCe kept an ear peeled for her mother. Even though she knew better, CeCe waited to hear her mother's voice croak above the rushing water to ask about her day, about the commencement ceremony, about how she was doing.

CeCe turned out the lights in the bathroom and living room. She double-checked the doors and window locks. She unfolded her sheet next to the couch and folded herself into the cool fabric. CeCe tucked away the long day, her weary limbs, and an utterly broken heart.

TWENTY-FOUR

PANCAKES

CeCe looked forward to spending the summer with her new family in Decatur, but the ordeal with Michelle had shaken her. She wrestled with her guilt and counted the days until she could surround herself with aunts and uncles and cousins who might listen to her. Talk to her. Give her a reason to smile or laugh.

CeCe climbed from the bus in Decatur on a Thursday morning and fell into an all-night movie marathon with her cousins. On Friday, they lazed around the house before meeting the entire family for dinner at Aunt Rosie's. Fried chicken and catfish, beef brisket, green beans, cut spaghetti, homemade rolls, macaroni and cheese, pound cake, and peach cobbler. Only here could CeCe ever see so much food in one place.

"Family" was still a fresh concept for her, this much family, anyway. CeCe tried to take it all in, testing every angle to see if she liked it as much as she'd hoped to. She put out the tableware and napkins with Aunt Rosie. She played tag and cards and checkers with her cousins. She read the liners of cassette tapes while the older cousins talked and shared their music. As she wandered in and out of the living room and porch, she caught snippets of the grown-ups' conversations: Dazz Band concert, tuition loans, gas prices, *Hill Street Blues*, *ET*, test-tube babies, car trade-ins, office backstabbing, John Johnson on the cover of *Forbes*, shopping for a class reunion.

"Girl, get outta grown folks' business," Coretta said, giving CeCe a start. Coretta laughed as CeCe sprayed playing cards across the dining room table. Apparently, she'd been doing more blatant leaning and "ear hustling" than card shuffling.

CeCe opened her mouth to protest but Coretta twisted her mouth and cocked her head to the side in a comic "don't even try it" expression. As Coretta passed through the dining room, CeCe grinned as she ducked her head, scooped the cards, and headed back outside with the other kids. Coretta playfully pinched at CeCe's arm as she walked past.

"Hey, CeCe," Coretta said, before CeCe reached the screen door. "How about pancakes tomorrow, just me and you?"

CeCe's elation plummeted when the idea of being in trouble invaded her mind. Maybe it was the cereal bowl in the front room. Maybe it was the second slice of pound cake. Maybe they hadn't wanted her back for a second summer. Maybe Coretta was going to give CeCe a list of restrictions, the way Mrs. Johnson had done once Michelle had started inviting CeCe to birthday parties and to spend the night. CeCe wasn't allowed in this room and wasn't allowed to touch that photo album and couldn't eat from these dishes at the Johnson house. Michelle wasn't, either, but Mrs. Johnson didn't leave those instructions to chance or to her children. She reminded CeCe of the rules every time she came to play with Michelle.

Michelle.

"You don't have to actually eat pancakes if you don't want to," Coretta was saying, concern contorting her expression. "You can eat what you want. I just wanted to have a girl time with you."

"I like pancakes," CeCe said quickly. She didn't want Coretta to uninvite her.

Coretta relaxed her face. "Good. Me, too. We'll go while the girls are at dance."

CeCe meant to merely smile, but knew her face was beaming. Coretta smiled, pinched at CeCe's arm again, and returned to the living room with the other adults.

Neither of them had been able to finish eating their tall stacks. CeCe and Coretta leaned back in their booths and made a show of rubbing their full bellies. CeCe liked the way Coretta fit all of her different pieces together, how the Fusser and the Fixer and the Funny Coretta were all different parts of her, but all the same. CeCe didn't think her own parts—the Nice and the Angry—could share the spaces inside her.

"So, junior high. Kind of a big deal," Coretta said, sitting up to sip her coffee. "Anything you want to know?"

CeCe hadn't thought about it. Valmore was a magnet school for gifted students and CeCe had earned a lottery seat and a scholarship. Ms. Patterson had given her the application and Mrs. Anderson had helped her fill it out. They'd been more excited than CeCe when she showed them her acceptance letter. CeCe looked forward to attending a school filled with kids who liked to learn like she did. No one to tease her about good grades and enormous library books. She couldn't know, however, what she didn't know about middle school.

"Like what?" CeCe asked. "Lockers? Algebra?"

Coretta laughed, more to herself. "I was trying for a segue. So much for that," she said. "Look, I wanted to talk with you about your body, CeCe. The changes that will happen soon. About your period. About sex. All of that. You up for it?"

CeCe's face grew hot. She looked at the tables and booths around them and shifted in her seat. Coretta laughed.

"How about this? Tell me what you know about sex and I'll tell you if you can opt out of this discussion," Coretta said.

"I know I don't want any," CeCe said, folding her arms across the buds on her chest.

Coretta dropped her head in laughter. "Good," Coretta managed. "You have plenty of time for that. Besides 'not wanting any,' tell me what you know. I mean, how does it work?"

CeCe furrowed her brow, feeling her thick bangs tickle her forehead. Carefully, she cited the diagrams and definitions she'd found in the library and surmised from novels. She described the two genitalia, how they interlocked, the function of sperm and eggs, and even a sketchy overview of the stages of pregnancy.

"You've done a lot of reading, huh?" Coretta said smiling. "So, what doesn't make sense?"

CeCe felt as if a cashier had invited her to shove a candy bar into her pocket. What CeCe knew most certainly about sex was how little she understood it. In her reading, CeCe knew she missed the core, like the back-story to an inside joke. In her head, she didn't understand the allure of sex. Especially if it leads men to their own daughters. CeCe considered her questions. She didn't want to sound like a thirteen-year-old.

"How does it really work?" she blurted, cringing at herself as Coretta grinned another amused smile.

"Well, when it 'works' right," she began, "it starts with a kiss."

Coretta drained a small carafe of coffee while telling CeCe about what gets inserted where, how sex differed from intimacy, how to clean her privates, the lies boys tell to get sex, and how long CeCe should wait before trying.

"The church wants me to tell you to wait until you're married," Coretta said, as they walked to the car. "And you should try. At minimum, no sex until you're at least eighteen. By then, you'll be mature enough to pick someone who's special, smart, and knows how lucky he is to earn such a gift. Don't rush just to say you've done it. So many girls do that and regret it. You only get one time to have a first time. Doesn't it make sense to make that one time as perfect as you can?"

CeCe nodded as she fastened her seat belt. All the way home, with the scent of maple syrup filling their conversation, CeCe imagined a humongous red bow underneath her sundress. She was also sad for her friend. CeCe turned to the open window and closed her eyes against the wind.

TWENTY-FIVE

TONIC

CeCe sipped her drink and glanced at her watch. She hadn't intended to arrive to the bar so early, but realized the cushion gave her time to safely return a call to Rocky. Rather, she logged into her voicemail and returned his message with a voice note. "Thanks for calling me back so fast," she said. "I wanted your opinion on something, your advice, I guess, but I think I got it worked out. Well, I'm working on working it out. Anyway, you don't have to call me back. I mean, you can. But if you can't, it's OK. OK. Bye."

CeCe slipped the phone into her purse, applauding herself and her timing. She pushed Rocky from her mind as Eric appeared in the restaurant window. Emerging from the rows of parked cars, his gait was athletic and graceful. As he approached, CeCe's chest thumped harder and harder.

This was her first date in more than a year. CeCe shifted on her barstool, spinning the wedge of lime inside her glass of tonic. She'd read online that ordering alcohol ahead of her date could send a negative subliminal. Perhaps she'd failed at dating prior to this most recent hiatus, she thought, because she hadn't known about "subliminals."

Eric disappeared from the window's frame to enter the building and CeCe pulled out her lip gloss for a quick, final swipe. In the closing second, she also reached into the bar well and popped a maraschino cherry in her mouth. The article also suggested subtle, fruity breath instead of overwhelming mint.

Eric saw her right away, smiling past the hostess. He was handsome, not gorgeous—less like a movie star and more like an "everyday-guy" movie extra. CeCe liked that. She had enough to be self-conscious about. He offered a pleasantry to the hostess as he continued past her and toward the end of the bar where CeCe and her tonic waited. CeCe gave a little wave as he drew near, forcing herself to breathe.

TWENTY-SIX

SPECTACULAR

CeCe never heard from Michelle again. Rumor had it Mrs. Johnson moved with Michelle and Michael to Milwaukee. CeCe never found out whether Mr. Johnson went to jail. She would never know if Michael had forgiven her.

With time, she felt less guilty about the experience. She never told Michelle's secret, but shared with Coretta how her friend had moved away without notice. Coretta would ask about Michelle during their phone calls for a while, and then the subject melted into bra cups, sanitary pads, hair grease, and Ronald Reagan.

"He is the beginning of the end for Black people," Coretta would say. "Remember I told you."

CeCe anticipated a beginning to several ends of her own that summer. She had completed middle school and braced herself for the ninth grade at Maclin High, one of the feeder schools for Valmore. She and Pam were already talking about their shared college dorm and bridesmaid dresses.

CeCe planned ahead for her mother's future, too. Dr. Harper assured CeCe her mother would be fine when CeCe went away to college. CeCe took into account the added chores and habits her mother had assumed over the past two years and realized she agreed with Dr. Harper. For the time being, CeCe was still the one to make sure their apartment had what it needed, when needed. She'd even forged a letter to the brokerage firm requesting an increase in their monthly disbursements. Even though they were petite, buying food and clothes for two women proved more costly than a woman and a child. The confirmation letter explained the restructured payments would exhaust her mother's trust fund four years sooner than scheduled. CeCe calculated she would be out of college by then and capable of picking up her mother's expenses.

CeCe faced only two new significant stressors during her middle-school years. One was the changing landscape of her neighborhood. The county had converted their apartment complex into low-income housing for anyone, not only veteran families or seniors. On Kennedy Boulevard, Mr. Curtis' newsstand was long gone. The corner store replaced its bread and penny candy with liquor bottles.

The second frustration was her father's continued silence. They had started trading letters after her mother's breakdown. For three years, he had penned CeCe long and winding letters, full of advice, glimpses from his past, affirmations for her future. In every letter, he proclaimed an undying love for CeCe and for her mother. CeCe asked why he didn't write her mother, too. He wrote that he felt afraid.

CeCe thought of that day sometimes, when she and her father had caught the bus together from the library to this apartment. Her father had found the listing by accident, he had told CeCe. Being drafted had made him eligible for the new housing just in time. He'd only slept three nights there, with his wife. CeCe calculated she had been conceived inside those three days. Inside a love so thorough between Quentin and her mother. She understood why her mother buried herself inside that bed every day.

She'd waited in the courtyard for her parents to push open the screen door and step into the sunlight beaming down on their porch slab. She waited to see them hand in hand, or with her mother curled girlishly into Quentin's one-armed embrace. Instead, Quentin had crashed open the door commanding CeCe to find phone numbers for her mother's doctor and family.

"One minute she had my face in her hands and the next minute she crouched on the floorboards, moaning," Quentin repeated to the paramedics, the intake nurse at the mental hospital, Dr. Harper, and Aunt Rosie. To CeCe, he kept saying he was sorry. So, so sorry.

CeCe's letters to Quentin after her mother's release described a vivacious recovery. She wanted him to feel at ease about returning to them soon. CeCe also wrote about Mrs. Anderson and training the new library assistant, as well as sleepovers with Pam, books she read, and all the places she hoped to visit one day.

From the very beginning her letters outnumbered his three to one, but CeCe didn't mind. Her father was busy getting better, just like her mother, without, she hoped, the mumbling, rocking, and staring. CeCe couldn't call him because their phone didn't have long-distance service. Her father placed calls to her on Christmas and her birthday. Both times, CeCe asked if he wanted to speak to her mother, and both times he said he didn't know if that was a good idea.

His letters came less consistently throughout middle school and to a complete stop before the end of her eighth-grade year. CeCe vowed if she didn't find a letter or postcard before she went to Decatur for the summer, she would go back to pretending he didn't exist. When she dragged her duffel bag from the house with no letter from her father, CeCe fumed for weeks, assigning every broken thing in her life to him. Their small apartment. Their fixed income. That she couldn't play volleyball or basketball or be a fashion model because of the short genes he'd given her. That her mother was broken, almost beyond repair. That he'd broken CeCe's heart.

Barely a week after arriving in Decatur, Coretta announced CeCe would stay with Aunt Rosie for a few days. CeCe wasn't surprised Aunt Rosie would want to be the first to offer advice about her upcoming year as a high-school student. At least her father had given her family.

CeCe and Aunt Rosie watched back-to-back episodes of *Jeopardy!*, worked the garden, cleaned and cooked mustard greens for Sunday dinner, and sucked Popsicles in the back yard. One afternoon, CeCe read in the porch swing when Aunt Rosie sat in the fanback chair next to her with a large brown envelope.

"Sometimes when we lookin' real close at a patch," she said, "we don't know we only seeing part of the quilt."

CeCe looked over the edge of her book at Aunt Rosie. She could rarely guess where these Rosie-isms might lead, but had come to trust they always held a nugget of wisdom. Aunt Rosie's eyes did not sparkle as she spoke, though. CeCe lay down her book, looking from Rosie's solemn face to the envelope in her hands.

"What's going on, Auntie?" she asked.

Aunt Rosie held CeCe's gaze before speaking. "Your daddy died, baby."

The inside of CeCe's chest constricted violently as she struggled to focus on Aunt Rosie's face. Rosie waited while CeCe tried to blink and twitch into understanding. Her mouth formed slow shapes, but ejected no words.

"I guess he been sick for a long time," Aunt Rosie said. "Your letters was gettin' sent from his apartment to a nursing home."

CeCe's chest convulsed again.

Aunt Rosie laid the square envelope on the swing next to CeCe. The flap was already opened.

"I saw your name on the envelope, but it didn't make no sense why it came here. So I read it," Rosie said. "Look like he been lovin' on you harder than he could say. We was all seein' his little patch, but the quilt is always bigger, baby. Always bigger."

Aunt Rosie lifted herself from the wicker porch chair and stood above CeCe for a moment. She used her thumb to wipe away the tears that sprang into CeCe's eyes, kissed the top of her great-niece's head, and shuffled back into the house.

CeCe stared at the yawning envelope. She recognized the return address as the Milton Olive Towers, the residential hall where her father had settled in Detroit. In the early letters he wrote to her, he described the facility as a kind of hotel for, mostly, veterans of color. CeCe slid a sympathy card from the envelope with a folded letter tucked inside. The card was signed in a florid script, Anna Schultz. The letter was typed:

Dear Crimson—

We've never met, but I feel as if we have. I've had the privilege of knowing your father for several years now. He was one of the men I cared for here at Olive Towers. Your father was special to me for many reasons. First, when he moved here three years ago, we were both new to this building. I loved the job right away, but there are always so many things to learn in a new place. He was one of the only residents to sit down and ask how I was adjusting and to encourage me on my rough days. Odd, it was MY job, to make sure HE was OK. I knew instantly he would be one of my special residents, and I was right.

He was a quiet presence, but when your father did speak he had wise advice, insightful observations, sincere questions, and wonderful stories about you. He told me all about your job as a library assistant, the straight As on your report cards, and what a big help you've been to your mother. He was so proud of you, Crimson. He saved all of his best words for talking about you.

When he started to get sick, no one knew what he had for a long time. His coughing and wheezing had gotten so bad he couldn't get out of bed. The doctors ran tests and learned he had a disease called pulmonary fibrosis, even though he wasn't a smoker. He said it felt like someone was trying to smother him. We moved him to a nursing home, and the front desk forwarded your letters to him there. This last letter landed on my desk because your father passed away in March, just before his birthday. Please forgive my invasion of your privacy, but I opened your letter because I knew something wasn't right. I don't know why you weren't informed of his passing by Carla Weathers (our contact of record). I also couldn't say why your father stopped writing you.

What I am certain of, though, is that your father loved you more than anything in this world. He kept your letters in a box on his nightstand all the time. All the time. It's not unusual for residents to withdraw from their families when they get sick, to protect them somehow. But I'm only guessing at what Quentin might have been thinking.

I am deeply sorry for your loss, Crimson. Not having your father will be hard enough (trust me, I know. My father died when I was just a little older than you). The last thing I would want is for you to go another day thinking he didn't adore you. His body eventually lost to the illness, but I want you to know that his heart was entirely devoted to you, his only daughter.

My prayers are with you and your family, Crimson. Thank you for bringing a spectacular man such spectacular joy.

Sincerely,

Anna Schultz

TWENTY-SEVEN

TETHERED

CeCe sat on Aunt Rosie's porch for the rest of the summer. Coretta's had too much light for her now. Laughter, movies, skating, pancakes, all of it too much.

Between her checklists of chores, CeCe gave small pushes to the swing with her bare heel. Sometimes she read. Sometimes she stared at the seam of field and sky. Sometimes she succumbed to violent weeping. And sometimes she watched the chase of wind through Aunt Rosie's pecan trees. Before summer ended, CeCe called Anna Schultz to thank her. They spoke for a few minutes, both admitting to feeling lighter in spirit before disconnecting the line.

CeCe next phoned Dr. Harper, who explained, again, that he could not divulge anything her mother had or had not told him about CeCe's father. CeCe began to unfasten. When the scream rocketed from her throat, vile and sick, Cece collapsed against the kitchen table and fell to the floor.

CeCe took the glass of water in Coretta's outstretched hand. She gave CeCe a soft smile and small nod before turning to leave the living room. CeCe sipped and placed the water glass on the couch's end table. The telephone waited. CeCe picked up the phone and balanced it on top of her legs. She wore a skort, convinced by another cousin that her shapely sprinter's legs were showcase caliber. The base of the blue Princess phone sat heavy and hard against her skin.

CeCe dialed her house number as Coretta and Aunt Rosie listened to the rotary's spinning clicks from extensions in the kitchen and master bedroom. Since CeCe had refused to wait for her return to Prescott and an appointment in his office, Dr. Harper insisted CeCe have family around when she called to confront Carla. CeCe would have phoned her mother the night before if the meds from the ER hadn't put her to sleep. Four stitches. She awoke stringing together beads of venom for this call.

CeCe sat on the edge of the couch, the phone cradled in her lap. Her sutures pricked at the hardening gauze. CeCe hadn't taken any medications that morning; she wanted all of her pipes and circuits to be open and clear. The phone clamored its first ring. On the fifth ring, they heard Carla's voice.

"Hello?" she said. Her voice was hollow and dry.

"It's me, Mama."

"CrimsonBaby," her mother said.

CeCe snorted, repelling her mother's shorthand affection.

"CeCe?"

CeCe scrambled to block the vicious words from leaping in front, moving them to rear flanks like she'd practiced. Everything in CeCe teetered, like wobbly table legs. She couldn't predict the wreckage of this collision, but resigned herself to fly directly into it.

"Daddy died," she said.

Silence.

"Four months ago."

Silence.

"You knew and didn't tell me," CeCe said, her voice climbing.

Carla cleared her throat.

"Why didn't you tell me?" CeCe asked, fervor flooding into her mouth.

Her mother hesitated again, and said, "I didn't know how."

"You didn't know how?" CeCe repeated, incredulous. She expected "I wanted to protect you," "There never seemed to be a right time," or "You're going through so much right now." But not this. Not a complete lack of effort. Another failure without even trying.

"What did you need to *know how* to do?" CeCe mocked. "I don't *know how* to keep us alive, but I do it. I figure it out, don't I? You couldn't figure this one thing out?"

"CrimsonBaby," her mother started, letting her voice trail away and fill the phone line with quiet.

"What?" CeCe demanded. "CrimsonBaby, what?"

All of them listened to Carla's silence. They could not even discern her breath.

"What, Mama? What could you possibly want to say to me right now?" CeCe asked. Volume pushed her vocal cords against the inside of her neck, blood against the inside of her veins, and a thick gurgle of rage against the inside her skull. CeCe bolted onto her feet, the powder blue base crashing to the floor.

"Exactly!" CeCe said again and again, louder, to a shrill scream. The tethered phone base tumbled alongside CeCe's feet as she stomped a furious circle into the living room carpet and emptied her venom into the receiver. By the time she screeched, "I hate you," Aunt Rosie stood in front of CeCe mouthing for her to hand over the phone.

"At least Daddy wanted to be here with me," CeCe screamed at her mother, the velocity pitching her forward onto her toes.

CeCe disassembled into hysterical tears while her mother kept mumbling her name. Rosie swiped the phone but not swiftly enough to dodge CeCe's parting words to her mother: "You should be the one who's dead."

CeCe spent the last three weeks of summer with her temples and flesh pounding. The rage eked from her pores like a film of sweat. She was furious with everyone: her father for leaving her alone for the last and final time, her mother for being inept at living, the social worker for not seeing the forest for the trees, Rosie and Coretta for not finding the legal loophole to retain her in their care, and her cousins for enjoying their tennis classes and mascara while she waited for two sets of failed genetics to implode inside of her.

TWENTY-EIGHT

SILENCE

CeCe got home from her date with Eric after 11 p.m., hours beyond either of their expectations. Changed into her nightshirt, CeCe padded to the kitchen and traded text messages about the date with Pam.

Pam teased about a grocery store wedding and CeCe joked about asparagus bouquets. CeCe poured a glass of juice and leaned against the counter as she sipped. The phone dinged an alert once. Twice. The first text was, indeed, a clever reply from Pam. The second message was from Eric.

"Got the 'great time' text," she typed to Pam. "Swooning."

"Leaving nothing to chance," Pam typed back. "Smart man. Me like."

CeCe toggled messages to Pam and Eric. She placed her empty glass in the sink, giggled at a text from Eric, turned off the kitchen lights and moved into the hallway. CeCe liked the way he gently teased about her enormous car, and she had liked the snow-soft kiss on her cheek. She typed and smiled when her mother's voice startled her.

"Nice?"

CeCe still started at her mother's voice sometimes. She was braced for their familiar silence when CeCe moved her mother into Terri's vacated room three years prior. The tradeoff for her mother's rediscovered speech had been the anxious phone calls triggered by spasms of panic over CeCe's whereabouts and well-being. CeCe decided the exchange had been an even one, but the sound of her mother's voice could still catch her off guard.

"Didn't hear you, Mama," CeCe said into her mother's darkened room.

"Your date," her mother's voice said. "Was he nice."

CeCe grinned a little. She had stewed in their early years here, at her mother's deliberate gall to ask about her days, after so much time, to remember a big client event or notice a new pair of earrings. CeCe admonished herself for scowling when her mother's voice would whistle from the dark bedroom.

"Yeah," CeCe said into the bedroom shadows. "He was really nice."

CeCe leaned her entire right half toward the doorway's yawning darkness, listening for speech or light snoring.

"Good," her mother finally said. "That's good."

"Good night, Mama," CeCe said, waiting. Her mother did not reply.

CeCe shuffled to the end of the hallway and into her bedroom. Her phone dinged with a new message. CeCe closed the door and switched off the lights. She gripped her phone and slipped into bed. After activating her alarm clock, CeCe felt along the ledge of her headboard shelves to find her charger cord. She plugged in her phone, anchored an elbow into her spare pillow, and smiled down at the small screen.

"Was at a conference," read the message from Rocky. "Sacramento. Call you tomorrow."

CeCe's heart lurched. She still had no idea how to make that stop.

TWENTY-NINE

BATS

ONLY FRESHMEN ATTENDED SCHOOL ON the first day at Maclin High. CeCe appreciated the early chance to navigate the enormous building, practice opening her very first locker, and share her new classmates' nervous energy. In their orientation assembly, their freshman guidance director, Mr. Meadows, introduced the head principal, the nurse and head secretary, cheerleaders, graduating seniors, class presidents, and yearbook editor.

CeCe kept turning to look at the sea of the freshman faces. Six hundred, the size of her entire elementary school and triple the size of her middle school. Her nerves settled a bit more each time she spied a Valmore face. They were blended into a population of academically strong students from throughout the district. Many of their classmates had advanced to private high schools, as expected, but CeCe looked forward to Maclin's honors classes and, of course, adjusting to the expanded social network of high school.

When CeCe spotted Jesse, she froze. She was pulling out her lunch bag and a library book but folded into her locker when she saw him. CeCe made a silent wish not to have any classes with Jesse, and to spend the next four years passing him in the halls as infrequently as possible.

In the cafeteria, CeCe sat down at an empty table with her brown bag and book. She was reading Toni Morrison's *The Bluest*

Eye, a title the public librarian had suggested. CeCe thought she might not enjoy the novel, but she was immediately engrossed.

"You like it?" a voice asked.

CeCe looked up to face another brown-skinned girl standing at her lunch table. CeCe recognized her from the assembly. The girl was tall and lean, with wide-set eyes and fleshy, pink lips. She looked, to CeCe, like a grasshopper.

"So far," CeCe said.

"I couldn't finish it," the girl said. "It was too depressing."

CeCe nodded in understanding. She noticed the girl had a book tucked underneath her arm, too. "What are you reading?"

"*Cujo*," she said, placing her lunch bag on the table, freeing her hands to show CeCe the book cover. CeCe nodded again. Stephen King was one of her favorites. "My name's Laurita."

"CeCe."

The girls sat together in a cocooning silence. They munched and sipped and turned pages with the din of their new cafeteria scattering behind them. Mr. Meadows' voice in the PA speakers jerked them from their stories and instructed them to prepare for the bell and their afternoon classes. The girls tossed their trash, but Laurita folded her lunch bag, just like CeCe.

"Which bus do you ride?" Laurita asked. CeCe was relieved that her new friend asked about the city bus. At Valmore, everyone else had a yellow bus, minivan, or Volvo to pick them up.

"Clark, then I change to the Kennedy," CeCe said, walking with her new friend out of the cafeteria.

"I take the Clark bus, too," Laurita said. "Then I go the other way, on the Fourth Avenue bus. Want me to meet you after school and we can walk together?"

CeCe nodded, hoping she didn't look as spastically excited as she felt on the inside. At the end of the day, CeCe stacked books into her locker when she saw Laurita at the far end of the hallway. Her new friend came toward CeCe, lanky limbs bending and knocking like a marionette. The two made their way through the ebb of students pouring out to school buses, bike racks, and idling cars and continued walking another block to the Clark Avenue bus stop.

In their short bus ride and while waiting at their shared transfer stop, Laurita managed to tell CeCe about a lethargic cat named Chitlin, her summer in the country backwoods of Alabama, the roller skating rink near her house, her straight As in math, a big brother in college, the time her father had gotten them lost driving to Busch Gardens, and the vacuuming she needed to do before her mother got home from work. As Laurita's Fourth Street bus came into view, she finished a story about Chitlin and paused to smile at her new friend.

"It's me and you," she said, placing a hand on CeCe's shoulder. "We're freshmen, we're black, we're kinda nerdy, we're small—well, I'm skinny and you're short—and we're not one of the cool kids. But we've got each other, OK?"

CeCe heard herself agreeing with Laurita, sharing a hug as the bus reached their stop and waving as Laurita boarded. CeCe's smile crashed once the bus pulled away.

Not one of the cool kids.

The next day was a madhouse. CeCe noticed an electricity in the hallways she hadn't felt the day before. Navigating her small form in between the hundreds of stalklike upperclassmen affirmed to CeCe that she was truly a high school student now. Nudging along to their lockers, CeCe thought of all the high school montages she'd seen on TV: girls walking in pairs, hugging textbooks to their bosoms; letterman's jackets raucously chasing each other through the halls; beautiful people with lip gloss and moussed hair; quirky-looking kids with black clothes and heavy boots; adult voices spiking above the roar of students to direct one to the office, another away from that locker.

CeCe and Laurita stood against the wall beside CeCe's locker before parting for their separate homeroom classes.

"You know where you're going?" Laurita asked.

"I think so," CeCe said. They did not face each other. They were watching the flow of students, timing their plunge.

"OK, but if you have to pull out your schedule, be sure to go into the bathroom," Laurita said. "You want to look like you know what we're doing."

CeCe nodded and the two girls scooted into opposite directions and fell into the stream of students. CeCe waited by Laurita's locker at lunchtime, as agreed. CeCe regarded her friend's burgundy-and-cream ensemble, at how the pants matched the cardigan and the polo matched her hair barrettes.

Hair barrettes.

The lunchroom was alive with chatter and shrieking, a cacophony of shoe soles and slammed books, and so, so many faces. Over sandwiches, CeCe and Laurita talked about the presence of the upperclassmen, the homework they'd already been assigned, and the characters in their classes.

"There's this one guy in my English class named Jesse," Laurita said, peeling the top from her fruit cup. "He's so ridiculous. He made fun of everyone when the teacher stepped into the hallway, but after class, out in the hall, he acted like a scared rat. He was really mean."

"I used to go to school with him," CeCe said. "He tries to be a bully."

CeCe did not mention her confrontation with Jesse on their last night at Neil Armstrong, because she would have to tell Michelle's secret to tell the story. Besides, CeCe didn't want to think about Jesse. She'd spent two years forgetting him, and figured she could stay out of his path for another four.

She was wrong.

CeCe, Laurita, and another new friend, a Puerto Rican girl named Sophia, were eating lunch at their usual table the next day. Sophia made them all laugh with her retelling of a French horn blare in band class that made the teacher blush for ten minutes. CeCe and Laurita were clutching their stomachs while Sophia acted out the scene. Jesse and two other boys were on their way out of the lunchroom, but swerved to stand at the end of the girls' table.

"What's so funny?" he asked, leaning on the table, looking from one girl to the next. His eyes danced with mean flames. None of the girls answered him.

"What's so funny?" Jesse repeated, straightening to his full, albeit slight height.

"Who wants to know?" Sophia asked, with a snap in her voice.

"Nobody," he said, glancing at his two sidekicks, seeming to cue their laughter. "Nobody cares what you three bats are talking about."

The girls replied in staggered sighs and mutterings. Jesse shoved his hands in his pockets and had turned his entire body to face CeCe only. "I just came over to remind *Crimson* that I'm still gonna get her back," he said. His small green eyes were piercing and cold. His consonants were sloppy along the letter "S," his mouth still full of metal braces.

"I had to spend the summer cutting grass for two old ladies on my block for free because you narced on me," Jesse said, sounding venomous.

"I didn't narc on you," CeCe said, hoping to be indignant instead of nervous. She pinched her sandwich between her fingers.

"She's a liar, too," Jesse said to the taller boy on his left. He turned his attention to Laurita and Sophia. "Did she tell you how she narced on her own best friend until the whole family had to move?"

"Shut up, Jesse!" CeCe said, her eyes wide. "That's not what happened!"

"So you admit *something* happened," Jesse said, mischief filling his eyes and grin.

"No—well, yes—but I didn't—" CeCe stopped, her words frustrated. CeCe's protests sounded like she was defending herself, and she didn't want her new friends to think she had anything to hide.

"Shut up!" she hissed at Jesse. "You don't know what you're talking about."

"Oh, yes I do," Jesse said. "You narced on your fat friend, you narced on me, and I bet you'll narc on anybody. I'm gonna hafta warn people about you. You're a menace."

A lunchroom monitor moved in their direction, but Jesse curled a wicked grin onto his face as he and his new clique of sycophants moved past CeCe's table and out of the lunchroom.

"Keep an eye on her, you bats!" he said in a stage whisper to Laurita and Sophia, his words slippery with spit.

The girls were silent once he left. CeCe felt angry and embarrassed, frustrated and upset. Her temples had begun to pound and her heart thundered in her chest. CeCe buried her face in her hands. Sophia placed a hand on her shoulder first, then Laurita reached from across the table to touch the back of her hands.

"Don't worry about him," Laurita said.

"Yeah, he's nothing," Sophia said. "Come with me to the home ec room. I'll buy you a cupcake from their bake sale."

"No, thanks," CeCe said, lowering her hands and looking at her friends. New friends who were already looking at her differently. Already wondering if they'd made a miscalculation. CeCe knew how it could be for kids on the fringe, like them. In middle school, she had thought all the outsiders would stick together. On the contrary, missteps or misjudgments were much more detrimental to their social survival, and the fringe kids had learned to cut bait fast.

At home, CeCe continued to think of Michelle. Not only their last night, but all of the memories they'd accumulated over the years. In actuality, Michelle and her twin brother Michael had been CeCe's oldest friends at Neil Armstrong. Now, her single remaining close friend was Pam, and CeCe needed to talk to her now. In the middle of reading her American history assignment, CeCe swung her feet stood up from the couch and went to the phone in the hallway.

Her mother sat at the kitchen table, staring into the usual nothing. CeCe looked at her mother as she lifted the receiver. Waiting, CeCe realized, for her mother to ask—even demand—just who in the world did she think she was calling?

Her mother kept staring.

CeCe looked away and punched Pam's number into the phone. She raised the receiver to her ear and waited. Silence. CeCe pressed the phone hook with her index finger, but still heard no dial tone. CeCe tapped the hook impatiently.

"Mama, where's the phone bill?" CeCe asked, looking down at the floor and not at her mother.

"What'd you say, CrimsonBaby?" her mother said.

"Where is the phone bill?" CeCe repeated, still looking at the linoleum floor. She kept one finger on the phone hook and the phone receiver in her other hand, as if the line might spring back to life. CeCe couldn't look up at her. She wouldn't be able to stand the slumped shoulders, the ever-present coffee mug, or her vacant expression.

"The phone bill?" her mother repeated. Eyes still on the floor, CeCe could hear her mother shifting in her seat, building momentum to stand, perhaps. CeCe imagined her mother standing and glancing around on the floor as if the bill might be there.

"Forget it," CeCe said, slamming the phone on the receiver. She went to the hallway desk and fished inside for the notepad she'd made in fifth grade to keep track of their account numbers for the phone company, the electric company, and the bank, contact information for the lawyer's office managing her mother's trust fund, and the address for Aunt Rosie and Cousin Coretta.

CeCe didn't understand how her mother could confuse such a short list of tasks. Sweep the kitchen. Clean the coffee pot. Bring in the mail. Leave it for CeCe. CeCe would have to take three buses downtown tomorrow for a money order and to pay the phone company. CeCe didn't look at her mother for the rest of the evening.

At school, Jesse continued to yell "narc" at CeCe in the hallways and call her friends "bats" in the lunchroom. Although, Laurita admitted he only acted that way around CeCe, ignoring them when the girls encountered him alone.

"I know you can't tell us what happened," Sophia said one day, "but this guy is really, really pissed at you. Maybe you should apologize."

"But I didn't do anything," CeCe said, surprised at Sophia's suggestion.

"Sometimes, you gotta take one for the team," Laurita said. Her tone was flat and she didn't look up from her pudding cup. CeCe had noticed how Laurita had started to wear her hair down now.

We're a team?

"I didn't do anything," CeCe said, more quietly. Laurita shrugged one shoulder, peering into the bottom of her snack cup. Sophia launched into a story about her little sister tanning a Barbie doll in the microwave.

For the next several weeks, Jesse would swerve out of his way to insert himself into CeCe's conversations, blurting that CeCe was a narc and couldn't be trusted with any secrets. CeCe saw him making an erratic beeline toward her one afternoon and closed her eyes in pre-exasperation. She tried to turn away but one of the varsity wrestlers walked by, blocking her path long enough for Jesse's voice to reach her.

"You gotta go narc on somebody?" he said.

"This is getting really old," CeCe said.

Jesse walked away laughing. "Maybe for you."

In late October, on picture day, someone handed a note to the girl waiting in front of CeCe in line. The girl giggled, looking around. She shook her head, sighed, and turned around to look pitiably at CeCe. CeCe looked at the girl blankly until she held up the square of notebook paper for CeCe to read: "There's a narc bat behind you. Watch your back!"

CeCe looked around, too, but saw no sign of Jesse. Her insides collapsed. He'd enlisted the entire school.

CeCe ate her lunch in the home ec room by the middle of November. The teacher, Mrs. Watson, didn't ask any questions or demand an explanation, and CeCe was grateful. Laurita and Sophia hadn't questioned her, either, and CeCe assumed they appreciated the relief. They would speak when passing in the hallway or chatter quickly at the beginning of the school day, but neither asked CeCe to slow down on the way to class or to wait for them on her way to the bus stop anymore.

CeCe would eat her lunch and read while Mrs. Watson graded papers or set up for her sixth-period class. She also taught the health class all of the freshmen had to take. They covered first aid, nutrition, hygiene, mental wellness, careers in health, and an odd review of epidemics throughout history.

"Mrs. Watson," CeCe asked one day, a random curiosity filling her mind. "I have a weird question."

"Weird questions are my specialty," Mrs. Watson chirped. She was a thin woman, with a long graying ponytail and bright hazel eyes. She wore lots of embroidered vests, long denim skirts, and clog shoes. She bounced through the room like a robin, placing gauze and bandages on each desk.

"I started my period this year and I want to make sure it's normal."

Mrs. Watson looked up from her fistfuls of gauze. "What makes you think it might not be?"

"My best friend started her period in the sixth grade and, well, I remember her talking about—," CeCe shifted in her seat, crossing her legs at the ankles and looking down at her feet. "The smell."

"There's an odor?" Mrs. Watson asked, moving from desk to desk.

"No," CeCe said. "That's just it. I don't smell anything. With all the Summer's Eve commercials and stuff, I thought it was supposed to smell, but it doesn't. I didn't know if that meant I was low on . . . estrogen or something."

Mrs. Watson laughed, birdlike. "The way these companies push that stuff, you'd think so," she said.

Mrs. Watson told CeCe a woman's body produces its own cleansing fluids and that douches were a marketing ploy. She also explained how the iron content in menstrual blood sometimes created a stronger scent than regular blood. She emphasized the importance of good hygiene and more thorough washing.

"Does that make more sense?" Mrs. Watson asked.

"Yes," CeCe said. "I wasn't looking forward to smelling like baloney."

"Baloney?" Mrs. Watson repeated, and howled with laughter. "Sweetheart, I think smelling like lunch meat would be adding insult to injury for us women!"

CeCe agreed and laughed, wondering why she found it so much easier to talk and laugh with adults.

Laurita appeared at CeCe's locker before their last class period. "Where were you at lunch today?" Laurita asked. CeCe noted an unfamiliar edge to her voice. Maybe her friend missed her after all. "Mrs. Watson's room," CeCe said. "She lets me eat in there since—"

"It was you!" Laurita screamed. Laurita looked around and clenched her teeth to constrain the volume of her voice. She stepped close to CeCe's face. "Lunch meat? You told her I smelled like lunch meat?"

CeCe's mouth gaped open and her mind raced to connect the explosive dots, but her mind couldn't focus as she stared up into Laurita's flaring nostrils.

"I didn't—," CeCe said. "I mean, I wasn't talking about you—I was asking—"

"Save it, CeCe," Laurita said. "I do *not* believe you. Why would Crystal come up to me out of nowhere and ask how my lunch meat was doing this month?"

"Crystal?" CeCe said, confused. "Jesse's girlfriend?"

"You can't blame this on Jesse," Laurita said. "It was *you* talking about your *friend* to Mrs. Watson, who thought it was so funny she told Ms. DiPaulo and guess who was retaking a test in Ms. DiPaulo's room?"

"But I wasn't talking about you," CeCe said, tears making their way to her eyes.

"Right, like you have another 'best friend,'" Laurita said as she turned to leave.

"Laurita—"

"Look, I'm already sick of having this crazy-ass kid calling me a 'bat' every day because of . . . whatever you did to him, and now his crazy-ass girlfriend is telling our gym class my coochie smells like lunch meat!" Laurita said, backing away. "Find a new best friend, *Crimson.*"

CeCe wanted to protest again, but the venom Laurita had coiled around the syllables of her name made CeCe stop. As her friend stomped away, CeCe knew Jesse had won.

By the time the weather chilled and snow threatened its return, Jesse had expanded his menacing enterprise to a small network of enforcers. Systematically, they made CeCe's name a damning expletive for any brand of unfavorable news:

"We had a pop quiz in Geometry. Crimson narced."

"We're getting apple slices instead of tater tots. Crimson."

"The Aerosmith concert got Crimsoned."

The slightest grace was that most of her classmates knew her as CeCe, if they registered her name at all. She sat in the back of their classes as they flung around her birth name like a booger. Laurita ignored her completely, but Sophia greeted her between classes, band practice, and forensics. CeCe tried sinking into the walls and floors inside Maclin High School. She didn't waste time rolling curlers into her hair and stopped laying out her clothes at night and agonizing over the makeup bag. She stopped it all and no one seemed to notice.

"CeCe, Mr. Meadows would like to see you in his office," said her homeroom teacher one morning. It was the last week before holiday break and everyone was anxious for vacation to start. As she gathered her books and stood, a few of Jesse's minions chanted quietly from the back of the room, "Narc! Narc! Narc!" A hushed rumble of laughter followed CeCe from the classroom.

She walked the wide hallways, listening to the slip of her flat shoes across the tiles. CeCe looked down at the gleam on the floors as she made her way to the office. She passed banks of lockers, intersecting hallways, and classroom doors with clips of the teachers' lessons lobbing overhead as she walked by. It was calming to move through the corridors alone.

"CeCe, come on in," Mr. Meadows said, standing in the doorway of his interior office. Mr. Meadows was a large man with a broad back and shoulders, as if he wore hooded sweatshirt beneath his plaid dress shirts. He also had a booming voice and an effortless smile. Like all the other freshmen, CeCe had liked Mr. Meadows since he had guided them through their first day as Maclin Vikings.

She felt uncomfortable now. She'd already had a midterm one-on-one with him, like all the other freshmen, and didn't know what this meeting could be about. CeCe hoped the trend of social workers hadn't followed her to high school. She sat at the small round table in the corner and waited.

"I like to be straight with you kids," Mr. Meadows said as he sat, lifting his ankle to cross his knee. "I don't like beating around the bush because we're too smart for that, right?"

CeCe nodded and swallowed, perching the tips of her fingers nervously on the table's edge.

"There's something going on with you, CeCe," Mr. Meadows said, "and I wanted to talk to you before things got out of hand."

CeCe's eyes widened and her brain searched for things she'd done or said that might "get out of hand."

Mr. Meadows released one of his rolling-thunder laughs. "Relax, CeCe. I forgot to say, 'You're not in trouble.'"

CeCe relaxed her shoulders and lowered her hands into her lap.

"Your grades are OK but, based on your marks at Valmore, we were expecting a bit more from you," he said. He considered his words before adding, "It doesn't seem you're making many friends, either. Is it true Mr. Kingsman found you eating lunch in the girls' shower?"

CeCe dropped her head. It sounded more pathetic when Mr. Meadows said it out loud. She'd started eating in the bleachers then moved to the locker rooms for complete seclusion. Once she realized girls still streamed in and out to retrieve forgotten folders, books, and hair bands, CeCe had moved to the shower stalls. Mr. Kingsman, the janitor, found her sitting on a pallet she made of clean towels with a book in her lap and sandwich in hand.

"Y'know, CeCe," he said. "I won't pretend like I know how you feel. A new school. New kids. New rules. A whole new obstacle course to master, right?"

CeCe pursed her lips, the closest she could offer to a grin.

"The bad news, kiddo, is that you have to figure it out. You have a great future at this school and I'd hate to see it squished in your very first semester." Mr. Meadows forced his torso against the small table to face CeCe. His mustache had streaks of gray, like his short, cropped hair.

"Tell me what I can do to help you turn things around next term," he said.

CeCe looked at his big face and kind eyes. She didn't know what to say. She didn't know what she *could* say. She couldn't narc about Jesse calling her a narc. She couldn't repeat the lunch meat misunderstanding without embarrassing Laurita again. She couldn't tell him about how coming to school was as agonizing as going home. CeCe wanted to tell him all of this, but she couldn't. Instead, she started to cry.

"Oh, CeCe, don't start crying on me," Mr. Meadows said, unwedging himself to stand and get a box of tissues from his credenza. "Then I'll start crying, and you don't want to see a big clumsy guy like me crying, not with this huge honker. Trust me, it's an ugly, snotty sight."

CeCe took the tissue and felt a small laugh escape.

"That's better," Mr. Meadows said, smiling back at CeCe. He sat and waited.

Finally, she said, "I don't know."

"OK, that's fair," he said. "If you had a solution, you would've done it already, right?"

CeCe smiled weakly and shrugged one shoulder.

"Tell you what," Mr. Meadows said. "How about you think about it over holiday break and we'll come up with a plan together."

"OK," CeCe said, scooting her chair back, sensing their discussion was over.

"I have one suggestion to start," Mr. Meadows said. CeCe turned from the door, her hand on the lever. "There's a little cubicle in the back of our office. You can eat your lunch there for a while. No one will see you, no one will bug you, and no one will swipe your pudding cup. Sound good?"

CeCe beamed, nodded.

"All right then," Mr. Meadows said, standing and following her through the door. "I've got to get upstairs and talk to the seniors about their winter sledding trip. You'd think they were taking a spaceship to the moon, as complicated as they're making things."

Booming laugh.

"Thank you, Mr. Meadows," CeCe said.

"You're more than welcome, CeCe," he replied. "No one expects you to figure out this high school stuff all by yourself. Then there'd be no reason for *me* to show up! You're not as alone as I know you think you are. We Vikings gotta stick together, right?"

"Right."

CeCe thanked Mr. Meadows again and went to her locker to get ready for her first period class. She could feel the goofy outline of a smile on her face, and it felt good. At lunchtime, she carried her brown bag to Mr. Meadows' office and the guidance secretary tucked her into a back cubicle, as promised. When CeCe left the office, the secretary gave her a blank sheet of school letterhead. CeCe held the sheet gingerly, looking quizzically at the empty page.

"Makes it look like you were here for something super official," the secretary said, giving CeCe a wink. Understanding dawned across CeCe's face and she gave the woman a bashful grin.

All at once, CeCe felt small and enormous. She'd spent week after week feeling more and more invisible in these halls. The students didn't speak to her, the teachers rarely called on her, even the bullies didn't expend much energy on her anymore. But she wasn't invisible to Mr. Meadows. Or his secretary. Or Mr. Kingsman. They saw her as a moving shadow, but at least acknowledged her dimensions and made their own efforts to help her begin to feel whole.

You're not in this alone.

The night before their first day back in January, CeCe laid out her clothes and rolled curlers into her hair. She smiled at her reflection in the bathroom mirror, "dressed, pressed, and fresh," as Coretta liked to say when they were all polished for church. CeCe felt buoyant walking up to the school, like having a second first day of school. Before heading to her locker, she stopped in to show Mr. Meadows her new look and let him know she'd worked on some good ideas to show him over lunch. When she reached the office, the secretary greeted her with a sad frown.

"Oh honey," the secretary said. "Telling you was going to be the most difficult."

CeCe stopped in the doorway.

This lead-in rang familiar.

"Mr. Meadows is out for the rest of the year," the secretary said.

CeCe's entire body went numb with this news. Muscle by muscle, thought by thought, she felt a familiar ache of loneliness begin to creep back into her bones.

"He had a troubling, private incident occur with his daughter and he's decided to take a sabbatical until next school year."

CeCe thanked the secretary and went to her homeroom class. She ripped the wish list into small, even squares and sank into her seat. The teacher handed out their new schedules and she knew the day would prove an end instead of a new beginning.

By the end of the week, sure enough, CeCe had random people—even upperclassmen—stopping to ask her what she'd said to get Mr. Meadows fired. One by one, her classmates had clearly decided Jesse had been right all along. Week after week, more "evidence" surfaced about CeCe's alleged whistle blowing: being called from class to Mr. Meadows' office, that she snooped through lockers, that the secretary created a "private family matter" story for fear that CeCe would get her fired next.

When they learned Mr. Franklin, the grisly and joyless sophomore counselor, was taking over, CeCe's position as the freshman class pariah was cemented for eternity. She had stopped protesting, stopped trying to explain, and stopped being angry at the doubting glances. She even stopped being scared about what barb might be hurled her way. Returning to her bleacher seat for one, CeCe found a permanent switch inside herself and slid everything to "stop."

THIRTY

SMIRK

CECE MUMBLED A TIGHT-LIPPED thank-you from the concrete. The tall woman extended her hand and pulled CeCe back to her feet. The waiting cluster of riders filed around her and onto the bus.

CeCe limped to the side, pretending to examine her ankle as the bus hydraulics sighed and pulled away from the curb. No scrapes, no strains, no embedded bits of glass, just a bruised ego after falling from a city bus, plowing down a small crowd of commuters, and smearing her white interview blouse with a stranger's chocolate bar.

She dashed a glance over each shoulder and pointed herself toward Carpenter Street. The crisp spring breezes coiled around her arms, pulling her along to Rocky's house. They became friends towards the end of freshmen year, her first semester at Linden. She'd transferred mid-year, unable to endure any more of Jesse's taunting. She'd been relieved to be free, but missed the rigor of her old school's curriculum. At Linden, CeCe breezed through her homework, wrote long notes to Pam in place of their regular sleepovers, picked up her mother's prescriptions, and crowded any remaining mental space with dense books like *Iacocca*, *The Sicilian*, and *The Color Purple*.

CeCe also waited for the crazy spores to erupt inside her. Rocky waited with her, although less patiently. He responded to her gripes and theories with stark truth and crude affirmations. He was like

Cousin Coretta in the form of a cute guy. Rocky was under-tall for a guy, just as CeCe was shorter than average for girls. He had a broad forehead with thick eyebrows and wise, auburn eyes that complemented his shock of russet-colored hair. Rocky, a fixture with their peers since elementary school, was often referenced as "the black kid with freckles," though he could also have been called "the honors student," the "track star," "Camille's boyfriend," or the "debate team champ." CeCe, on the other hand, existed as the "quiet new girl with the big booty."

CeCe absorbed Rocky's friendship like an essential nutrient. She regularly rode the Kennedy bus to hang out at the blue house on Carpenter Street. Most visits, Rocky focused on some necessary task—homework, ironing, or shaping the hairs of his struggling mustache—while she rambled along some stream of consciousness or blurted out random comments about the latest book she was reading. CeCe spoke few words to the rest of the world, but unleashed them all inside the walls of Rocky's room.

Only Rocky's room did not have meticulous designs from Africa and Harlem like the rest of the blue house on Carpenter Street. Instead, faraway ambitions, like Mali, Belize, New Guinea, and Fiji, were held in place with clear thumbtacks. Above his work desk was a framed trinity of Malcolm X, Michael Jordan, and Mahatma Gandhi. "Consciousness, Excellence, and Righteousness," he had explained to CeCe.

"Pick up a guidebook next time you're at the library," Rocky said, interrupting CeCe's report. He did not look up from the Adidas cradled in his lap.

CeCe sighed and leaned back against the wall. They'd been debating the subject of college since they met. Rocky's parents had impressed upon him the question of where he might go, not whether. For CeCe, the prospect of college seemed implausible.

Her life assignment—tending to her mother—had been cemented in her after middle school. CeCe had resigned herself from the habit of dreaming.

"College isn't part of my plans," she lied. "I'm not gonna pretend to be hell bent about it now."

"Lame," Rocky said, eyes still on his polishing job.

CeCe bristled and snapped, "Just because you get a hard-on whenever someone says 'college' doesn't mean everybody else thinks the same way."

Rocky gave a labored sigh and said, "Not unless that someone can read a novel a weekend. Solve the Sunday crossword in one afternoon. Make sense of Robert Harris *and* Robin Williams. Or calculate the recipe for three-quarters of a batch of brownies in her head. *That* someone should be thinking about college."

"Maybe *that someone* doesn't want to go to college."

"Maybe *that someone* is full of shit."

Rocky returned to his polishing. CeCe sat on his bed, looking at the back of his head.

"And *that someone* will regret being so full of shit one day," he added.

When CeCe left, she refused Rocky's offer to drive her home or to the bus stop, or to walk her to the corner. She ignored his smirk as he walked her to the door.

"This hurts me more than it hurts you," he said as she exited. CeCe flashed her middle finger before the heavy door closed.

By the time they reached their senior year, CeCe and Rocky had developed an eerie symbiosis. They weren't joined at the hip as they had been in the beginning, but they were elemental parts of each other's lives and everyone knew it. CeCe still wasn't invited into the cool social circles, but she could sense their sniping comments dissolve outside of her earshot. In so many ways, Rocky had become her protective force field.

It was their first day as seniors and the hallways pulsed with feverish excitement. Their classmates and underclassmen greeted her as they passed in the halls, and CeCe returned awkward head nods and weak smiles. She felt as if someone had yanked off her cloak of invisibility after all these years.

After third period, CeCe stood washing her hands in the girls' bathroom mirror when a dark-haired girl she knew to be on the track and field team with Rocky rushed in to fix her hair in the mirror. She was tall and lean, a pole-vaulter and long-distance runner. She pulled a small brush through her long, coal-black hair when she recognized CeCe wringing her hands beneath the faucet.

"You must be having the best day ever," the girl said, with a punchline in her eye.

"The last day will be the best day," CeCe said, reaching for a paper towel. The girl, she believed, was a junior.

"Not the senior thing," the girl said, dismissing CeCe's reply with a wave of her brush. "I mean, yes, *that*, and you finally get to have your crush all to yourself. Camille and Rocky broke up."

CeCe wouldn't see Rocky until lunch hour. Throughout their junior year, while he dated Camille, CeCe and Rocky would chat while loading their trays and then separate to their respective tables. This time, Rocky followed CeCe to her seat. She raised her eyebrows dramatically and looked searchingly about the lunchroom.

"Stop it," Rocky said, a grin on the corners of his mouth. "I know you heard about me and Camille."

"Why'd I have to hear about it?" CeCe said, snapping the small pepper packet in half and shaking small dashes across her mixed vegetables and her pasta.

"The rumor mill just moved faster than I could think," Rocky said, peeling the paper from his straw.

CeCe laughed, in spite of herself. "Nothing moves faster than all that thinking you do."

"I'm going to take that as a compliment, if you don't mind," Rocky said.

"Knock yourself out," she said.

CeCe quieted while Rocky bowed his head to bless his meal. Watching his lips part and bend around his prayer, CeCe considered how they might look to others in the lunchroom now. They'd had lunch together most days since sophomore year. CeCe loved Rocky but not romantically, at least not the way she thought romantic love should feel. She'd loved him like family, like a promise, like salvation.

While Rocky blessed his food, CeCe let herself wonder for the first time how it might feel to adore him. With Camille as a constant all these years, CeCe hadn't been confronted with the fantasy before now. When Rocky looked up, CeCe's eyes were fixed on him.

"Man, chill," he said, twisting his face into mock irritation. "Can a brotha finish talking to God first?"

CeCe rolled her eyes. She felt the small idea sink as quickly as it had appeared.

Rocky talked about his summer with Camille as they ate their lunches. CeCe wrinkled her nose as Rocky noisily shoveled spaghetti into his mouth. For all his refinement, CeCe marveled at what a *boy* he still was.

"We agreed things had gotten dumb with all the back-and-forth," Rocky said, between smacks. "Plus we didn't want to burn our entire senior year knowing we weren't gonna last after we graduate and move away. "

CeCe's head shot up. *Move away? We?*

"I thought you were applying to U of I?" CeCe said.

"I am," Rocky said, stuffing a corner of bread into his mouth.

"That's just a backup. Northeastern has always been the goal. Their education school is one of the best and I feel pretty good about getting in. I might even qualify for this fellowship program that gets me experience in the classroom as early as next summer . . . "

CeCe heard his words, registered the mounting enthusiasm as he explained the program, the rigorous selection process, the boarding academies that recruited from among the school's graduates. CeCe knew Rocky hoped to teach at elite private schools. He wanted to expose privileged children to brilliant people of color. As he explained it, he wanted to be their Great Black Hope, the same way young, white teachers expect to rescue their new inner-city classes. *Aren't there rich white kids in the state of Illinois who need cultural awakening?* CeCe thought.

"I talked to one of the program administrators a few weeks ago," Rocky said around another full mouth of spaghetti. "I'm heading out there in October."

"Oh," said CeCe, poking at her food, her appetite now gone. "This is serious business."

Rocky nodded, swallowed, gulped at his soda, and went on about his scheduled interview. CeCe's head bobbed up and down and her stomach flipped over and over.

"What's up with your applications?" Rocky asked, forking the last mound of pasta into his mouth.

CeCe shrugged. "I'm gonna work for a while first."

"Don't be stupid."

"Don't be an ass."

"Noted," Rocky said.

When CeCe got home from school that afternoon, she still had Rocky's news itching in her ears. *Boston.* "Moving away" gripped CeCe in the throat much more viciously than "going away." Going away, at least, felt more closely tied to "coming back." CeCe was annoyed with herself. Now that she'd let the idea of "them" peek above her surface, she couldn't keep it submerged.

Drown, drown, drown.

THIRTY-ONE

WISHES

CeCe stood with her wrist draped over the open refrigerator door. She stared at the containers and bowls covered with aluminum foil, measuring the depth of her hunger against her willingness to cook. She decided to finish the rest of the sloppy joe mix, even though there were no more hamburger buns. CeCe had a civics paper to write—well, to start—for the next day. She would read a chapter of her novel instead. From the first day of school, her mood had soured from foul to rancid. Schoolwork was an evil she managed. Humans, on the other hand, persisted in chafing her nerves.

She heard her mother's slow shuffle in the hallway as she set the range dial to medium. CeCe picked up her library book from the counter and leaned against the sink to read while dinner warmed. Her mother stopped in the kitchen archway, a weathered elf in sweatpants. Her mother was present most days now, sweeping and rinsing, but CeCe still didn't hold the lunar strength to draw her mother far enough away from those dark shadows.

"Here," her mother said.

CeCe looked up, puzzled at the sound of her mother's voice. Her mother floated about the house to "lay eyes" on CeCe, as Auntie Rosie would say. She floated in the hallway while CeCe prepared for school in the morning, in the afternoon when she read or did homework, and, again, at night before most of the windows in their apartment complex went dark. Aunt Rosie urged CeCe to see the love in those efforts. CeCe saw nothing inside of nothing.

"Here," her mother said again. Her tan cardigan sagged from daily wear and constant tugging. She clutched it closed with one fist. With the other hand, she held out to CeCe a fifty-dollar bill.

"What's that?" CeCe said, her book spread open between her fingers.

"For your pictures."

"What pictures?" CeCe asked, closing the book over one thumb to stir the bubbling meat sauce.

CeCe's mother stepped one foot into their small kitchenette and stretched an arm toward the table. She always seemed uncertain about being allowed in their kitchen. She laid the bill on the table and returned her feet, side by side, to the hallway carpet.

"Senior pictures," her mother said, turning her shoulders to return to her bedroom. It was 7 p.m., and CeCe knew this would be the last time she'd see her mother until morning. CeCe had never known her mother to stay up later than 8 p.m. It wasn't odd when they were going to bed at the same time. As CeCe grew older and needed to stay up with her homework or finish a book, she slept in the living room until the couch became her regular bed.

CeCe turned off the stove and moved the pan to a cool eye. She opened a cabinet next to the fridge and pulled down a bowl.

"I didn't order any pictures, Mama," CeCe said as she spooned the mix into her bowl.

"Thursday," her mother said.

CeCe turned to look at the fifty dollars, wondering how her mother knew about picture day, of all things. CeCe planned to sit for her photo, like every year, but had no intention of hauling wardrobe changes, testing alternate sweeps of her bangs, or allowing herself to be excited. Her yearbook photos were little more than record keeping. Since Neil Armstrong Elementary, CeCe knew that photographers' props and cheerful attention were reserved for the kids who purchased the photo packets.

She pulled a fork from the dish rack and remembered the mail. Her mother usually didn't open it, but the school logo might have enticed her, or maybe the envelope had been oversized. CeCe exhaled to push away the annoyance.

"Yeah, I know," CeCe said, dismissing the topic. She took a seat at the table with her bunless sloppy joe and flattened the paperback on the table with her forearm.

Her mother remained fixed in the doorway. "Get the big one," she said. "The eight by ten."

"I'm not ordering pictures," CeCe said, already sinking into the lines of her book. She lifted several heavy forkfuls to her mouth. Her mother continued to loom.

CeCe sighed and looked at her mother. Her mother cast her gaze down the hallway, as if deciding whether to escape back into her bed.

"Please get them," her mother said, clearing her throat and turning to CeCe again. "For me."

The hairs on CeCe's arms lifted.

"For you," CeCe repeated. Her mother lowered her eyes to the carpet.

"Order *my* senior pictures for *you*?" CeCe said. A scream began to claw from her gut. She closed the book, harder than she intended, and its force ignited a fuse.

"You, too," her mother said.

She sat back in the chair, her hands clasped over her stomach. "How are you doing this for 'me, too,' when I don't want the pictures?"

"You'll wish you had them," her mother said, planting herself for the tsunami crash.

"Pictures. That's what you think I'll wish for?" CeCe said, straightening in her chair. Her brows crumpled into a scowl and her neck grew hot. CeCe felt the pressure of combustion beneath her skin.

"What about a birthday party, Mama? Why didn't you wish me one of those?" CeCe said icily. Her mother turned to face the bedroom, but did not retreat. CeCe swept aside her book and nudged the bowl of sloppy joe mix to the center of their table.

"How about real cooking?" CeCe continued. "No? Then how about having a *parent* at parent-teacher conferences? Or maybe having a parent show up in the emergency room when I'm getting stitches? How about showing up for anything?"

CeCe leaned her forearms against the table edge. She moved to the edge of her chair with all of her weight on the balls of her feet. CeCe made tents on the table with her fingers, the table keeping her from springing into the air.

"You should wish me a few more strangers to help me understand tampons and racism and sales tax and bra sizes and incest and gentrification and mascara and yeast infections and—"

Her mother mumbled and CeCe stood, pushed back her chair. Her fingers were still pinned to the table. "What was that?" she asked her mother. Her voice filled the kitchen. "What? Were you wishing me Easter eggs and Christmas presents? Were you wishing me Santa Claus, Mama?"

"Crimson, I said I'm sorry!" her mother croaked, her voice dense and dry, like prying open an old shed door. She remained in profile, she kept her eyes and her words pointed away from her daughter's unwinding fury.

"You're not *sorry*," CeCe said, spitting out each word. The pressure beneath her skin and throbbed. "You're *pathetic*."

CeCe's mother lowered her head.

"All these years, I've waited for you to apologize for all this,"

CeCe said, her voice cracking. She looked at her mother shrinking in the hallway, disappearing in front of CeCe's eyes. CeCe
thought of all the times she blinked and the light in her mother's
eyes would be gone, giggles and sing-alongs forgotten. CeCe had
learned to continue their games and songs without her mother.
She was incensed that her mother was cowering now in the hallway. Her mother had no right to be sad or angry. She had no right
at all.

CeCe slammed her palms onto the table. The thunderous sound
radiated from the kitchen into the hallway, the living room and,
CeCe hoped, beyond the moon. She continued to slam her hands
on the table as she screamed louder and louder at her mother.

"You left me to figure this out all by myself!" CeCe screamed.
"You left me all by myself! You are not allowed to be sorry! You're
a goddamn coward and a quitter! You are not allowed to ask me to
forgive you for that!"

Her mother's shoulders shuddered and CeCe watched her sink
onto the floor. CeCe picked up the bowl of sloppy joe and hurled it
where her mother's profile had been.

"Shut the fuck up!" CeCe said. A smear of tomatoes and grease
glistened down the wall. Her mother lay on the ground, turned away
from the meat sauce, her face messy with tears.

"Don't you dare stand there and cry for me now," CeCe hissed,
pulling back her shoulders and staring down at her mother. "You
didn't leave any options other than this life you made for us, and I'm
stuck here in it until I go crazy too or you decide to completely give
up and die."

The words leapt from CeCe's lips and rolled across the floor tiles
until they rested in front of her mother. CeCe glared at her mother
and her mother gawked back at her. CeCe's entire body remained
rigid with adrenaline.

Her mother slowly rolled herself to her feet. She did not survey the mess of meat on the wall and carpet. She did not hold her daughter's gaze for long. CeCe waited for guilt to begin gnawing at her, but remorse did not come. Instead, she felt sated. Like eating Sunday dinner at Pam's house. She turned away from her mother to lean against the countertop.

Her mother's voice sounded like a gargle at first and she said, "Just wanted you to have them." She gathered the collar of her worn cardigan sweater with both hands and stared at the floor. "Always wished for mine."

CeCe kept her eyes on the money as her mother retreated to her bedroom. Her mother would cry for hours inside that little bedroom, CeCe knew. She thought, then, about sedatives, therapy, emergency clinic admissions, Dr. Harper, and progress. She pressed her fingertips to her temples, hoping to squeeze the last of the thick sludge from inside her mind. CeCe stood there for some time, leveling her breathing. Allowing her rage to drain away.

CeCe lowered herself into the kitchen chair and watched a clump of ground beef travel down the wall. Her screams still seemed stuck in the air, and she thought and she thought about the absurdity of choices. CeCe folded her arms across her chest and fixed her eyes on the overturned bowl in the hallway. She let out a slow breath and decided she would wear a lavender top for picture day.

THIRTY-TWO

LURE

"I don't want to get in over my head, Pam," CeCe said into the receiver, exasperated with her friend's relentless campaign about the types of jobs CeCe should pursue. Pam's voice sounded stripped and compressed to CeCe from so far away. Their conversations had become clipped and sporadic in Pam's first few years in Seattle, but they had settled into a satisfying rotation of bimonthly phone dates. CeCe knew her friend missed her, but CeCe would always miss and need her much more.

"I just want to find a job, Pam, not win a lifetime achievement award," CeCe said, pressing the receiver against her ear with one hand and stacking clean bowls in the kitchen cupboard with the other.

"That's the dumbest shit I've ever heard," Pam said. "I'm done with you."

"Fine," CeCe said, grinning. "Talk to you this weekend."

Pam ended the call.

CeCe had started job hunting toward the end of spring when she learned the frame shop where she'd worked since high school was going out of business. She'd worked full time as an office assistant there for two years. She had less than two weeks until her last paycheck and no prospects in sight. In addition, her apartment building had devolved into thug-land; Rocky and Pam had moved even farther away; and her mother had adopted a new slate of troublesome habits for CeCe to monitor and manage. Picking at the tender flesh around her nail bed. Subsisting on cups of coffee unless CeCe made her eat. Napping in cooling baths with the door locked. CeCe was in a foul mood most days, a storm cloud visible above her head.

She half-heartedly scanned the papers and responded to want ads with defeat heavy on her voice. Her job search didn't become earnest until midsummer, and she found herself standing slack-jawed in the lobby of their apartment complex.

"Coretta?"

Her cousin leaned against the lobby desk flipping through a magazine. She wore a gray suit, brilliant white shirt, large pearl studs, and shiny kohl heels. Coretta checked the time beneath the peek of her shirt cuff when CeCe called her name.

"Thank God," Coretta said, standing up straight. "I've been leaning on this buzzer for twenty minutes."

"Mama doesn't ever expect company, so she doesn't answer the bell," CeCe said.

Coretta furrowed her brows. "You know that's crazy, right?"

CeCe cringed a little, but shrugged her shoulders.

"I figured you wouldn't be gone too long," Coretta said resting one manicured hand on the desk and the other on her hip. "Since you're not doing much with yourself these days."

CeCe's eyes rolled before she could harness them. Coretta laughed.

"Suck it up, sister," Coretta said, crossing her arms. "You're going to take this chin checking, and then you're going to get your shit together."

CeCe stared and let her handbag fall to the floor. She knew Coretta well enough to know there would be no way to shorten or sidestep whatever speech she'd planned.

"What the hell is on your mind right now?" Coretta asked. "Why are you sitting around with no job, no classes, not doing anything?"

"I have a job," CeCe mumbled.

"For about ten more minutes, the way I understand it," Coretta said, crossing her arms to mirror CeCe's defiant stance. "What's your plan, CeCe?"

CeCe tried to form a rebuke. Her cousins must have reported her situation back to their mother because CeCe hadn't spoken at length with Coretta or Aunt Rosie in months. She'd grown weary of the random pep talks about her potential and questions about her goals. As if she didn't know she could be a college graduate like Pam and Rocky and her cousins. As if her fate hadn't been carved for her.

"I'm looking. I just haven't found anything," CeCe said.

Coretta unfolded her arms and returned a manicured hand to her tailored hip. "Crimson Celeste Weathers, don't give me that bull-shit," she said. "You can't be looking too hard. Uncle Frank's son found a job in less than a month, and you know he ain't good for a damn thing."

With her sassy cadence, crisp lipstick, and an elegant wag of her finger, Coretta reminded CeCe in that moment of Phylicia Rashād's character on *The Cosby Show*—classy, professional, lovely, and not one to be played with. Except Clair Huxtable didn't curse at her kids.

"Of course I'm looking hard," CeCe said, snapping her hands to her hips.

"I interview applicants every week and you cannot tell me you're not able to outshine half of the weed-heads trying to find jobs all of a sudden."

"I'm looking, all right?" CeCe said, letting her arms fall. "How you gonna tell me what I'm not doing?"

"Because I know better," Coretta said. "You can do better."

"Stop trying to tell me what I can do!" CeCe yelled. "I can't do anything! Why am I the only one willing to face that? I am not going to do anything more than what I've always done, stuck in this apartment with my fucking mother."

CeCe stopped yelling before she realized Coretta had slapped her. She'd never been hit before. Her cheek burned and her eyes sprung with tears. CeCe put her hand to her face and stepped back from her cousin.

"What the fuck is wrong with you?" she screamed. "You can't put your hands on me!"

"Hush," Coretta said stepping boldly to CeCe. "Don't you ever disrespect your mother like that. Ever. I don't care what you think she's done or hasn't done. Don't you ever fix your lips around her name that way again, do you hear me?"

CeCe's face and entire body twitched with rage. She still held her cheek. Coretta reached out and swatted CeCe's hand away from her own face.

"Do you hear me?" Coretta said.

CeCe nodded and began to cry.

Coretta took a deep breath and took a step back. She backed herself all the way to the check-in desk, leaning back on her elbows.

"Look, CeCe, your life hasn't been fair. I get it. Now, get over it," Coretta said. "Your father is dead, your mother is sick, your friends have moved away, you're shy and awkward, and now you're out of a job. And you're only twenty years old. None of that shit is fair, but you have to find a way to get over all of it."

Coretta patted the counter space next her and CeCe walked reluctantly to stand beside her.

"You're not the first person to get dealt a fucked-up hand, and you won't be the last," Coretta said. "But you have to keep playing the game, sister. You have to figure out how to keep playing the game."

CeCe opened her mouth to protest, but Coretta raised one silencing finger. She lifted herself from the counter and brushed at the back of her jacket. She hefted the strap of her leather work bag to her shoulder and moved toward the door.

"More than anything, CeCe, you have to figure out how to live your life. I know Carla doesn't want you trapped in this little apartment with her forever."

"How do you know that?" CeCe said, her voice small.

"No mother would," Coretta had said.

CeCe redoubled her search efforts after Coretta's visit. Pam had even teased in their phone call about tattling to Coretta. CeCe laughed when Pam disconnected their call. Immediately, the phone rang again. CeCe smiled at the receiver, laughing at her friend in advance.

"Bitch, don't make me stop this car," CeCe squealed into the phone, parroting a line from one of their favorite movies. There was no laughter or sassy comeback, just a heartbeat of silence.

"I'm sorry," the un-Pam voice said. "I'm looking for Crimson Weathers."

CeCe gasped, smashing her own forehead with the palm of her hand.

"Oh, my God," CeCe said. "I—um, this is—um, oh, God. This is—um—Crimson."

"That's a little disappointing," the woman said. "This is Margaret Sorensen from Capitol Properties. I'm a district manager for the Hip Pocket."

CeCe wanted to hang up the phone, but her hand wouldn't cooperate.

"Ms. Sorensen, I am so sorry. I was talking to my best friend . . . and she . . . I thought," CeCe stammered, stunned as the broken words continued to tumble from her mouth. "Ms. Sorensen, if you would please bear with me, I'm a little mortified right now. I was really hoping to hear from your store. I could really use a do-over right now."

"That's not usually how life works, Crimson," Ms. Sorensen said.

"Better than anyone, I would know," CeCe said, "but I'm positive I could redeem myself."

CeCe heard the woman take another heartbeat pause. Then she heard a dial tone.

She returned the phone to its cradle and dropped her head, sputtering curses down to the floor.

The phone rang.

CeCe's heart jumped. She crossed the fingers of her left hand, hoping it wasn't actually Pam this time, and picked up the phone again with her right.

"Good afternoon, Weathers' residence," CeCe said brightly, adding the foreign salutation in hopes of scoring a few extra points.

"Yes," Ms. Sorensen said. "May I speak with Crimson, please?"

"This is she."

"Hello, Crimson. My name is Margaret Sorensen."

When CeCe received the call, three weeks and two interviews later, to join the company's management training program, Ms. Sorensen confided that the "Weathers' residence" line had won her over.

CeCe's mother sat outside watching the courtyard when the call came in. Her mother had broadened her realm from the kitchen table to include the square slab of concrete outside their back door. CeCe never knew what prompted her mother's change of habit, but was glad to see her getting fresh air and nodding to the neighbors passing by.

CeCe pushed open the screen door and it whined on its springs, making CeCe cringe. She spent so many years as a kid being careful not to let the door bang shut, careful to maintain quiet for her slumbering mother. CeCe sat down beside her mother. She knew her mother appreciated these visits, for their sentiment and their brevity.

"It's not bad out here today," CeCe said. "We don't have many more of these days left."

Her mother raised her eyebrows, nodding in slow agreement.

"Guess what?"

CeCe's mother turned to face her. Her eyes were so weary now. They seemed distant from this apartment slab, from this moment. Growing up, her mother's eyes had always been far away from their life. Sitting here now, however, it wasn't terror that leapt and rolled in the back of her mother's gaze. Now, her eyes were emptied. CeCe didn't allow herself to wonder what her mother thought about now that her mind seemed cleared of the brush and thorns that had consumed so much space.

"I got the job," CeCe continued.

She had stopped sharing her news with her mother a lifetime ago. Knock-knock jokes, poems, A-plus papers, herself, they all garnered the same blank reaction. Even with a canon of research, DSM definitions, and properly affixed labels of major depression disorder, dysthymic disorder, and catatonia, CeCe could never shake feeling of profound rejection. The therapists tried to help her cope. The books tried to help her understand. CeCe could never accept that her love and devotion would never be enough to lure her mother from such a consuming sorrow.

With deliberate effort, CeCe refused the hateful thoughts that once claimed so much of her mind and heart. With deliberate effort, she refused.

"I start next week already," CeCe said, stretching out her legs in front of her. Her mother took a sip of coffee, and watched her daughter without expression.

"There are six of us, I think," CeCe said. "We'll each get placed as assistant managers and then, if we're good, we'll be managers of our own store within two years."

CeCe saw something brighten against the shadows of her mother's eyes. Just a flash, and it was gone. CeCe looked at her mother for a long, long moment. The color of her skin reminded CeCe of baked bread, but now looked dry and textured like bread, too. She worried for her mother, in spite of herself. It had always been this way. CeCe admit to herself that her worrying was a crutch of its own. Coretta had been right. Living with her mother in their tiny, starter-sized apartment would not keep either one of them safe. Sane. Alive.

CeCe felt a bolt of resolve rocket through her gut.

THIRTY-THREE

NUGGETS

CeCe slipped her key into the lock. She turned her wrist and the tumblers fell away. She pushed open the door and the morning sun poured over her shoulder and onto the hardwood floor. She thought of how the light had dappled through the trees the afternoon of Doris' party. CeCe was encouraged to see the sun continuing to pour its affection on her new house.

Her heels clapped against the flooring, trailing loud, slow steps through the living room and dining room and down the hallway. She bounced with a clacking cadence into every room. Returning to the living room, she jumped to see Rocky standing in the front hall.

"Shit!" CeCe blurted, slamming one hand against the wall and the other to clutch her chest. "You scared me."

"It's a gift," Rocky said coolly, his eyes settling on her. After an empty moment, where CeCe had no clever retort, Rocky pointed questioningly to the open door.

"Yes, please," CeCe said, shaking from her trance. Rocky closed the front door and stepped into the heart of her new home.

"This is your place?" he asked, sweeping the naked space with his eyes. He wore a cardigan vest over a loose dress shirt and caramel leather shoes. His hands rested inside his blue jean pockets, with his thumbs relaxed on the outside. Still with those hands in his pockets, CeCe thought.

When they confirmed this meeting, CeCe hadn't offered any specifics about the house address and Rocky hadn't asked. He toured the house now, room by room, until he leaned on the windowsill framing her tree. His gaze fell from the curve of her domed ceilings down to her eyes. CeCe's heartbeat pulsed in her ears.

Rocky shook his head and smiled at her, his full mouth still framed by a goatee of russet hair. She'd never met a redheaded Black person before Rocky, and had only seen a handful since. She'd marveled in high school over the anomaly of his paprika-colored waves, sienna skin, and splattering of freckles. How he made it all seem so normal, irrelevant. So much about Rocky had seized her attention then. She'd spent most of their years since high school trying to unlove him.

"This is a dope spot," he said, his baritone filling the empty room. "Congratulations."

CeCe couldn't help but beam. "Thanks," she said. "And thanks for coming."

"No problem," Rocky said, pulling his hands from his pockets. "Can a brotha get his hug now?"

CeCe stepped into Rocky's outstretched arms, ignoring the glimpse of gold on his left hand. Their embrace was careful but strong; they had so many fragile and unspoken words suspended between them. Since moving back from Nashville, where he'd gone to graduate school and started his teaching career, they'd caught up with one another in sparse patches of phone calls and over rushed cups of coffee. Rocky never asked CeCe about missing his wedding and CeCe never asked Rocky about missing their friendship.

His return to Prescott was triggered by his mother's failing health. After years of gracefully managing a late-life onset of multiple sclerosis, her condition began to plummet and his father had become overwhelmed. Rocky came home to help them both. He said he'd also grown weary of blithe boarding school students and the insufferable pretensions of his faculty peers. In his first four months of being home, Rocky had negotiated a new dean of students position at their old high school.

Since he initiated their contact once he got settled, CeCe felt hopeful about their "new normal." She had been a swirl of emotions in anticipation of that first lunch. As the weeks unfolded to months and, now, into two years, her giddiness soured to embarrassment and bitterness as Rocky routinely rushed her from the phone or dodged another invitation for tea.

Once, CeCe had opened the door of her apartment quadruplex to find Rocky standing there with two large cups, coffee for him and tea for her. She'd been decorating the apartment for the holidays and Rocky had made a detour to her place during his route of errands. He hadn't stayed long, but managed to prickle her ire.

"So, have her come with us, then," she had said, flinging her hands into the air and spinning to face him. Rocky flinched as CeCe whipped the Scotch tape roll at him. She hadn't felt comfortable hanging Christmas decorations when Terri shared the apartment. Her roommate had always welcomed CeCe to put up her tree and wreaths, but CeCe felt it disrespectful somehow to Terri's altar, shells, and pantheon of ancestor guardians. With her mother moved in to Terri's old room, CeCe had been looking forward to draping the entire apartment with holiday cheer for the first time. Rocky was ruining her afternoon.

"We can go see another movie," Rocky had said, still shielding himself.

"I don't want to see another movie," CeCe said, turning back to her garland. "I want to see *Good Will Hunting*. I'll go by myself. That won't be anything new."

"Hold up," Rocky said. "I'm trying to make it work."

CeCe let the sparkly rope float down to the floor and lodged her hand into hip. "What's to make work, Rocky?" she said. "Your wife has decided not to like me and is doing a good job of convincing you to do the same."

CeCe knew this last part was merely dramatic flair, but felt justified in her oncoming tantrum. She'd waited eight years to have Rocky back in Prescott, stretching herself beyond dignity to revive, and even redefine, their friendship. She'd volunteered to help sit with his ailing mother, but was told that wasn't "necessary." She offered to share his wife's photography portfolio with the event managers at her office but was told events weren't his wife's "genre." CeCe stopped trying. She tried to stop caring, too, but couldn't deny her wounded feelings.

Rocky pursed his lips and gave CeCe a familiar "C'mon, now" face. He crossed the living room, breaking off a strip of Scotch tape and handing it to her. CeCe glared at Rocky's outstretched index finger and then at Rocky. She took the tape with an exasperated breath and returned to her measured and meticulous swags.

"Ronni doesn't like the idea of you," Rocky said, standing a distance from her as if she might swing. "She's never said anything negative about you as a person."

"The *idea* of me?" CeCe said, shaking her head as if she could shake off his words.

Rocky handed her another strip of tape. "She comes from a completely different world," he said. "If you could meet the women in her family, you'd understand. She's the only one not interested in 'regulating' her man."

There was a foreign earnestness in his voice, but the empathy was for his wife, not for CeCe.

"It was different when you were an abstraction, miles away. It's harder than she thought, now that she's here. You're really here," Rocky said. He followed her small steps, as she traveled the wall with her garland. "I promise she's tried, Crimson, but my relationship with you goes against everything she was raised to accept."

An abstraction, she thought.

CeCe was silent as she retraced her steps to affix modest red bows in the pattern of garland arcs.

"I know this is wack, but I need to you to help me on this," Rocky said, handing her more strips of tape as they circled the room again.

"I know it's a lot. And I shouldn't ask, but I'm asking. Begging, really, Crimson. Like I said, I'm trying to work it out. I just don't know how yet."

CeCe fastened the last ribbon in place, looking around to inspect the room. There would still be a tree, holiday cards, angels in the doorways, and poinsettia plants on the tables.

Without turning away from her work, she asked, "How many times did you rehearse that little speech on the drive over here?"

"Got it down in three," Rocky said.

CeCe shook her head again.

"Fine," CeCe said, layering her irritation for effect. "I'll go see the movie with my new best friend."

CeCe hadn't turned around. She could hear Rocky let out his slow breath, and shaking his head.

Rocky shook his head again now, standing in front of the window that looked out on her new back yard. The stubs of dreadlocks Rocky had sported two Christmases ago were now brushing his collar in thick, brandy-colored cords. He reached up to tie two locks into a convenient hair band while CeCe told him about Doris, the house, and her mother.

"It's not like it used to be," CeCe said, facing the window, "where she wouldn't eat or bathe or talk or get out of the bed if I wasn't around. It feels wrong, though. Like I'm turning my back on her. I know I'm not, but I can't shake it."

CeCe's cell phone chimed. She crossed the empty room and picked it up from the floor, next to her purse and keys.

Rocky watched her examine the phone and asked, "Is that Mother?"

CeCe looked up, with a sideways smile. She hadn't heard it in forever. Coretta and her family called her mother by name, and Pam had always asked about Ms. Carla. Rocky, the one who absorbed the volume of her ranting and angst back then, always referred to her as "Mother."

"No, it's an email alert," CeCe said, sliding a finger over her phone screen. "I'm giving the online version of my *Sports Illustrated* subscription a try."

Rocky's eyebrows shot up. "*Sports Illustrated*? What in the hell? I didn't think there would ever be any hope for you and sports."

"Don't plan a parade," CeCe said, smiling back. "I flip through for sporty nuggets. They come in handy with clients sometimes."

"Sporty nuggets?"

CeCe nodded, retracing the wood floor to lean against the window again. "Once," she said, "I was at a reception and worked in something about Chad Dawson being one of the most underrated fighters in the game. I only remembered the name because I thought 'Chad Dawson' sounded more like a pop star. Anyway, the guy wasn't a client yet and he agreed with me. He went on and on about how boxing has changed, the last fight he'd bet on and how we should all travel to Vegas for the next main event match. All I was thinking was, 'Sign the contract.'"

"Did he?" Rocky asked.

CeCe turned to him and said, "You gonna get tired of questioning my fabulousness."

CeCe laughed. Rocky did not.

"I've never questioned that," he said, his topaz eyes fixed on her, serious. CeCe felt weak.

"I'm proud of you, Crimson," Rocky continued softly. "Not surprised, in the least, but still really proud to be standing here with you."

CeCe felt a familiar stretching inside her chest. She folded her arms across herself, trying to prevent the blush and fat tears from escaping her chest.

"Thanks, Rocky," she said. She couldn't risk any more language than this. Rocky returned a small knowing grin and turned them both around to gaze at her tree.

THIRTY-FOUR

DENIM

CECE COMPLETED HER HIP POCKET training and started at Morgan's Crossing, the smaller of Prescott's two malls. She'd been placed there with the only other black female in their management program, Terelle. CeCe didn't know how to take Terelle at first, with the lace camisoles beneath her suit jackets, buckled knee boots and long, fire-red nails. She was sharp-edged with a sharper tongue, causing the trainers, their peers, and CeCe to regularly wince throughout the five-week program.

They hadn't become a cozy cohort, like CeCe had expected. The fourteen of them were friendly and cohesive during the long days, but scattered like pollen seeds as soon as they were released from the conference room. CeCe had been pleasantly surprised when Terelle invited her out for a drink on their last day. They talked openly and traded easy laughs. CeCe admitted she looked forward to starting the job, officially being a grown-up. Terelle shared her goal of owning a Cookie Factory or Auntie Anne's franchise someday.

"Don't let the hoochie gear fool you," Terelle had said, stirring her drink with gleaming pink talons. "I got plans."

After more than a hundred happy hours together, Terelle and CeCe had been promoted to store managers and progressed to being good friends.

"You should come to this party with me tomorrow," Terelle said, her nails clipped short and the waves of shiny hair weave gone.

CeCe hadn't been to a party in more than a year, again at Terelle's invitation. CeCe counted their happy hour rituals as her social life because Terelle's antics tended to draw interesting strangers. Young professional women with their chignons and tongues loosened from vodka. Silver-haired men clenching their virility and bottles of beer. Waitresses and bartenders pounding tequila shots through their final hours on the clock.

And men.

Terelle attracted every stripe, like clumsy moths. CeCe could claim better looks than Terelle. Softer features. Better bones. Smoother skin. But Terelle's personality filled a crowded room when CeCe offered only complicit quiet and nervous eyes from behind her tumbler of sweet booze. They sought her out sometimes and she could squeeze conversation from her mouth if they were patient. Most often, though, anyone lingering at CeCe's seat simply wanted a turn for Terelle's attention.

"Should I bring anything?" CeCe asked, taking down the party address.

"Yeah, bring the hype version of you," Terelle said, dropping single bills on the bar top and standing to leave. "And wear something to show off all that booty. Always some fine ass men at Terri's parties."

CeCe feigned a knowing chuckle, and her chest tightened behind the button-down blouse. She hadn't thought about her clothes. At twenty-three, CeCe would've been self-conscious enough trying to outfit herself for a party filled with people their age, but Terelle's friend, Terri, was getting her doctorate in art therapy. CeCe had always been comfortable with seasoned grown-ups, like Doris, Mrs. Anderson, and Mrs. Castellanos. Nothing in-between. Regret began its slow coil around CeCe's nerve.

She arrived to the party at 8 p.m. sharp. She wore green denim pants with a matching denim shirt, a black belt with a dazzling buckle, black boots, and big, sparkly earrings. Pam had approved the outfit in another long-distance consultation call after directing CeCe to find something sexy, but not too sexy. Comfortable, but not too casual. Flattering but not too fitted. Stylish but not trying to be too trendy. CeCe blushed a little when Terri opened the door and right away said, "Ooh, I like your outfit!"

Terri was tall and lean and moved like a dancer. She had a fair complexion and a tangle of brown spiral curls. She wore a long skirt with patchwork denim, corduroy, and kente fabrics. Her long-sleeved top was dark brown, comfortably fitted, and slung low from one shoulder. She was small breasted and CeCe could tell she wasn't wearing a bra.

Two other people were helping, lighting candles, unloading bags of ice, planting serving spoons in pans of food. CeCe insisted on helping, too, taking off her jacket to help Terri move a loveseat into the spare bedroom.

"This would be your room, if I pass inspection," Terri said, once they lowered the couch in the empty room.

CeCe looked up at Terri and shook her head. "I thought I was the one under inspection," CeCe said. "Besides, Terelle told me not to say anything."

"I've known Terelle since she was in the second grade," Terri said, nudging the sofa against the wall with her thigh. "I love her like my own sister. But I'll be the first to tell you, that girl can't hold water."

They heard the door open and the rumble of a man's voice. CeCe and the other three women had finished shuffling the furniture, and were laying out floor pillows and bowls of snacks.

"Woman, I told you I would help move the furniture." CeCe looked up to see a handsome man standing at the end of the hallway. His skin was so richly dark that it gleamed. He wore crisp black jeans, a Wu Tang Clan concert tee, and a fitted green camouflage jacket. Both his style and his movements suggested a deliberate ease but, to CeCe, his presence instantly overwhelmed the room.

Terri replied, "Then you should have come *before* 8 o'clock."

"Why, so I could stand around waiting to move furniture *after* 8 o'clock anyway?"

"Boy, hush," Terri said.

CeCe and the other women followed suit when Terri lowered herself to a floor pillow. The man walked to the sofa instead and pulled it away from the wall.

"Dub!"

"Terri, don't get brand new. You know I ain't sittin' on the floor."

The women groaned and shook their heads. Dub batted back their teasing comments as he pulled the couch closer to the circle. They all laughed, including CeCe.

Dub froze on the edge of the couch and glared at her. "Where'd you come from?"

CeCe's laughter was replaced with a stunned and gawking silence. She intended to introduce herself, but no sound came out as her mouth clammed open and closed.

Dub leveled her with a satisfied smile and said, "I don't speak guppy, sweetheart."

"Don't start," Terri said, shooting him the side eye. She pulled a stick of incense from the plastic champagne flute next to the stereo and lit it. "Dub, this is CeCe. Be nice. We want her to stick around for a while. CeCe, this is Dub. We all made a pact to love him in spite of himself."

CeCe looked timidly at Dub. Dub scaled her with his sultry eyes and smiled.

"Party before the party," Terri said, shifting the mood and attention to the Aretha Franklin discography set she'd slid from CD rack behind her. She slipped her fingers into what turned out to be an empty box and pulled out a sack of weed and rolling papers. CeCe looked to the women and smiled.

"Can I move in tonight?" she asked.

THIRTY-FIVE

INEXHAUSTIBLE

CECE ENTERED THE APARTMENT, SO full of afternoon sun that even the hallway glowed. She'd decided not to head back to the office after visiting the house. Her steps were still full of hardwood music as she padded their carpeted hallway humming, intoxicated, all over again, with Rocky.

Tossing her purse and keys on the kitchen table, she floated moth-like toward the sunlight humming through the front-room windows. Her mother's voice met her in the hallway.

"You could've told me."

CeCe stopped flying, guilt and stomach plummeting to the floor. Then quiet, both women expectant.

"Crimson?" her mother called.

CeCe lifted her feet, like cement blocks, to the end of the hallway. The few steps weakened her. She could feel her breath and heartbeat thrusting back at her blouse. CeCe stopped at the archway. Her mother, in profile, sat in her armchair. Her face was expressionless, even now, but weary. CeCe looked at her mother's features, how they were loosening their moorings. Her mother had set herself free too late, and now she was getting old. She carried her years less gracefully than other fifty-year-old women she had met, but CeCe forgave her mother this thing.

CeCe wouldn't describe the years she'd given her mother as forgiveness. Inside, a small part of her still had its arms crossed, convinced her mother could have gotten better if she had tried. The more reasonable parts of her understood her mother's unwinding. CeCe had satisfied her resentment with selfish martyrdom. Self-pity had also proven to be an inexhaustible distraction. Her mother hadn't chosen this life, regardless of how she believed her mother could have raged back at it. CeCe couldn't persecute her mother for the defects in her chemistry, the shredding her soul has endured.

"Hey, Mama," CeCe said apprehensively. Her mother didn't turn to face her.

She repeated, "You could've told me, CrimsonBaby."

CeCe stretched out her fingers, the only part of her able to move. She wanted words to find her. She wanted her mother to look at her. CeCe balled her fingers. Her mother turned.

CeCe's lips remained closed. Her eyes opened and closed. Her mother looked away. CeCe crossed into the room. An explosion of flowers sat on the coffee table. Starbursts of primrose, saffron and sugar petals clustered into loose knots, sprouting into towers, and curling in all directions.

CeCe stared at the bouquet, unmoving. Her heartbeat resumed its pace and her face unfastened a smile.

"They just came," her mother said. "Maybe thirty minutes."

"Who are they from?" CeCe asked, moving toward the flowers.

"You tell me," her mother said. "You didn't want me to know you were seeing somebody?"

CeCe laughed, reaching for the card. "I'm not seeing anyone, Mama."

Hardly beautiful enough, the card read, *but I'll keep trying. Much, Eric.*

CeCe's mother hummed a little from her chair. "Maybe you are now."

THIRTY-SIX

WORTHY

CeCe sat at the small kitchen table as Terri shuffled around the apartment, dusting, vacuuming, and moving stacks of notebooks and mail from one room to another.

"What is wrong with you?" Terri asked, stopping in doorway of their kitchenette.

CeCe looked up at her, puzzled. "What?" she said. "I'm reading."

"No, you're not reading," Terri said, waving her dust rag at CeCe for emphasis. "I can usually hear you flipping six pages a minute. You must be staring at the words. What's up?"

CeCe adored her roommate. It had been just over a year and she'd come to look at Terri like a big sister. In spite of all her cosmic-astrolology-energy-community-power talk, Terri knew how to get at the core of things and still be gracious with her raw honesty. CeCe closed her book.

CeCe reached for the stack of mail resting near the kitchen phone and tossed a large, square envelope toward Terri's end of the table.

"I've been cordially invited."

Terri picked up the envelope and slid the thick invitation from inside. CeCe watched her friend's eyes scan the calligraphy text.

"Greg Rockwell?" Terri said. "Is that Rocky?"

CeCe nodded. Terri clucked.

"Aww, sweetie, I'm sorry," she said. "You know it's for the best, right? This sets you free to fall in love with someone else now."

CeCe glared. Terri laughed, clutching the dust rag in mock deference.

"Too soon?" she said, teasing.

CeCe's sobs erupted from her core. She heard the stuttering sound against the linoleum as Terri scooted the other kitchen chair closer. CeCe fell limply into her roommate's slender embrace. Her forearms were wet with tears. Terri loosened her soft harness and slowed her cradling rock when CeCe's crying begin to subside. CeCe pulled away, eyes on her lap. Terri leaned back in her chair and crossed one leg over the other. She wore long biker shorts and an oversized T-shirt that was plain blue, except for the huge, wet stain CeCe had left in the center of her chest.

"You don't have to stop loving him," Terri said. "You just have to release him. I take it he was your first?"

The words crashed into CeCe's fragile chest. "No, he's not my first."

Terri hooked her hands around her bent knee and leaned back.

"Really?" Terri said with genuine surprise, "I would've bet money—"

"I don't, um, have a first," CeCe interrupted. She saw curiosity melt over the concern in Terri's eyes.

"So . . . " Terri said, her eyebrows raised into questions marks and her elegant almond features filled with knowing.

"Yes," CeCe said, slumping back against her chair. "Yes."

Terri was quiet, nodding, trying to restrain an impish smile.

"On purpose?" Terri asked, still wrestling with the corners of her grin.

"On purpose?" CeCe repeated, her eyes sweeping the cabinet

doors and appliances for a suitable response. "I—I guess so. I mean, it just never happened."

"Did you ever want to?" Terri asked, giggles gone from her now.

"Yeah," CeCe said. "I guess."

Terri gazed, patient while CeCe began to fidget. "You wanted your first time to be with Rock?"

"Rocky," CeCe corrected. She looked into Terri's eyes and said, "Yes."

Terri gave another slow nod and leaned forward in her chair.

"There are no mistakes," she said. Her eyes were filled with compassion and warmth. CeCe didn't always connect with Terri's flower child-speak, but she appreciated her cosmic advice today.

"The universe knows exactly what it's doing," Terri said. "Whether he was meant to stay in your light or not, destiny always finds its way."

CeCe gave Terri a weak smile and Terri stood to leave, picking up her dust rag from the table.

"If everything works out," Terri said, "destiny will find its way into them drawers."

CeCe raised her book with a threat and a grin as Terri scooted into the hallway.

"I'm ready," CeCe announced one Sunday, while Terri perched on the edge of her huge blue bed filing her toenails. CeCe had been on a string of dates with a former store customer named Raven. Once his invitation jumped from chicken wings at the sports bar to taking a ride on his motorcycle to stealing away to a bed-and-breakfast, CeCe had rushed into Terri's room to verify whether his plans were to have sex with her.

"You're ready because you're twenty-four and it's time for sex to happen or because it's time for sex to happen with you and Raven?"

CeCe lay on her back watching the slow spin of the ceiling fan.

"Both?" she said, more a question than a confirmation.

"I think you might have different expectations depending on your real answer. First times are all about expectation," Terri said.

"It can't be both?" CeCe said. "About me and about Raven?"

"Of course it can," Terri said. "But, trust me, deciding whether the priority is you or whether it's *y'all* will make a difference."

Me or us.

"Sounds like a lot of thinking around whether to fuck or not," CeCe said.

"Trust me, fucking is worth thinking about," Terri said. "That's how you own it." She pointed her emery board at CeCe for emphasis.

Own it? CeCe thought. *I'm supposed to own fucking?*

"Does Raven know it's your first time?" Terri asked.

CeCe took a deep breath and exhaled, making a long motorboat sound with her lips.

"Mmmhmm," Terri said.

CeCe rolled over onto her stomach, closing her eyes and listening to the *scrish scrish scrish* of Terri's nail file.

"How do you even bring up something like that?" CeCe asked.

Terri looked to the ceiling, thinking. "Hi, Raven," Terri offered, "I'm looking forward to Saturday. I have something special I want to share with you."

CeCe groaned.

Terri laughed. "You'll be fine," she said. *Scrish. Scrish. Scrish.* "You'll be just fine."

Terri taped a note to CeCe's door when Saturday morning came: "Own it!"

CeCe put on her Soul II Soul CD and packed her gray duffel bag with toiletries, an Anita Baker CD, and a sundress for brunch. The last item CeCe packed was a satin fuchsia camisole she'd purchased on one of her lunch breaks. CeCe thought it flattered her figure well, embellishing her small bosom while amplifying her ample derriere. CeCe pulled off the price tag and tossed it into the wastebasket. She decided it would be less overwhelming for Raven if her lingerie and her vagina weren't glaringly brand new.

When CeCe emerged from the apartment with an overnight bag, she could see Raven's face burst open with excitement. CeCe wondered why he seemed so surprised, as if he suspected she might change her mind. The trunk to Raven's car popped open as he bounded up the steps to take her bag. He kissed her hard on the cheek.

"You look beautiful, Beautiful," he said, giving her elbow a soft squeeze.

He held her hand through dinner and grew increasingly affectionate at the martini bar: standing particularly close behind her in lines, a thumb tracing the curve of her back, a warm palm resting on the inside of her knee. CeCe thought she might hyperventilate before the end of the night, not from Raven's touches, but because of his electricity. She'd read of "sexual energy" in her novels, but she hadn't expected it to be literal. Visceral. Magnetic. Intoxicating.

Raven held her hand while they waited for the restaurant valet. They were quiet, comfortable, enjoying the live jazz spilling from the upper-level lounge. Without fanfare and without pretense, Raven raised their clasped hands and pressed a kiss into the back of CeCe's palm. Her heart fluttered.

When Raven pulled into the parking spot of his apartment, he turned to face CeCe before killing the engine. He leaned in for a quick peck on the lips. CeCe felt herself blush again at this slow and focused attention.

"This was an amazing night," he said. CeCe smiled in agreement as he leaned in for another slow kiss.

"I have a feeling I'm in for more 'amazing,'" he added with a sly, sexy smile. That dimple, CeCe thought.

He kissed her again, deep and passionate. CeCe drew in a deep breath once their lips parted and she began to assemble Terri's words in her head.

"I'm a virgin," her mouth blurted instead.

The smile lingered on the left, dimple-less corner of Raven's mouth while he searched CeCe's face for a punchline.

The smile faded.

"You're for real?" he asked, retreating to his side of the sedan.

CeCe nodded.

"Aww, man," Raven said. He turned from her and looked straight, into the indigo night. CeCe couldn't turn away. She watched him as the flutters in her stomach elevated to quakes.

"CeCe," Raven began, turning to face her again, "I, um, I don't know what to say."

Although CeCe knew his following words would be devastating on one level or another, she was more alarmed to see this fissure in his composure. In the past month or so that they'd been going out, she'd never seen him get flustered or overly dramatic or lose his poise.

They had sat in the car for nearly twenty minutes, two quiet islands in vastly new waters. When Raven spoke, he explained that he'd never been anyone's first and was nervous—no, "unnerved" was the word he'd used. He asked the typical questions: had she waited for religious reasons, had she ever tried, was she sure. CeCe matched his low tone. The entire exchange felt like a prayer.

They sat some more, the stars out in the distance each taking their turn to spin against the night.

As he put his hands back on the steering wheel, Raven assured CeCe that he genuinely liked her and was humbled she would consider him so worthy.

"But I guess I'm not so worthy," he said, more to himself than to her, "because I don't know if I've ever been this nervous in my life."

The drive was quiet. As they stood at the bottom of her apartment steps, Raven pulled CeCe close into his body. She felt the tangle of tears at the back of her throat and refused to release them. Not out here. Not on the cement steps she'd expected to mount in the morning as a bona fide woman. Not next to her gray duffel bag with the brand-new nightie still folded inside.

CeCe politely declined his usual escort into the building. Entering the dark apartment, CeCe was grateful that Terri was gone on a retreat with her doctoral cohort. No doubt, CeCe thought, Terri was listening with her body and beguiling the group with her lyrical thoughts. CeCe gave herself permission to fold her body into her roommate's blue bed and let the tears go.

THIRTY-SEVEN

LOBBY

WITH EACH WEEK THAT PASSED, CeCe withdrew from every social ritual, except visiting the library and her mother. She skipped Thursday happy hour with Terelle, payday pancakes with Doris, a few phone check-ins with Pam, and only half-heartedly dished the tabloids with her cousin, Tremaine.

Raven had left one awkward message a week after their fateful night. CeCe and Terri played and replayed the recording, trying to analyze his stumbling unease. CeCe theorized the call simply proved his proper upbringing, not that he wanted to hear from her again.

"Give him a chance," Terri had said.

"Fuck that punk," Terelle had said.

"Wait to see if he calls again," Doris had said.

He didn't.

After another fruitless week of voicemail checking, CeCe stopped waiting to hear from Raven. She reassured her small tribe of girlfriends that, yes, she understood Raven's issue with her virginity was no reflection on her. Still, CeCe imagined herself emitting a radar signal to all men, warning them to keep their distance. A twenty-four-year-old virgin was, apparently, a young-adult brand of cooties.

"Maybe I'll just buy some sex," CeCe had broadcast to her friends. "Order myself a full-body massage with a generous side of 'happy ending.'"

"Rent-a-dick? Your scary ass?" Terelle had said, howling at the prospect. "I'm sorry, but I'd pay to see that go down!"

"Just do me a favor and stay off that Craigslist thing," Doris had said.

Pam had lathered them both into breathless laughter about crotch catalogs, toe-curling money back guarantees, and bring-your-own-lube specials. Before hanging up, she had said sweetly to CeCe, "It'll happen, girl. It will."

Terri appeared in the doorway of their bathroom a week later and said, "I have a proposition for you."

CeCe stood in front of the mirror, using a small-toothed comb to part her hair into narrow sections and scratch and lift the dry flakes from her scalp. Aunt Rosie had told her to always give her scalp a thorough scratching before washing it. CeCe looked at Terri's reflection warily. Whatever the proposition, CeCe already knew she would ask Terri to do her laundry in exchange.

"Let me help with your first time," Terri said.

CeCe's hand froze, the red comb hovering above her scalp. She leaned against the vanity sink, close to the mirror, wearing a tattered tee and faded gym shorts. Instantly aware of her protruding ass pointed at Terri, CeCe watched her roommate through the mirror and formed her reply.

Now she was supposed to consider becoming a lesbian?

"I appreciate it, Terri, but I don't see how—umm—sleeping with you would help—"

Terri's pensive expression swung open with a laugh. She pushed at CeCe's hip with her foot. "Not with me, girl," Terri said. "I mean, let me help you, maybe, set something up. I know Operation Gigolo was a joke, but it might not be a bad idea to take fate into your own hands."

After a quiet moment, Terri asked, "So, what are you thinking?"

CeCe could see her tousle of frizz and curls leaning into her peripheral vision. CeCe let her chin drop to her chest, her own hair unbound, wild and falling into her eyes. Her chest heaved a sigh and she felt her entire body tense.

CeCe opened her mouth and waited for the tangle of words to find their way. "I'm thinking that sounds desperate," she said. "I'm thinking my friends believe I'm a lost cause. I'm thinking I want to cry right now . . . "

Terri entered the bathroom and leaned against the counter, her back to the mirror and her earnest face to close to CeCe's.

"OK," she said, pausing for a moment. "And what are you thinking now?"

Terri's eyes searched her friend's face while CeCe's expression was incredulous.

"I don't know," CeCe said, a quiver in her voice nipping at the edges of her words. "I don't know if I'm thinking. This is all feeling. Feeling embarrassed, feeling foolish, feeling broken, feeling—"

"No, none of those feelings are welcome here," Terri said, with a slow shake of her head. "I hear you, little sister. We can let this go right now. I'm sorry to set any of those feelings into motion. You have nothing to be embarrassed about. Nothing at all. After listening to you joke about the stripper all week, this just started to sound like a rational alternative in my head. I feel badly for even suggesting it. Please forgive me?"

CeCe stepped into the open arc of her friend's arms, with her own arms still folded. She wanted to weep when Terri enveloped her, but no tears fell. She was empty, through and through.

The two of them moved in their own quiet circles for the rest of the day. Terri in the living immersed in a constellation of index cards, Post-It notes and charcoal sketches and CeCe engrossed in the true crime bestseller, *Midnight in the Garden of Good and Evil*. As roommates, Terri and CeCe rarely needed to negotiate one another's need for space or quiet. As friends, they stayed in tune to the other's orbits and moods.

"I choose," CeCe said, standing in the archway of the living room. The afternoon sun was fading in the windows. Terri's cards and sketches had been stacked into a system of neat piles and she was writing in a notebook. She looked up from her seat on the floor, confusion drawing her face into a squint.

CeCe threaded her fingers together as she leaned against the doorway. She could bail on the idea right now. She could say that she wanted to choose takeout or the next DVD rental and dismiss her past forty minutes of contemplation, rationalization and self-motivation. She could be done with this foolishness and continue with life as she knew it, but the words sprang from her mouth before her nerves could wither.

"I choose the guy," she said.

Terri grinned. "Of course."

CeCe took one step into the living room, leaning her back against the doorway arch now. She looked down at her clasped fingers and asked meekly, "Did you have suggestions, though?"

"Of course," Terri said, smiling broadly as she rolled onto her side to prop her head on one hand and count off prospects with the other. "Marcus, from the co-op. Corey, who works at the rental office. Sabian, the grad assistant you like. The one with the infinity tattoo on his neck? And Dub."

"Dub?" CeCe said, her arms falling to either side. "Dark-skinned Dub?"

Terri let her counting hand drop to the floor and fixed her eyes on CeCe.

"Yes," Terri said. "Are we really about to have a conversation about dark skin and light skin?"

CeCe flapped her arms and shifted her weight in the doorway "No!" CeCe replied, offended. "But we could have a conversation about what an asshole he is!"

A smile pulled itself across Terri's face again. "Oh, that," she said. CeCe's insides began to sink. She felt a red flag wanting to pitch itself in her gut. Terri sat up and gestured to the couch. CeCe slouched over and sat, crossing her legs and her arms. Terri crossed her legs, leaned forward and told CeCe Dub's story. She didn't suggest that Dub hid a kinder, softer side or was masking the scars of childhood tragedy with some false bravado. When she first came out in college, Dub was one of the few friends who grilled her with relentless questions and stood by her side while she sorted them out. Terri said Dub was crude and arrogant even then. Still, she credited that cockiness for every success he'd earned, from his tender days as a chess prodigy to becoming a pint-sized all-conference linebacker to negotiating himself into executive offices before turning thirty.

"He's an ass," Terri said. "But he's an unapologetic ass, who's honest, loyal, consistent, about his business, and *perfect* for a job like this."

CeCe heard herself laugh. "Job?" she repeated.

Terri covered her face with her hands and shook her head. "I'm sorry," she said giggling.

CeCe waved away her apology and let herself sink into the couch. Dub was arrogant as hell but Terri was right, he wasn't mean. He also wasn't hard to look at, with his glistening skin and muscular frame boasting behind his designer clothes. Besides, Terri trusted him and she trusted Terri. The other options were guys with whom CeCe had never held a full conversation.

"When?" CeCe said.

"He's free tomorrow."

"Terri!"

Terri held up hands with a shrug. "Entirely your call," she said.

After a long silence, CeCe said, "You haven't led me wrong yet."

Terri reached out to rest her hand on CeCe's foot. "Little sister, I don't intend to start now."

When CeCe arrived at the Phoenix Hotel, she chanted affirmations under her breath. *You deserve this. You deserve this. You're not a desperate reject. You deserve this. You deserve this. It's going to be fine*... Still, she'd insisted on meeting Dub at the hotel, in case the expedition exploded into flames.

CeCe had read about swanky events held at the Phoenix Hotel, but she had never been inside the building. When the parking garage elevator slid open onto the lobby, CeCe took in the boutique hotel's elegance. The lower level was spacious and decorated in harlequin patterns of fuchsia and tangerine. A shelf traveled the lobby walls and CeCe's eyes followed the eclectic collection of statuettes, pewter candlesticks, copper balls of twine, antique tin boxes, empty wine bottles, a vintage radio, and a purple chaise where Dub sat.

Dub stood and walked toward her. In the enormous framed mirror mounted on the wall behind him, CeCe saw herself. She looked different, womanly, already. Terrell had sculpted her hair into a small ocean wave that tapered at the nape. Soft hues of berries and spice were dusted on her full features. Pam had coaxed her to buy a new dress, and Terri had calmed her about the price. It was a strapless dress, the color of ripe plums. Strips of plum-colored leather trimmed the bodice in a corset effect, highlighting the contours of CeCe's curves. The crepe fabric felt like a promise with each soft swish across the back of her thighs.

CeCe took a deep breath and returned Dub's smile. He dressed to a precise fashion, as usual, in straight gray pants that looked to CeCe like a couture kind of canvas.

"Look at you," he said. "I hope you know how remarkable you look."

Dub's compliment slid over her bare shoulders warm and true. She had been prepared for a critique, an opinion, or an annoyed commentary, but saw none of that in his eyes tonight.

He smiled at her, seeming to read her thoughts.

"Let's go," he said, cradling her elbow with one hand and resting the other on the small of her back. With the pads of his fingers, Dub guided her across the hotel lobby and back to the elevator. He pressed the button at the top of the panel and CeCe commanded her stomach not to lurch.

At least I'll lose it in the penthouse, she thought.

Dub stayed close to her without actually touching her body. In her periphery, she could see him smiling at his shoes. Her panic began to break apart and float to every limb and region of her body.

What if it hurts? she thought. *What if he's really rough? What if I'm really, really bad? What if this was just a horrible idea?*

The elevator buttons illuminated the third floor, fourth, fifth, all the way up to ten. CeCe swallowed hard as the last button, the P, filled with light. Dub's hand returned to her back.

The doors opened and CeCe stopped in her tracks. The room that faced them was not a lavish penthouse suite, but a resplendent supper club with islands of purple tablecloths and high vases filled with long, red feathers. CeCe didn't feel Dub's hand push at the small of her back but, rather, intuited him urging her forward. Her body responded and, at that moment, CeCe knew she would trust his guiding hand throughout the night.

"Welcome to the Phoenix," the hostess said.

"Reservation for Williams," Dub said. The hostess scanned her oversized ledger and nodded approvingly.

"Yes, Mr. Williams, your table is ready." She picked up two red, leather-backed menus. "This way, please?"

CeCe felt Dub's hand leave her back. She glanced over her shoulder and he gave a small smile and a nod toward the hostess. CeCe followed behind the hostess, her sleek black hair swaying in easy rhythm with her hips. CeCe realized her own hips swiveled differently inside her plum dress.

The hostess placed menus at their seats and wished them a great evening. Dub thanked her and stood behind CeCe as she seated herself. The sommelier arrived immediately and Dub ordered a bottle of Sauvignon.

"I hope you don't mind," he said.

"No, not at all," CeCe said. "I don't know anything about wines."

"As long as you can remember merlot, sauvignon, chardonnay, and Shiraz, you'll be fine," Dub said. "Most folks ask for white zinfandel and think they're doing something. Zinfandel is the Tang of wine."

CeCe laughed. He was clever. She could never deny him that.

"Did you take a class or something?" she asked.

"Nah. I had a roommate in grad school who worked at these high-end joints," Dub said. "He hipped me to the basics. Trial and error from there."

"You consider yourself a connoisseur, then?" she teased.

"I'd just as soon have a beer or vodka sour," Dub said.

"Vodka sour?" CeCe said, propping her elbow on the table then quickly removing it. "I would have pegged you for a cognac or scotch guy. Something to put hair on your chest."

"Shit, it only took one night curled next to a toilet to learn my lesson about dark liquor," he said. Dub told her about his fraternity brothers challenging him to "upgrade" his liquor to the tune of a dozen shots and how he'd spent the rest of the night hurling in the bathroom.

Laughing at his antics, CeCe said, "I can't imagine you huddled in the bathroom, let alone sleeping on the floor."

Dub shrugged his shoulders. "Even Batman has a rough day."

The waiter came to take their order and CeCe was impressed at Dub's knowledge about cuts of meat, seasonality of vegetables, and seasoning in Béarnaise. Once their orders were placed, Dub raised his wineglass to her.

"Here's to brand new," he said.

"To brand new," she repeated, clinking his glass.

They chatted about college and the mall and diets and Walter Mosley books and Terri's art and vacation dreams and birthday wishes. Their meals were delicious and filling. Her anxieties were relaxed and quiet.

"This was really nice, Dub. Thank you," she said.

A familiar mischief appeared at the edges of his grin. "Are you thanking me for choosing this place or for treating you to dinner before I sex you down?" he said.

The waiter's cheeks reddened as placed the red portfolio on their table. CeCe's face hardened. This version of Dub was familiar. Still, they'd had a great evening so she tried to process his crass statement as a reasonable question.

"Both, I guess," she said. "I didn't really know what to expect. It was really nice."

Dub sipped water as she spoke and watched her for a steady moment over the edge of his glass.

"You're surprised I'm not an asshole all the time?" Dub asked.

CeCe flushed and commanded her body not to squirm. She cocked her head to the side and looked Dub directly in the eye. "Yes," she said. "I was even more surprised you agreed."

Dub was signing his name to the bill. "Why?" he asked, without looking up.

"I had the impression you only date tall, glamorous women."

"You've seen me with these tall, glamorous women?"

"Well, no, but you always go out of your way to broadcast your high standards and your premium tastes and your trendy friends and your tailored clothes," she said. "A guy like you is only going to have high-end women."

Dub measured her and she cursed herself for letting Terri talk her into this. CeCe had witnessed Dub dismantle more than a few debaters, including herself, and knew this conversation was about to take its fatal dip.

"How would you describe a guy like me?" Dub asked, reaching for his wineglass.

When CeCe had experienced Dub's verbal challenges in the past, she always bailed from the exchange before he could fillet her pride. Tonight, she had nothing to lose. She was at a fancy restaurant, dressed up in sexy clothes, full of wine and leg of lamb, holding her own with a worldly, sophisticated, bona fide grown man. Even if the sex part didn't happen, she was already ahead.

"You're an ass," CeCe said. "That's how I describe a guy like you. You're rude, self-absorbed, self-inflated, and cruel. An ass."

Dub spun the base of his wineglass, and his eyes landed on hers as she continued to speak.

"I listen to you talk down to Terri's friends, like you're doing them a favor to be in their presence. You even treat me like peon most of the time. 'Did you mean to wear two different shades of black, CeCe?' 'Are you still letting that white girl talk crazy to you at work, CeCe?' 'Why don't you get some real hip-hop in your life, CeCe?' What makes you think you know every fucking thing?"

Dub leaned back in his chair. CeCe wondered if he was crafting a response or letting her vent without listening to her at all. He reached for the bottle of wine and poured what remained into her glass.

"I didn't think you'd get all that out. Impressive," he said, smoothing the front of his slacks as he crossed his legs. "CeCe, I've known you for almost two years now and this is the first time I've heard you stand your ground on anything. I've heard you whine. I've heard you bitch and moan. And I've heard you ask questions you already knew the answers to, but you've never spoken your mind. Congratulations."

"Kiss my ass, Dub," CeCe said, her brows furrowed with irritation.

"Bonus point," Dub said with a smirk. "Now, back to me. CeCe, I know how I come off to people, but I can't concern myself with your perception, can I? If I don't think I'm the shit, who's going to? If I don't define standards for myself, how can I complain about the quality of my life? If I can't give people pure, unfiltered truth, how can I expect to hear it? If all that makes me an ass, I'll be that. And I sleep like a baby every night. You know why, CeCe? Because I'm not fake. I'm not shady, and I put in the effort to try and be fucking phenomenal at everything I do. Do I know 'every fucking thing'? Of course not. But what I *do* know and what I *do* believe, I stand on it."

CeCe waved away his response and said, "That's not how you act, Dub, all noble and shit. You act like you're never wrong."

Dub sat up, anchoring his elbows on the table. "That's what I'm talking about," he said. "I didn't say anything about never being wrong. I said I stand on what I know. You learn shit when you know how to shut up and pay attention. You should try it."

"What the fuck is that supposed to mean?" CeCe asked. She pressed against the chair back with her arms crossed.

"It means you should spend more time listening to what people are saying instead of being so afraid somebody might hurt your little feelings," Dub said. "You're not in high school anymore, CeCe. Why would you give a fuck what I think about your clothes or your job or what CDs you buy? Just because somebody has an opinion doesn't mean you have to make it yours. You decided I was an ass who wouldn't think much of you because you're an ass who doesn't think much of yourself."

CeCe sat motionless in the fancy chair, in her pretty dress, fighting the tears that wanted to spring from her expert eye makeup. She could not cry. She could not deny the truth in what Dub had said. CeCe felt an anchor lifted from each shoulder. He was right. She still felt people's eyes staring through her rainbow dress, reading some other little girl's name written on the tag. CeCe had not been protecting her story from the world; she'd been hiding behind it. She leveled her eyes on Dub, who watched her coolly.

"So," she began, "you admit to being an ass?"

Dub laughed aloud, ignoring the heads turning their way. "I don't just admit it; I embrace it."

The waiter breezed past their table, sweeping the portfolio as he went.

"Know who the fuck you are, CeCe, and stand on that shit," Dub said. "Never, ever, ever discount yourself. To anyone. Not a man, not a friend, not a supervisor, not a cashier at McDonald's, not anyone. Not ever. You are worth everything you've decided you're worth."

"I guess I deserved that," CeCe said as the weight of his words framed themselves around her thoughts.

"I don't know about what you deserved, but I know what you needed to hear."

CeCe looked at Dub and nodded somberly. "Thank you."

Dub unleashed a sly grin. "Don't thank me yet," he said. With a full smile Dub stood and walked around the table to extend his hand. His eyes were locked onto hers and CeCe felt tiny explosions begin to pop and tickle beneath her skin. CeCe took Dub's hand and rose to her feet.

"Thank me in the morning," he said. He held her gaze while he planted a tiny kiss on the back of her hand. CeCe inhaled his skin, his bravado, and the sweet smell of wine on his lips.

"I hope you give me reason to," CeCe said. She heard Dub chuckle as she turned to walk away. His eyes were on her hips, she knew, and so she worked them. CeCe didn't look over her shoulder for him when she reached the elevator. She pressed the call button and smiled when Dub's baritone rumbled behind her just before the doors slid open.

THIRTY-EIGHT

CINNAMON

CeCe clasped and unclasped her hands underneath the table. Her mother sat on the other side, arcing her head back and forth to look at the hanging sculptures and exposed-pipe decor of the restaurant. CeCe marveled, instead, at the two of them. When her mother noticed CeCe's stupefied expression, she raised her eyebrows.

"We're at a restaurant," CeCe said, amazement continuing its dawn over her. "I'm twenty-eight and this is the first time you and I have gone to a restaurant."

CeCe's mother curled the edges of her mouth, less of a smile and more of a nod. Evolution, they knew, was not a speedy affair.

"Glad you asked," her mother said.

They each squared shoulders. CeCe shifted in her seat, bracing for an annoyance to ripple through her small joy. She felt nothing, no irritation, no reflexive flair. Like unfaithful lovers, CeCe and her mother gazed at one another as silent accusations passed.

"From your date?" her mother asked. "The flowers?"

CeCe had started to tell her mother about Eric back at their apartment. She found herself wanting to gush to her mother for the first time in a long time and suggested they go out for dinner. Her mother had accepted easily, simply. CeCe filled their ride with radio songs and nerves.

Their waitress had a sprawling tattoo that screamed in full color from beneath her folded, white sleeve. Her smile was honest. Her eyes were sharp and heavily lined in charcoal. She said her name was Pearl. CeCe hadn't expected a name so polished, so smooth. She didn't carry an order pad. CeCe ordered a shrimp skewer appetizer and a glass of Riesling. Her mother ordered coffee.

"Would you like a cinnamon stick for your coffee?" the waitress asked.

CeCe and her mother both opened their mouths to speak, CeCe to dismiss the suggestion, but her mother's soft voice clung to the air more firmly.

"Sure," her mother said.

All three women grinned a little.

THIRTY-NINE

JAZZ

CECE KEPT HER EYES ON the seam that halved the elevator doors as Dub stood behind her. The elevator pulleys began to hum and CeCe watched the winks of steel, cinder, and fluorescent light as the elevator passed each floor. Every other cell in her body and her full attention were focused on Dub, standing close, like a floating neutron. He didn't speak or touch her, but simply exhaled against her skin.

Eighth floor. Seventh floor.

An electricity surged from Dub's body to hers. His breath across her neck and bare shoulders was titillating. CeCe felt his breath close enough to kiss her nape, but his lips only hovered there. He made her curves vibrate beneath the plum dress.

Sixth floor. Fifth floor.

Dub traced her forearm with his thumb—slowly from her elbow to her wrist—resting his hand on her hip and brushing that kiss across the back of her neck. When Dub touched her, a bolt rocketed from the tingle beneath her skin to the gasp in her chest to a flash of fire between her thighs.

Fourth floor.

The elevator car slowed, suspending them in place. CeCe closed her eyes and tried to will her heart to stop its thumping. The doors slid open and they stepped onto the carpet. Dub fished the keycard

from his jacket pocket, checked the numbers against the wall plac-
ards, and took CeCe's hand.

"This way," he said. "We're in room four-sixteen."

CeCe let Dub lead her down the carpeted hallway, defeating the
urge to crowd their quiet walk with comments on the hotel decor,
trivia about hotel housekeeping trends, compliments on his shoes.

410. 412.

Dub's thumb stroked the outside of her palm.

414. 416.

Dub gave her hand a small squeeze. He slid the keycard into the
lock, swinging wide the door.

"Miss Weathers," he said with a bow. CeCe intended to laugh
walking in, but giggled instead. She did not want to be juvenile
tonight, even if she was a rookie. CeCe walked across the room to
look out the window. Gazing at the view of the mercantile docks and
the river dancing with the neon lights from the jazz district, CeCe
gave herself a quick pep talk. She was ready, she kept thinking. She
was ready.

"Take off your clothes now," Dub commanded. CeCe spun
around with her eyes wide, catching the window sheers.

Dub trotted the length of the room to rescue her from the curtains.

"I'm kidding, I'm kidding," he laughed, moving her from the window. "Come over here and relax."

"See?" she said, pointing an accusing finger up at him from the
sofa. "Ass."

Dub laughed again. "I earned that one," he said. "I apologize."

CeCe took in the room while Dub hung his jacket and turned
the knobs and dials on the stereo. The suite had a kitchenette and
a cozy sitting area. She tried to ignore the king-sized bed recessed
behind them. The lights were off in the sleeping area, but the white
pillowcases and folds of the sheets still seemed luminescent. CeCe

would be sprawled across that bed soon. Or pinned to it. Or dangled over its edge. Or curled in a fetal position.

Dub found a jazz station, filling the room with snare drums, trumpets, and bass. A knock sounded at the door and Dub moved across the room to let in room service. The waiter carried a bottle of wine and two glasses. Dub directed him to the dinette table where the young man uncorked the bottle for them. Dub thanked him, tipped him as he left, and locked the door behind him.

"Join me?" he asked, pouring two glasses.

"Yes," CeCe said. This was happening. Maybe she should have lots of wine.

Dub brought CeCe her glass and sat in the red chair to the right of the sofa. She waited to see if they were going to toast again, but when Dub sipped she nervously sipped, too. CeCe wasn't sure what to say. At the restaurant, it was easy to forget why they were on this date in the first place. The conversation was effortless, as usual. It wasn't like Dub was a stranger. They'd logged hours of dialogue in the past few years, even if they were tense at times. CeCe tried to regain the ease they'd enjoyed during dinner, but found herself distracted by the 500 thread-count elephant looming in the space behind them.

"Oooh, baby, that's good," Dub said, breaking the silence. He looked at the glass of wine in his hand.

"This is the same wine we were drinking earlier?" CeCe asked. Dub nodded.

"Yeah, I like this," CeCe said, grateful to have actual words hanging in the air.

"Where could you imagine sipping this wine?" Dub asked, leaning deep into the chair. "Where would you like to travel?"

"Greece," CeCe said.

"Take a minute and think about it," Dub said, teasing.

"Don't need it. I've wanted to visit Greece since I was thirteen." CeCe told Dub about discovering *The Odyssey* in middle school and reading all of the mythological stories attached to the tale. Dub admitted he hadn't read either of Homer's epic works and only had a surface knowledge of Greek myths. He asked CeCe to summarize the story and by the time she'd woven in the tangential tales of Aphrodite's apple, sirens, Cyclops and Lotus-eaters and the rest, they were pouring out the last of the wine.

As Dub walked the empty bottle to the trash, CeCe dropped her head into her hand. She had rambled for more than forty-five minutes about mythical creatures when she was supposed to be having for her first sexual experience.

No wonder nobody's ever asked for any ass from me, she thought.

Dub took her wineglass and said, "Maybe we're all good with the wine."

CeCe cradled her head with both hands then, tears trying to push through her fingers. She wanted to speak, to tell Dub that it wasn't the wine, that she wasn't drunk, but she feared her voice could make the tears spill. She did not want to cry. Not now.

She heard the coffee table move and felt Dub lower himself to the carpet. He circled two fingers around each wrist and gently pulled her hands from her face. CeCe stared down at her feet. Pam had scolded her into getting a salon pedicure and CeCe was comforted by the ten glossy, peach toenails gleaming back at her. Still, a tear tumbled onto her bare foot.

Why do I keep trying? CeCe thought. *Why?*

New tears dotted the tops of her feet, and CeCe couldn't fight back the onslaught. She cried and heaved and sniffled and cried some more. After a moment, she found her forehead resting against Dub's chest. She straightened to pull away from him and sit up, keeping her eyes on their hands. Dub stroked the tops of her fingers and walked away from the couch. CeCe didn't look up, not wanting to watch him flee their posh hotel suite. When his gray shoes returned, Dub straddled her small naked feet and lifted her head. He held a pinch of tissues and her glass of wine. CeCe accepted them and blew her nose.

"Better?" he asked once she'd wiped her eyes and calmed her heaving shoulders.

CeCe nodded, holding their silence. Instead of pressuring her to speak, Dub reached for his wineglass.

"Toast," he said. CeCe raised her glass reluctantly. Dub held her weary gaze for a long moment.

"To the long version," he said. "My favorite kind of story."

CeCe inspected Dub's face, and his smile was warm and not the least bit mocking. She felt her chest patter.

"To long stories," CeCe said in a small voice. "Probably the only kind I have."

They both sipped from their glasses, Dub drinking until his wine was gone. CeCe emptied her glass, too, following his lead. Dub placed their glasses on the end table. When he turned to face her again, his eyes were certain and inviting. CeCe watched his eyes get closer and closer until her own eyes crossed and closed. Dub pressed his lips against hers slowly, again and again.

CeCe opened her eyes to look down at his mouth when Dub stopped planting kisses. His lips were moist, plump and waiting. CeCe leaned in to kiss him first and felt his mouth smile. Dub kissed her hard, his tongue finding hers. CeCe's plum dress had rolled back to her hips and Dub wedged between her knees. CeCe was sure he could feel her thong panties beginning to throb. She kissed him like soul food, losing herself in the rhythm of their consumption. The pricey plum dress bunched around her waist and CeCe didn't care. Instead, she pressed her bare legs back against Dub's hands as they gripped at her waist and thighs and he gnawed hungry kisses into her neck and cleavage. Tiny firecrackers exploded along her skin wherever Dub touched her. Dub tore away from her, his chest heaving a bit. CeCe breathed heavily, too, almost forgetting she didn't know what she was doing. She was not immediately aware of her legs wrapped around his thighs, her champagne-colored thong exposed, warm with wanting, and one cup of her matching convertible bra peeping above the dress bodice.

Dub pulled his shirt over his head and tossed it to an armchair. He still wore an undershirt, the mark of a well-groomed man, her Aunt Rosie had once told her. He leaned in for a quick kiss before standing to peel away his T-shirt. CeCe hoped her mouth wasn't actually gaping open at the sight of Dub's body. He was fit without being obscenely muscular. His skin was rich and supple, in deep hues of violet and brown. She wanted to touch it, trace her fingertips along the precision of his abs and biceps. CeCe expected him to be toned, but she couldn't have imagined wanting to put her hands and mouth all over him.

Dub took CeCe's hands and guided her to her feet again. He led her away from the sofa, toward the king-sized bed. Dub took CeCe's face in his hands and placed the softest kiss to her lips. She returned Dub's kiss, covering his hands with hers. He flowered petal-soft kisses to her nose and forehead, turning her away from him to plant more slow kisses at the nape of her neck.

CeCe felt the zipper on her dress slide open. Her head bowed, she flung open her eyes. *This was really happening*. Her shiny peach toes rooted into the carpet, keeping her steady. Dub's hand appeared at her hip. CeCe watched his fingers outline her silhouette. His body was solid against hers, and it felt good. He held the top of her bodice between his fingers and folded the dress down from her body, over her waist and thighs, and into a collapsed hoop around her feet. Stooping next to her, Dub kissed CeCe's thigh. He was unhurried and deliberate, making a pattern of kisses around to the front of her knee and up her inner thigh. As his mouth reached the champagne-colored patch of satin, CeCe held her breath. The kiss he planted there seared through fabric and skin.

CeCe looked to the top of Dub's head, holding his shoulders. When he looked up to her, she panicked. She didn't know whether to return his gaze or look away. *What's the etiquette here?* she thought. *Do I say something? Pet his head? Close my eyes?*

Dub smiled and returned to his work, laying down his kisses along her other inner thigh, knee, and hip. As he made his way around to the backs of her knees, CeCe caught sight of their blurred reflection in the flat-screen across the room. Her body was taut and compact, like a sprinter's, and the thong-and-bra set she'd purchased flattered her curves beautifully. CeCe had thought her physique too short or too stumpy at times. Tonight, she felt perfect.

Dub stood and helped CeCe step from the crumple of her dress. He navigated them closer to the bed, guiding her onto her stomach. CeCe felt the weight of him depress the bed next to her. He caressed the muscles in her back, the roundness of her backside, the back of her thigh, and her back again.

CeCe drifted away with the jazz music floating above them. When Dub unhooked her bra, she didn't jump or startle. The mattress shifted again and CeCe heard the light clink of his belt buckle, the yawn of his zipper, and the soft tumble of pants down Dub's legs. *Really happening.*

CeCe squeezed closed her eyes, but was too enveloped in bliss to be afraid. She listened to the lift and pulse of the music. Dub's hands were on her ass again, groping and caressing, hard and soft. He turned her to her back and his hands were firm on her small breasts, squeezing and caressing them between his nuzzles and kisses. CeCe's eyes remained closed. Her confidence was not strong enough to look him in the face. Not yet. Maybe not at all.

He felt good against her, the heat and strength of his hands and bare chest. CeCe floated her hands to his back, but Dub would lift them above her head each time, leaving them to hang over the edge of the bed. CeCe wasn't accustomed to receiving, but liked the task of trying.

Dub hooked a thumb into the side of her thong and, reflexively, CeCe lifted her hips from the bed. He slid the panties down, down, down, over her peach toes. She heard him step down from the bed to remove his own briefs. In that instant, CeCe was utterly naked and ashamed. An Eve moment, she thought. Dub's hand graced her stomach and a kiss brushed her breast, before CeCe heard the crinkle of foil and the stretch and smack of latex.

Really.

Her stomach tightened and his body slipped next to her. They were naked, skin to skin. Dub folded CeCe into the curve of his body, curling his arms around her and kissing the back of her neck. He molded her body into a loose letter S, scooping her hips with his. CeCe got lost in their body music, breathing and rocking together, and the inside of her thighs went from moist to wet.

Then she felt him. Dub parted the wet heat of her with only the tip of himself and CeCe sizzled with anticipation. A small part of her was nervous about the pain, but the rest of her felt complete pleasure. His arms were firm about her—one around her waist and the other around her shoulders—and his breath was warm against her neck. CeCe pressed her back into Dub's chest and her hands across his forearms. She opened her eyes, waiting to cross the meridian of pleasure and pain, before and after.

Dub continued to trail kisses and nuzzle her neck as he circled his hips behind her. The slick between her legs felt decadent. He slid in and out of her, reaching farther inside with each slow stroke. He pulled back and relaxed his embrace, turning CeCe onto her back again. She looked up at him, wondering if she had missed a prompt or instruction, but he just gave a little smile before kissing her on the mouth.

Dub pulled back the bedding and ushered them inside. He moved on top of her, sliding his arms around her. He angled her knees wide and he pressed his body between them, easing himself back inside the warmth of her.

"You OK?" he asked low against her ear, as if there were others in the room he didn't want to disturb.

CeCe gave a small nod. Dub anchored his feet beneath her heels and began dipping himself in and out in a smooth, easy cadence. CeCe looped her arms around his shoulders. The glide felt unworldly good to her. A random punchline raced across her mind, a crude one-liner by a standup comic about "dead fish," "dry hooch," and the women who "just laid there." CeCe wasn't naive enough to think she might impress Dub, but she didn't want to rank at the absolute bottom of his roster, either.

Closing her eyes in concentration, CeCe synced her body with the piano keys and saxophone chords that filled the room. She tried to visualize a ribbon unfurling from her neck and through her torso and hips. The image made CeCe snap her hips from side to side and caused her feet to keep scooting from under them. When CeCe fell completely out of rhythm with Dub, panic climbed her stomach. Desperately, she hunched and jerked her shoulders, trying to arch and grind a response to his body.

Dub stopped moving. "Relax," he whispered in her ear. He planted a single kiss on her naked shoulder. "You're doing fine."

He resumed his slow grind and CeCe allowed herself to think

only of the slippery welcome between her thighs. The radio music danced above them and Dub moved deeper inside of her. CeCe could feel his pelvis flush against the inside of her thighs and the space behind her navel filled with his mass. She pictured the carnival game where the swing of a mallet could sail a metal floater clear to the top of a marking post to strike a winning bell.

CeCe clanged inside and thought, *I'm not a virgin! This feels amazing! I'm not a virgin! This feels amazing...*

"OK?" he whispered again.

"Yes," she was able to whisper back this time.

The weight of him wasn't uncomfortable or heavy, as CeCe had thought it would be. She'd often wondered how the women in big-screen sex scenes were able to breathe. Her body took in more and more of him. Dub suckled the crook of her neck, circling his hips faster and wider. He maintained his slow rhythm, and CeCe heard herself moan.

"Like it?" he asked in her ear.

"Yes," she said in hollow whisper.

"Feels good?" he asked, his voice less steady.

"Yes," CeCe said, her breath quickening.

"Yeah, feels good," Dub said, pushing every inch of himself fully into her. CeCe tightened her circle around Dub's neck.

"Yeah," Dub said. "Yeah, yeah."

He thrust into CeCe a little deeper, a little harder. The added force didn't hurt her at all. In fact, it felt even better. CeCe was so wet between her legs. As Dub rocked in and out of her, CeCe felt something ignite in her depths. The ember grew with each stroke, growing brighter and larger and brighter and larger until CeCe burst into a shower of light and fire.

CeCe called out *Oh! Oh! Oh!* and rushed with warm, silky fluid. Dub grunted and cheered them as his hips pumped faster and faster until he climaxed with a low growl. His entire body went rigid, and then he let himself deflate on top of her. When Dub rolled away, CeCe heard the roll and snap as he removed the condom. She wiggled beneath sheets, looking up the ceiling. Stunned and smiling.

Dub lay flat on his back and CeCe expected them to separate to their respective sides of the bed now that their task was done. Instead, Dub slid his arm beneath CeCe's shoulders and curled her into his chest. CeCe rested her head there, listening to the boom of his heart and the lilt of a standup bass.

"Well done, little sprout," Dub said. CeCe laughed and pinched his side. He chuckled and kissed the top of her head.

"You good . . . ?" he asked. CeCe could hear sleep creeping into his voice. She gave a final small nod and wrapped her arms around his waist.

When CeCe pulled out of the parking structure the following morning, she wished she hadn't driven her own car. Her limbs were too weak and every inch of skin still tingled. The last thing she wanted to do was operate heavy machinery. She wanted to lie naked on expensive bed sheets all day. She wanted to mount him again, like she'd done after breakfast. She'd required minimal coaching that time.

Driving home, CeCe replayed how Dub had suckled her collarbone, his slow and certain kisses, the way he'd clutched fistfuls of her thighs and folded her body into proper angles. She did not mistake their night together as a budding of any kind. She also accepted that sex in the future would not always be perfect and holy. Aunt Rosie had once told her story about saving her money as a young girl to buy her first church hat. Girls couldn't wear hats to church until they turned fifteen. A tradition, Aunt Rosie had said, dating back to when marrying fifteen-year-olds was common. Aunt Rosie hadn't wanted a store-bought hat. She didn't want any duplications towering above the church pews. She wanted her first of many church hats to be the most special of any she might own.

Terri stood in the hallway with hands covered in paint when CeCe entered the apartment. She eyed CeCe nervously.

"I love you," CeCe said dreamily and Terri smiled back.

CeCe dropped her bag on her bedroom floor and lowered herself to the bed. Her face still stretched into a smile as she drifted to sleep. As the sun poured over her in her slumber, CeCe dreamed of beautiful girls in a rainbow of church hats.

FORTY

OPAQUE

THEIR MEAL ENDED QUICKLY. HER mother, still barely a nibbler, only ordered a cup of soup. CeCe had been ravenous, gobbling her pasta, and they finished at the same time. CeCe joined her mother in ordering a coffee. They stirred the black liquid with their cinnamon sticks.

"This is new," CeCe said.

"Different," her mother said.

They laughed.

"He sounds nice," her mother said, wrapping back to their exchange of short sentences about Eric.

"So far," CeCe said.

CeCe's mother looked down into her emptied mug. "Two ways life consumes you," she said. Her voice was weary but sure. "Swallowed or swept away. One way happens to you, the other happens because of you. Love can go either way."

CeCe looked at her mother's small fingers curved around the coffee mug. They were bony, frail.

"Which is better?" CeCe asked.

Her mother lifted her eyes and looked at CeCe. "Neither," her mother said. "Both make you fight for air. Both require small blessings. Both make your life . . . yours."

CeCe considered this. "I think I'd rather get swept away," she said.

Her mother smiled. "If only choosing were an option."

They let the barbed and weighted truth hover above the table for a moment. Both of them quiet.

"You were my one blessing, CrimsonBaby," her mother said into the void. "Thank you. I love you so much."

"I know, Mama," CeCe said. "You don't have to thank me. I love you, too."

"Carried such a heavy load," her mother said. "Hurting so much. Couldn't help you. Wanted to. Couldn't. Want you to know that."

"Mama, I know," CeCe said, swallowing the lump in her throat.

Her mother leaned back against her chair's metal-pipe backing, spent from her confession. Her eyes were clouded and resettled on her mug.

"I'm thinking about getting a house," CeCe said, shifting in her seat at the half-truth. Her mother met her eyes. A shadow of a smile hinted in her gaze.

"You should," her mother said.

"Actually, I have a house," CeCe said, the admission flying from her mouth like a trapped bird. They let the words flutter for a moment. CeCe continued, telling her mother about Doris' living will project with an unexpected nervousness making her tongue skip and speed.

Her mother nodded.

CeCe took in her mother's peaceful expression, the soft skin colored like warm bread. Neither of them had chosen this life; it had chosen them. They both had been swallowed, she decided.

CeCe leaned back in her chair and said, "We need to figure out how to get you back and forth to the Springer Center, but you're gonna love—"

CeCe cut her words short, as her mother's head moved side to side in a slow, somber swivel.

"Not going, CrimsonBaby," her mother said. "It's time."

CeCe's mouth fell open, while her mind tried to process. She started to protest but her mother shook her head more sternly.

"What?" CeCe said.

"It's time," her mother repeated. "Now. We'll both be fine."

The tears gave no warning. They fell as quickly as CeCe could wipe them away. CeCe did not dare language, knowing words would push a tidal wave. Her mother laid an open hand on top of the table and CeCe laid her hand inside. They used to sit this way on the courtyard bench, when her mother could excite her about gathering dandelions.

CeCe cried and, this time, her mother did not.

FORTY-ONE

WITHERING

IN BED THAT NIGHT, CECE stared up at the darkness. A rectangle of muted moonlight usually glowed on her bedroom ceiling, but the sky had been crowded with ominous clouds. Charcoal shadows crawled across her room and the night outside her window.

Walking from the restaurant to their car, CeCe's mother said she had always liked the eager smell of coming rain.

"And matches," CeCe had replied.

Her mother had grinned faintly, disappearing into the passenger side. The air was, indeed, heavy with the promise of a storm, but CeCe looked up to the sky with a smile. It had been so long since her mother had made her smile, CeCe felt like she was being transported in time. Or, perhaps, she was being projected forward, since nothing in this moment with her mother felt familiar. The cords between them for so long had been tenuous and steady, anchored and fraying.

CeCe climbed into the driver's side and fastened her seat belt. The Lincoln pulled them under traffic lights, past retail stores and along refreshed pavement. They listened to music sliding in and out of the CD changer. Her mother watched through the windshield as the city approached and slipped past them. Her arms were crossed tightly at the waist and she cupped an elbow with each hand. Her mother relaxed this containment of herself once CeCe pulled the car under their carport. She tried to imagine her mother traveling back and forth to this apartment on her own. Getting groceries. Paying utilities. Remembering the renter's insurance premium. *Your mother took care of herself before everything fell apart,* Pam had once reminded her.

Her mother started her bedtime ritual as quickly as CeCe could unlock the apartment door. It was two hours past her usual bedtime, and CeCe knew her mother was exhausted. CeCe walked the length of the hallway to the front room and let herself fall onto the sofa. She was spent, too, but didn't want to surrender to her exhaustion yet.

CeCe was flipping through channels when her mother appeared at the edge of the couch. CeCe jumped, asking her mother if she'd been taking ninja classes at the center, too.

Her mother, eyes heavy with sleep, coughed a single, weary chuckle. CeCe swallowed the foreign sound, feeling sated and light all at once. CeCe could smell the fresh scents of her mother's soap and body cream. She held closed the modest vee of an oversized nightgown, her bare arm protruding like a small wing.

Looking at the bones and chords of veins that patterned the back of her mother's hand, CeCe marveled, for the second time in so many days, at how time and age were circling about them. Withering her mother's hands. Softening her own resolve.

Fixed on the hands, CeCe didn't register her mother's forward lean until the kiss landed on her forehead. It was more of a light press of flesh to skin than a puckered kiss, but CeCe was too captured by shock to criticize her mother's technique.

"Love you," her mother said, her voice quiet and light. "Proud of you."

CeCe's heart exploded. She looked up at her mother and said, "I'm proud of you, too, Mama. I love you. So much."

Her mother's free hand landed on her shoulder and CeCe sat motionless, as if a butterfly had alighted there. Her mother patted her shoulder two slow times before turning to walk the hallway back to her bedroom. CeCe stared at the space where her mother had stood, her ears listening to the familiar clicks of the light switch, ceiling fan cord, and lamp, then the moan of the mattress. CeCe switched off the television and padded to her room, too. Even though every nerve ending in her body vibrated with joy, she knew she had to get some rest, too.

CeCe waited for sleep to find her, watching thunderclouds trace her ceiling and the sky. In an instant, she was gripped with the prospect of possibility. No longer elusive or theoretical, CeCe pushed back her approaching slumber and sat upright in her bed. She fumbled along the headboard shelf for her cell phone. Its screen illuminated her small face in the darkness.

She listened to its mechanical ringing. Two. Three. He greeted her by name.

"Hey, CeCe," Eric said. "I was just thinking about you."

"That's good," CeCe said, holding down her inhibitions for a moment and letting her idea flood into the phone.

"Listen," she said. "There's something I'd like to share with you."

FORTY-TWO

MOON

CeCe's mother didn't visit the house for months, long after autumn chills laced the morning air. She'd insisted that CeCe first felt fully settled in her new space.

"No rush," her mother had said via text message. CeCe had been unrelenting about having her carry and use a cell phone.

Eric had been mindful of CeCe's new space, too. He kissed her in front of the picture window after his first tour of the house, touched that CeCe had called to share such a special moment with him. She had looked up at him, wanting him to never take his gentle hands from the sides of her face.

Once CeCe had the house cleaned and a general layout in place, she redeemed Eric's offer to help by having him caravan the last of her boxes from what was now her mother's apartment. CeCe looked on, with a catch in her breath, as Eric cupped her mother's small hand and coaxed a girlish smile into her eyes. When she would retrace her lifetime with Eric, CeCe would mark the effortless glow in her mother's face as the moment she knew she would love this man for the rest of their lives.

Eric kissed her beneath her tree that evening, both of them tacky with dust and sweat. Inside, he pulled her through her the rooms and hallways, crisp with the smell of oil soap and newness, and into her bedroom. CeCe opened her limbs and her full heart as she and

Eric enveloped one another for the first time. As he tightened his embrace around her body, CeCe cried out, listening to her freedom music sing against the walls of her moon-washed room.

ABOUT THE AUTHOR

DASHA KELLY is a nationally-respected writer, artist and social entrepreneur. As a spoken word artist, Dasha has performed throughout the U.S., in Canada and appeared on the final season of HBO presents *Russell Simmons' Def Poetry Jam*. Dasha holds an MFA in Creative Writing from Antioch University. She is an alum of the iconic Squaw Valley Writers Community, the former writer-in-residence for the historic Pfister Hotel, and founder of Still Waters Collective, an arts education and community-building initiative. In 2014, Dasha was selected as a U.S. Embassy Arts Envoy to teach and perform in Botswana, Africa. She is the author of one chapbook, *Hither*, and three books: *All Fall Down*, *Hershey Eats Peanuts*, and *Call It Forth*. She lives in Milwaukee, WI.

ON THE WAY

STORIES BY CYN VARGAS

"In these fresh, sensual stories, Vargas bravely explores family, friendship and irreconcilable loss, and she will break your heart nicely." —**BONNIE JO CAMPBELL**

Cyn Vargas's debut collection explores the whims and follies of the human heart. When an American woman disappears in Guatemala, her daughter refuses to accept she's gone; a divorced DMV employee falls in love during a driving lesson; a young woman shares a well-kept family secret with the one person who it might hurt the most; a bad haircut is the last straw in a crumbling marriage. In these stories, characters grasp at love and beg to belong—often at the expense of their own happiness.

CRAZY HORSE'S GIRLFRIEND
A NOVEL BY ERIKA T. WURTH

"Crazy Horse's Girlfriend *is gritty and tough and sad beyond measure; but it also contains startling, heartfelt moments of hope and love.*" —**DONALD RAY POLLOCK**

Margaritte is a sharp-tongued, drug-dealing, sixteen-year-old Native American floundering in a Colorado town crippled by poverty, unemployment, and drug abuse. She hates the burnout, futureless kids surrounding her and dreams that she and her unreliable new boyfriend can move far beyond the bright lights of Denver before the daily suffocation of teen pregnancy eats her alive. *Crazy Horse's Girlfriend* thoroughly shakes up cultural preconceptions of what it means to be Native American today.

ALSO AVAILABLE FROM CURBSIDE SPLENDOR

MEATY

ESSAYS BY SAMANTHA IRBY

"Raunchy, funny and vivid . . . Those faint of heart beware . . . strap in and get ready for a roller-coaster ride to remember." **—KIRKUS REVIEWS**

Samantha Irby explodes onto the page with essays about laughing her way through a life of failed relationships, taco feasts, bouts with Crohn's Disease, and much more. Written with the same scathing wit and poignant bluntness readers of her riotous blog, Bitches Gotta Eat, have come to expect, *Meaty* takes on subjects both high and low—from why she can't be mad at Lena Dunham, to the anguish of growing up with a sick mother, to why she wants to write your mom's Match.com profile.

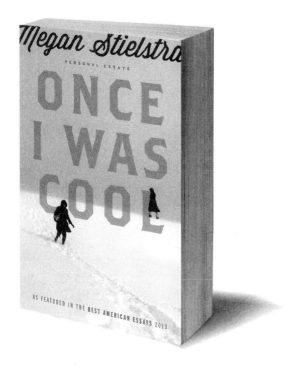